Madeleine Sutte~~r was~~ once the belle of the ball at the popular resort town of Misty Lake, New York. But as the sole survivor of the community's worst tragedy, she's come under suspicion. Longing for the life she once enjoyed, she accepts a rare social invitation to the event of the season. Now she will be able to show everyone she's the same woman they'd always admired—with just one hidden exception: she awoke from the accident with the ability to heal.

Doctor Jace Merrick has fled the failures and futility of city life to start anew in rural Misty Lake. A man of science, he rejects the superstitious chatter surrounding Maddie and finds himself drawn to her confidence and beauty. And when she seduces him into a sham engagement, he agrees to be her ticket back into society, if she supports his new practice—and reveals the details of her remarkable recovery. But when his patients begin to heal miraculously, Jace may have to abandon logic, accept the inexplicable—and surrender to a love beyond reason…

Soul
Survivor
#
/

Books by Thomasine Rappold

The Sole Survivor Series
The Lady Who Lived Again

Published by Kensington Publishing Corporation

The Lady Who Lived Again

A Sole Survivor Novel

Thomasine Rappold

LYRICAL PRESS
Kensington Publishing Corp.
www.kensingtonbooks.com

Lyrical Press books are published by
Kensington Publishing Corp. 119 West 40th Street New York, NY 10018

All Kensington titles, imprints, and distributed lines are available at special quantity discounts for bulk purchases for sales promotion, premiums, fund-raising, and educational or institutional use.

Special book excerpts or customized printings can also be created to fit specific needs. For details, write or phone the office of the Kensington Special Sales Manager:
Kensington Publishing Corp.
119 West 40th Street
New York, NY 10018
Attn. Special Sales Department. Phone: 1-800-221-2647.

Kensington and the K logo Reg. U.S. Pat. & TM Off.
Lyrical Press and the L logo are trademarks of Kensington Publishing Corp.

First Electronic Edition: December 2015
eISBN-13: 978-1-61650-991-0
eISBN-10: 1-61650-991-0

First Print Edition: December 2015
ISBN-13: 978-1-61650-992-7
ISBN-10: 1-61650-992-9

Printed in the United States of America

For my mom, Lorraine DeBonis Mancino, whose love for romance novels lives on in me.

Acknowledgements

Thank you to my awesome agent, Stefanie Lieberman, for loving this story and for all your efforts in seeing it published. My deep appreciation and thanks to my editor, Paige Christian, whose keen eye and stellar skills helped make this a better book. To my wonderfully ruthless critique group, Bonnie, Chris, Colleen, and Jean, thank you for never blowing smoke and always giving it to me straight. I couldn't have done it without you. Thanks to my daughters for their patience with a mom who spends half her time in an imaginary world. To my real-life hero, John, thank you for all your love and support, and for always having more faith in me than I have in myself. And lastly, my heartfelt thanks to you, dear reader, for sitting down to spend time with my characters. I hope you enjoy their story.

Chapter 1

Everyone wished she had died with the others. Maddie Sutter had accepted this truth long ago. But much to the small town's dismay, she insisted on living and breathing despite it.

Straightening her shoulders, she lifted her chin against the barrage of eyes watching her every move as she forged down Main Street. After three years of suffering this unwelcome attention each time she ventured to town, one would think she'd have grown used to the assault.

Maddie had resigned herself to many things since the accident, but she'd never adapt to the dread her presence induced in those she had known all her life—those who had once loved and cared for her.

With a fortifying breath, she approached a cluster of young boys on the corner. The same wretched imps had greeted her earlier when they'd spied her arrival in downtown Misty Lake. She braced herself for a repeat performance of the cruel rhyme they'd composed in her honor.

"Four dead girls on the slab, on the twelfth day of May. On Friday the thirteenth, one girl walked away."

Refusing to alter her course, Maddie strode straight toward them. Her lungs swelled with triumph as the alarmed little brats scattered like mice. With another fractional lift of her chin, she swept onward and rounded the corner.

She entered the general mercantile, the jingling bell on the door her only greeting as she stepped inside. Along with a handful of patrons, the store housed a hodgepodge of scents. Aromas of charcoal and beeswax mingled with the sweet smell of cinnamon and apples. Renewed by the boon to her senses, she enjoyed the whiff of fond memories that came with it. She shopped quickly, spurred on by the hushed whispers echoing through the aisles as she browsed the shelves.

Gathering a bag of sugar, a tin of baking powder, and the other items on her list, she headed to the front of the store, then placed them on the polished counter.

"Good morning, Mr. Piedmont," she said with a smile.

He wiped his hands on his bibbed apron and took a step forward. "Madeline."

With a curt nod, he lowered his somber eyes to the items on the counter and began to tally her purchases.

Maddie's smile faded, her mind drifting back to the days when Mr. Piedmont's face would light up to see her and her friends bounding into the mercantile. The Fair Five, as they were known back then, had charmed everyone. The girls had hardly put away their pinafores when they first learned to use their collective wit and beauty to full advantage. The Five always left Mr. Piedmont's store lapping at complimentary peppermint sticks, pressed upon them by the kindly merchant with a playful wink.

Maddie took a deep breath, forcing away thoughts of the past and the accident that had snatched her friends from this world. At twenty-four-years old, Maddie was a living reminder and the sole survivor of the worst tragedy in Misty Lake's history. People could barely stand to look at her. And Maddie couldn't blame them. She could barely stand to look at herself.

Mr. Piedmont worked swiftly, the sound of crumpling paper filling the awkward silence as he wrapped her purchases and bound the tidy parcel with string. By rote, his freckled hand reached to the nearby jar of candy. Placing a single peppermint stick on top of the bundle, he slid it toward her, then turned to face the shelves lining the wall behind him.

Tears blurred Maddie's vision as she stared down at the red-striped treat, the simple reminder of who she once was—who she still was, if only one of her neighbors could manage to look her in the eye long enough to see it. She swallowed hard.

"Thank you," she murmured to the shopkeeper's back before he walked away.

Maddie left the store and proceeded to her final errand. As she'd anticipated, a letter from Amelia awaited her at the post office. Maddie would wait until later to open it. Their recent correspondence had rattled her to the bone, and she knew any public display of emotion would be ripe fruit for hungry local gossips.

Not that maintaining decorum could help her cause now. People already believed the worst about her. These rare trips to town only served to remind her that nothing had changed.

Shoving the letter into her skirt pocket, she headed south on Main Street. To her relief, the band of young hooligans that had taunted her earlier was nowhere to be seen. She hurried out of town nonetheless. Each dreaded trip was a tax on her nerves, and when added to the anxiety of what awaited in Amelia's letter, Maddie yearned for the comfort of home.

When she reached the outskirts of town, she took the path through the woods that opened to a large field. She welcomed the sound of chirping crickets and birds. As always after she exerted herself with a lengthy walk, her leg was beginning to ache. She slowed her pace, then stopped to rest at her favorite spot on her grandfather's sprawling property. Sitting on a felled birch log in the broad clearing, she stretched out her leg. The cramped muscles unfurled as she enjoyed the serenity of the surrounding forest, the gentle spring breeze through the swaying trees. The sun felt heavenly, and she lifted her face to bask in its glow.

She'd avoided town all winter, hibernating like a bear in a cave. She'd emerged from seclusion renewed by foolish hopes, but the first outing of the new season had been just like the last. A bear would be better received.

Maddie sighed in defeat, dug out the letter that was fairly vibrating in her pocket, and unfolded its pages. The bold strokes on the delicate cream sheets conveyed Amelia's confident tone and dramatic style.

My dearest Mads,

I received your response denying my request, but I refuse to take no for an answer. I simply cannot get married without you!

You swore an oath to one day serve as my bridesmaid, and it is time for you to honor it. My deep love and concern for you force me to hold you to your promise.

The past is the past, my dear friend, and you must lay it to rest. Eventually, the town will follow suit. Consider attending my wedding as your first step toward getting on with your life.

We arrive in Misty Lake in three weeks. I look forward to seeing you then.

Forever yours,
Amelia

Maddie's breakfast turned in her stomach. How on earth could she attend? No one, save Amelia, wanted her there. Certainly not Daniel. The mere thought of facing her former fiancé and all the others who'd blamed and abandoned her...no. Maddie hadn't the courage. Amelia didn't understand. How could she? She was not present when it happened. Nor was she here for the aftermath.

Something rustled in the woods across the field. Squinting against the sun, Maddie scanned the trees. A deer hobbled into the clearing, took one final step, then collapsed to the ground. Maddie gasped at the arrow protruding from its shoulder.

Without a thought, she ran to the deer and dropped to her knees at its side. Blood flowed, a crimson stream from the gaping hole around the arrow. The trembling doe stared up at her, eyes wide with pain and terror.

Maddie glanced around to ensure she was alone. The arrow was a direct hit to the vitals, and the poor creature couldn't have traveled far. Someone might be tracking it. Glancing into the deer's desperate eyes again, Maddie tossed caution to the wind.

She grasped the arrow, clenching it as hard as she could. The blasted thing was in deep. Mustering her strength, she pulled, grunting as the arrow ripped through the torn muscle and flesh in which it was lodged. She fell backward, arrow in hand. Blood gushed everywhere. Tossing aside the arrow, she leaned over the deer and pressed her hands to the wound. Blood oozed between her fingers. Life drained from the deer, the warm flow filling her nose with the acrid scent of looming death.

She squeezed her eyes shut, swallowing against the bile rising in her throat. Behind her closed lids, pictures flashed in the darkness. The wagon careening out of control. The approaching tree. The bodies hurling through the air. Sounds of terrified screams filled her ears. Tears poured down her face as she opened her soul. All the pain, all the guilt, manifested inside her, raging through her veins. Heat radiated to her hands, transferring everything onto the dying deer.

Her hands grew hotter and hotter. Her heart pounded and she could barely breathe. She opened her eyes, watching through her scalding fingers as the stream of blood slowed and the torn hide around the wound began to close. The deer stirred, and Maddie sat back on her haunches, panting for air.

The deer sprang to its hooves. Its wide eyes met hers before it darted across the field, white tail raised like a flag as it hurdled the birch log, then disappeared into the forest. Maddie exhaled a shaky breath. The thrum of her pulse waned in relief. Once again, she felt worthy, if only for a moment, of surviving when no one else had.

She'd awakened after the accident with the ability to heal, and the absolution implied by this power helped her cling to her sanity. The mysterious gift was her only justification for living now, a token she'd smuggled back from some place between heaven and earth. One she had to keep hidden if she hoped ever to regain any semblance of a normal life.

"Hey, there!"

Maddie spun toward the voice in the trees. A man charged into the clearing, a large bow in his hands. With a curse, she pushed to her feet and turned her back to him as she gathered her wits. Wringing her bloody hands furiously between the folds of her beige skirt, she fought for composure, concocting her lies.

She inhaled a sharp breath and turned to face him. He stopped, startled by the sight of her. "Are you all right?" He rushed toward her. "Did it hurt you?"

"I'm fine," she said, backing away from the tall stranger.

He glanced down at the pool of bright blood at his boots, then looked around for the deer. "What the devil happened? Where is it?"

Maddie pointed toward the trees. "It ran into the woods."

"It's still running?" His blue eyes narrowed. "Impossible. I struck a kill shot."

"Unfortunately for the deer, your aim was not so precise." She gauged his wary reaction. "Nor is your eyesight if you thought you struck the vitals," she added, pinning her lies firmly in place with an angry nod. "Your clumsy shot to the gut will prolong the poor animal's misery. I dislodged the arrow to lessen its suffering."

His brows shot up. "You dislodged… Are you addled?" He stared in disbelief. "What possessed you—?"

"Senseless torment possessed me," she shot back. "And I assure you, my mind is quite sound."

The man was not convinced. Lowering his chin, he yanked off his hat and scratched his dark head. "I could have sworn I hit the…" Tousled black hair gleamed in the sunlight as he bent for the arrow. "You dislodged it, you say?"

He analyzed the bloody hair on the arrow, clearly distracted. She could see the questions forming in his bewildered eyes. She had to get rid of him.

"Your deer bolted, but it won't get far." She gave a nod toward the trees. "You should hurry."

Ignoring her suggestion, he took a step forward. "What's your name?" He dropped the arrow, his gaze fixing on her bloody hands. Reaching into his coat, he pulled out a handkerchief. He grabbed her wrist and attempted to wipe at the blood.

Maddie yanked back her hand. "My name is Madeline Sutter, and I can do that myself."

With a frown, he relinquished the cloth and let her proceed with the task.

"I'm Jace Merrick, Miss Sutter. I've taken over Doctor Filmore's practice in town now that he's retired."

The news surprised her. Doctor Filmore was eighty years old, if he was a day, and she'd always assumed he would die wearing his stethoscope. She was equally surprised by the youthful mien of Filmore's replacement. And by this new physician's obvious appetite for hunting. Weren't doctors supposed to be devoted to preserving life? Not that Doctor Filmore had gone out of his way to preserve hers. He'd pronounced her dead for God's sake. She slapped the cloth between her palms.

"It's about time that old fool retired," she muttered.

Pushing her disdain for the elderly doctor aside, she focused on the man before her. Jace Merrick possessed a palpable confidence, but dressed as he was, he didn't look like a doctor. His brown trousers were tucked into large boots, and a green flannel shirt peeked out from his open tweed coat.

And yet, even in his casual hunter's uniform, the man was impressive. The words ruggedly appealing sprang to mind. He stood taller than most, surely taller than Daniel. Doctor Merrick's build was broader than Daniel's as well. A twinge of longing fluttered in the pit of her belly.

The queer sensation took Maddie aback. She straightened her spine, steeling herself against her attraction to the handsome stranger. As she knew only too well, a man in the medical profession could destroy her. The doctor's stern voice snapped Maddie out of her reverie.

"Wild animals can be dangerous, Miss Sutter. Especially when they're wounded. You were fortunate in this instance, but I'd advise you against taking such risks in the future."

"I appreciate your advice, Doctor Merrick, and I have some for you." She took a step toward him. "There is no hunting allowed on Sutter land, so please do your murdering elsewhere." She finished wiping her hands, then handed him back the bloodstained handkerchief. "Now take your belongings and get off my property."

* * * *

Jace blinked, staring at the woman. Whatever he'd done to earn her hostility, he'd obviously done it well.

"This is your property?"

"My family owns twelve acres. Hunting is restricted on all of it." Her spine stiffened like a broomstick. Beneath her simple straw bonnet, wisps of dark hair fringed her pretty face. Specks of hazel and gold sparked in her brown eyes, along with an annoying tinge of righteous indignation. "My grandfather makes exceptions in cases of necessity only." She eyed him from head to toe. "Since there are several eating establishments in town, and you're clearly not starving, you can pursue your sport elsewhere."

"In my defense, Miss Sutter, this hunt *was* necessary."

"Is that so?"

His business was none of her concern, but the challenge in her skeptical tone got the best of him. "Your elderly neighbor, Mrs. Tremont, is a patient of mine. Her weight has dropped drastically, and her appetite continues to wane."

Her smug tone faded. "I'm sorry to hear that," she muttered, looking genuinely distressed.

"The woman has a craving for fresh venison. I apologize for trespassing, but I intend to provide it."

She lowered her eyes, and Jace couldn't help enjoying her contrite response.

"Had you not intervened with my deer, I'd have no reason to dally here. On *your* property," he added, just for the hell of it.

"Well, don't let me keep you," she snapped. "Good luck with Mrs. Tremont." Her hard look softened again, as did the harshness in her voice. "Please send her my regards."

With a lift of her chin, she collected her market basket from where it sat beside a log, then hurried away. Jace stared after her, absorbing the view. She held her head high, her stance rigid and aloof. Her frame was small but curvaceous, possessing the perfect measure of female proportions. Ample breasts, narrow waist, pleasing backside.

Of course, one had to get past the bloodstained dress to appreciate what lay beneath, but as a doctor who'd seduced dozens of nurses whose aprons were soaked with far worse, this posed no problem for Jace. Her slender form moved swiftly as she made her way down the path through the field, but her pace was slowing. He detected a slight limp in her gait, though from this distance, he couldn't be sure.

"Madeline Sutter," he mumbled, shaking his head. What kind of woman went about pulling arrows from dying deer?

Jace had met some odd people during the month since he'd arrived in town, but he'd yet to meet anyone like Miss Sutter. Dragging his gaze from the fading view of her, he squatted before the patch of blood in the grass where his deer had fallen.

From the amount of blood and crimson color, Jace agreed with Miss Sutter's assessment of the situation. The animal was certain to bleed to death before getting far. It had to be dead on its feet to have allowed her anywhere near it, let alone remove the arrow. How it summoned the stamina to move on, Jace hadn't a clue, but he knew it would bed down in dense cover as soon as it could. Like any diligent hunter, Jace was obligated to recover it.

He reexamined the arrow. The hair attached was coarse, dark gray with dark tips, and two or so inches long. This evidence indicated a perfect kill shot behind the shoulder, not in the gut, as the girl had claimed.

With a shake of his head, Jace stood, preparing to track the deer. He would find out the truth soon enough, though with a wounded deer, one could never be certain as to how soon that might be. Mrs. Tremont was in dire need of protein. Since the old woman had no husband or sons, Jace would do what he must to provide it.

It had taken only one house call to discover that the duties of the country doctor entailed catering to each patient on a more personal level than was possible with the human wreckage he'd treated at Pittsburgh Hospital. Although his office had yet to open officially, he already knew the hell of the emergency ward—and the endless misery that flowed through its wide double doors—was a stark contrast to a small-town practice. He could make a real difference in Misty Lake, and not just to the wealthy summer visitors. Here he'd have the time to focus on each patient case without the patch-them-up-and-ship-them-out approach of the hospital. The change would be just what he needed to replenish his spirit from the toll of the daily tragedy that had sucked him dry.

Inhaling deeply, he forged past the memory of his internship in the city and the suffocating despair that came along with it. The pine-scented breeze coursed through his senses, anchoring him back to the present. The beauty of his current surroundings lifted his mood. There was nothing like a walk in the woods and reconnecting with nature to remind him that he was alive.

Perhaps if he'd found some comparable diversion from his rote existence in the city, he might have fared better there. Not that it mattered now. He'd made a decision to build a practice in the country, and he intended to succeed come hell or high water. Even so, he knew that, as a stranger, he should expect some initial hostility and skepticism from Misty Lake's residents. Miss Sutter had merely acted upon the resentment that a lot of her neighbors were nursing privately.

Swatting at a horsefly, he took a few steps in the direction in which the deer had bolted, searching the ground for the blood trail that would lead to his prey. Bloody hoof prints led from the scene. Hunching down for a closer look, he followed the tracks to a birch log, scanning the ground as he moved. "What the…?"

Not a single droplet of blood lay anywhere in the vicinity of the tracks. Had the deer's wound simply stopped bleeding? He scratched his head, glancing around. The blood flow might have ebbed somewhat, but to cut off entirely without leaving a trace? Preposterous. There had to be a logical explanation. There always was. As a man of science, Jace was curious to know what the devil that explanation was.

He inspected the peeling bark on the decaying log, then saw something flutter on the ground behind it. He reached for the discarded leaf of paper trapped in the weeds. Miss Sutter's? He collected the thing, then read with interest the letter that was, indeed, addressed to Madeline Sutter.

The past is the past, my dear friend, and you must lay it to rest. Eventually, the town will follow suit.

Who was this strange woman he'd encountered in the middle of nowhere? The woman who refused to attend her friend's wedding, but had no qualms about dislodging an arrow from a wild animal or ordering a man twice her size off her property?

Madeline Sutter intrigued him, and few women accomplished that feat. Jace looked forward to meeting her again. He glanced toward the path through the field. Locating her residence wouldn't be difficult. And her dropped letter gave him the perfect excuse to pay her a visit. For the moment, though, he had a deer to track in the opposite direction.

He gathered his things, then headed into the woods. When he returned to town, he would ask around about his latest acquaintance. Whoever she was, he couldn't wait to find out more.

Chapter 2

Thankfully, the house was quiet when Maddie returned home. Since it was Saturday, Rhetta would be elbow-deep in laundry, and the echo of Gil's axe confirmed he was splitting wood out back. Grandfather took his daily nap promptly at noon, so Maddie was confident she could make it to her room undetected. She needed to change her clothes, as she hadn't the energy to explain her bloodstained dress either to her grandfather or to the loyal household staff.

Despite her aching leg, she raced up the wide staircase to her room at the end of the hall. Closing the door quietly behind her, she exhaled in relief. Sunlight poured through the windows, drenching her in golden warmth. Inside this room she always felt safe. During her recovery, she'd spent months confined to her bed, staring at the walls of her private infirmary until she knew each tiny rosette on the floral wallpaper, each curve of the glossy wood molding by heart. This room knew her just as well, for it had seen her at her worst.

The plush carpet had cushioned the impact of the numerous falls she'd suffered while forcing her shattered leg to support her weight, despite Doctor Filmore's orders to accept her lameness and resign herself to using a cane. The down pillows on the brass bed had absorbed her tears of pain and frustration when she'd feared he might be right. They'd muffled her screaming nightmares and cradled her head while she'd cried herself back to sleep. The thick draperies had shielded her from the world outside and the light of day she'd been too despondent to face.

In the safety of this room and the familiar furnishings, time stood still. Memories of her life before the accident, the friends and the moments she missed so much, lingered like cobwebs in every corner. Within the solitude of these walls, she could revel in the happy memories and wallow in the ugly ones without moving forward. This room held her past. Her lost dreams. Her secrets.

After undressing quickly, Maddie balled up the soiled dress and shoes and stuffed them into a pillowcase. She pushed the bundle into the back of the tall armoire, then closed it tight. She'd discard the mess at the first opportunity. Of course, Rhetta wouldn't make the task easy. The vigilant maid didn't miss a trick, but Maddie would concoct some way to dispose of the evidence.

She scrubbed her hands, then changed into a clean day dress and shoes. Exhausted, she plopped into the large chair by the window. The ache in her leg had intensified, but she'd grown used to the chronic pain. Leaning back in the chair, she closed her eyes. Her thoughts returned to Doctor Merrick. Jace. Her breath hitched. The vivid picture of his striking face filled her mind. Thoughts of his muscular body quickly followed.

For a moment in the forest, through eyes untainted by the story of her past, he had noticed her as a woman. She'd sensed his awareness—that certain glint that sparked in men's eyes when they saw something they liked. Of course their squabble about the deer had quickly doused that spark, but she'd felt his brief attraction nonetheless.

It had been ages since a man had looked at her that way. And twice as long since she'd enjoyed it. The unexpected encounter reminded her how much she missed the attention—how truly starved she was for it. Even now, she found herself savoring that morsel of a moment and how delicious she had felt in the warmth of his desire.

Maddie opened her eyes, frowning. Why on earth was she still thinking of the man? He was a doctor. A threat. She supposed it might be this very fear of him that attracted her. She'd seen the doubt in his intelligent eyes when she fed him her story about the wounded deer. The way he'd analyzed the bloody arrow spoke of a man who questioned things, a man who sought answers. A man who'd do what he must to get them.

For all she knew, he was still trudging through the woods, trying to track the animal. She'd sent him on a fool's errand when he was attempting to help Mrs. Tremont, and she couldn't ignore her nagging guilt for his wasted effort.

For the first time after using her gift, Maddie questioned her actions. She'd never before considered the possibility that her strange skills might hurt others as much as help them. She'd never given it much thought at all. Instead she'd acted emotionally, by instinct, when she'd revived the deer, and the sparrow that had crashed into the parlor windowpane, and the kitten that had gotten caught in the stable door and broken its neck. Could these acts of compassion have unknown consequences? And what of her attempts to heal Grandfather?

Her spirit sank as she mulled the problem. Damn Jace Merrick for dimming this one ray of light in her life. Her talent for healing was all that she had, but suddenly, thanks to the trespassing doctor, she was beginning to question whether it was truly a blessing.

An hour later, Maddie headed to the dining room for luncheon. Grandfather was already seated at the head of the long table, enjoying his afternoon glass of port. He looked so small in the high-back chair that had once made him seem like a looming Titan. He was a withered colossus now—fragile and alone.

She swallowed her grief and a lump of guilt. His failing health was beyond her control, but there was no denying she was the reason they'd eaten each meal of the past three years with empty chairs at their elbows.

"Good afternoon, Grandfather," she said, slipping into the chair at his right.

He lifted his glass in greeting, then took a quick sip. His hollow cheeks were pale. She resisted the urge to ask how he felt, remembering his request that she limit such inquiries to once a day at most. Honoring her promise was becoming increasingly difficult as her worries for Grandfather's health intensified. Whatever would she do without the stubborn old goat?

For a moment she was tempted to try to persuade Grandfather to seek treatment from the town's new doctor. But the household help kept him well informed of town news, and she strongly suspected that the clever man already knew plenty about Jace Merrick and had decided he would have less nagging from his beloved grandchild if the doctor's arrival remained a secret from her.

"Ah, Maddie. I can tell from that sour face of yours that you finally received a response from Amelia," he said.

She nodded, thankful to be diverted to a less frightening topic. In the face of Grandfather's failing health, the Amelia dilemma was but a small thing.

"She refuses to accept my regrets."

He smiled. Beneath his bushy gray brows his eyes twinkled with ageless wit.

"That doesn't surprise me." He set down his glass, his fingers trembling with the effort. "What does surprise me is that the Hogles allowed her to extend an invitation to you at all."

"Oh, you know Amelia," Maddie said with a sigh. "She probably refused to hold the wedding in Misty Lake unless I was included in the party. She loves Lester Hogle, but she wants me there. And Amelia always gets what she wants."

"Too true! She'll run that boy ragged, for sure." Grandfather's burst of laughter was strangled by a fit of deep coughing. Despite his claims to the contrary, these spells were becoming more frequent. His heart was weakening, and his condition was deteriorating at an alarming rate. She'd tried her best to heal the unsuspecting man, but each day it became more apparent that her nightly ministrations were ineffective against his disease. Poor circulation left him sallow, fluid swelled his chest and limbs, and now this chronic cough.

Maddie waited on tenterhooks until Grandfather finally caught his breath. He despised being coddled. In fact, he barely allowed the application of the salve she used to disguise her healing attempts. At seventy-two, he still had the same pride that helped him amass a great fortune as a young man. Wiping his mouth with his napkin, he cleared his throat, then continued as if nothing were amiss. "So it's settled then. You're attending."

"I must. For Amelia." She took a long breath. "For the girls."

He reached for his drink. Maddie rarely mentioned the accident to him anymore; it simply wasn't worth the effort. Grandfather had mourned the tragedy in his own way, in silence and denial—and he'd insisted she do the same. While he'd been a constant presence as she recovered from her injuries, she'd had to manage her grief in private.

She hated that she still harbored some resentment about this silly code of silence. Especially now, when Grandfather's health was so poor. She loved the man with all her heart, but he had imposed a critical distance between them by refusing to discuss what happened. Try as she might to ignore it, Maddie continued to feel the ache of their unsaid words through every crevice of her lonely soul. Several long moments passed before she spoke again.

"Pastor Hogle will be at the wedding."

Grandfather frowned. "To hell with Pastor Hogle."

"And Daniel."

"To hell with him, too." He took another sip of port. "You'll have to find your guts, girl, but you'll find them."

He spoke the truth with his usual curt elegance, and she was grateful for his support.

"I suppose you may go ahead and send for Cousin Marvin," she said.

He lowered his weary eyes to the drink in his trembling hand.

"About Marvin…" He studied the glass as though searching for words in its crimson contents. The lengthy pause signaled that the forthcoming news wouldn't be good. "Marvin is unable to escort you."

Her heart sank.

"He left for Paris last week. But perhaps I can—"

"No, Grandfather, you cannot. I love you to pieces for offering, but I won't have you jeopardizing your health by escorting me. This affair will be crowded and filled with people you loathe."

He didn't argue. He didn't have the strength to argue, let alone attend the wedding and the string of events leading up to it. Amelia had written of her plans for a shopping trip, a lakeside picnic, rehearsal dinner, and dance. In another lifetime, Maddie would have swanned happily through twice that number of parties without a second thought. Now, it all sounded so overwhelming.

Grandfather nodded in surrender. "My dancing is not what it used to be, anyway," he teased. "We'll devise a different plan."

Thanks to Cousin Marvin, they'd have to. Not that she could blame Marv for choosing the glitter of Paris over waltzing with his poor pariah cousin at a sleepy upstate wedding.

"Of course we will." She smiled with feigned optimism. *And we have a mere four weeks to do it.*

* * * *

Jace was pleased to see Mrs. Tremont eating the venison he'd procured from Les Toomey. After giving up his search for the deer he'd hit that morning, he'd resorted to accepting two pounds of venison in lieu of payment for stitching Les's finger. Had Jace known Les always had an ample supply of fresh venison on hand, he'd have asked for it earlier instead of wasting an entire day in the woods in pursuit of an animal that had vanished into thin air. But then he wouldn't have met the young woman he couldn't get out of his mind.

There was something so haunting about her. Those soulful brown eyes and flush cheeks. Those lips. Her delicate visage opposed the stiff pride in her shoulders, the brusque lift of her chin. Jace couldn't recall ever being so intrigued by a woman. Fearlessness was a rare quality in a woman, but one Miss Sutter seemed to possess in spades.

From her angry reaction, he'd obviously struck a nerve by questioning her sanity. But what the devil had she expected after her reckless behavior with a wild and wounded animal? Their strange encounter, while memorable, hadn't gone well. Stranger still was that Jace had been in Misty Lake for a month before crossing her path. Literally.

While the town would soon fill with summer guests from the city, Madeline Sutter was a local. Even the residents on the far outskirts of town had managed to sate their curiosity about the new doctor by stopping by his office or "accidentally" bumping into him somewhere.

Jace glanced around the kitchen of Mrs. Tremont's remote cottage in the woods, wondering if Madeline Sutter called such a place home. His curiosity became too much to contain.

"I met your neighbor this morning," he said. "Madeline Sutter."

Mrs. Tremont stopped chewing, then swallowed hard. "Oh, that one."

Not exactly the response he'd expected. "She asked me to send her regards."

With an unpleasant twist of her lips, she speared a piece of meat with her fork, then popped it into her mouth.

Jace waited as she chewed, but she offered nothing further on the subject. Her silence intrigued him.

"She lives with her grandfather?" he pressed.

She frowned, her eyes sinking into a sea of deep wrinkles. "Adam Sutter should have sent her away after the accident. Would have been better for everyone, the girl included."

"Accident?"

"Wagon accident, three years ago. Worst misfortune ever to strike this town." Her voice dipped low with the weight of her sorrow. "Madeline Sutter was one of four girls inside the wagon when it crashed into a tree." Mrs. Tremont set down her fork. "All four were killed."

Jace tilted his head, wondering for a moment if he'd heard her correctly. "But you said she was one of four—"

"She died, too."

Jace blinked.

"Mrs. Tremont, that doesn't make sense," he challenged, shaking his head.

"Sense or no sense, the girl was as dead as a doornail and laid out with the others until the next day."

He leaned forward. "What happened the next day?"

"She opened her eyes."

Christ Almighty. Jace sat back in his seat. He'd read of such extraordinary cases, where comatose patients awoke after days, sometimes weeks. Of course those patients weren't pronounced dead. Thinking on it, Jace supposed he could understand how it might happen, given the circumstances and Misty Lake's remote location.

Accidents involving multiple victims were always chaotic. The distraction of hysterical relatives and bystanders often hindered treatment. Especially in a small community like this one, where the physician knew the victims and their families personally. In all the confusion, Doctor Filmore had obviously missed Madeline's pulse. Jace blew out a breath as he imagined the scene. "That must have been quite a shock."

"It was terrifying," the old woman agreed. Closing her troubled eyes, she shuddered for effect. "To see her awake from the dead like she did…"

The words stopped him short. Mrs. Tremont didn't strike him as one prone to theatrics, but surely she couldn't be serious.

"Ma'am, you do realize that the doctor made a mistake." Jace paused. "Don't you?"

She pointed a bony finger.

"You, young man, are a stranger to Misty Lake. Doctor Benjamin Filmore is one of us. For over thirty years, he took care of this town, nursing us through typhoid and cholera and the worst times of our lives. He delivered our babies into this world and eased the suffering of those he ushered out. He wouldn't make such a mistake as this, and you'll not tell me otherwise. Not in my house." She rose from the table with a swiftness he hadn't thought she could muster. She returned with the coffee pot and refilled her cup. "Doctor Filmore was as stunned by her resurrection as the rest of us."

"Resurrec—" Jace stopped himself before his angry disbelief got the better of him. "Is that really what Doctor Filmore called it?"

Mrs. Tremont shrugged. "That's what everyone called it. At first."

"What do you mean?"

She picked up her fork and poked at the bits of meat on her plate. "Her leg was so badly broken Doctor Filmore said she'd never walk properly again. Doctor Reed from over in Stephentown agreed. No one saw her for months after the accident. Not even the doctor, since she refused any more treatment from him. Then one day, she comes parading into church, fit as a fiddle."

"She recovered?" Jace's surprise faded as he gathered where this line of argument was leading. "And?"

Releasing a huff of impatience, Mrs. Tremont clarified what her guest was obviously too thick to comprehend.

"Lightning doesn't strike twice, Doctor Merrick. Neither do miracles." She gestured with the fork. "There's something plain unnatural about the whole thing. Pastor Hogle even said as much when the girl first came back to service. The Lord may work in mysterious ways, he told us. But so too, does the Devil."

* * * *

Jace was still furious when he returned home hours later. After asking around, he'd discovered the entire town shared Mrs. Tremont's opinion of Madeline Sutter. And to think that Misty Lake's esteemed pastor had encouraged the slander! The rumors of Madeline's odd recovery were poisonous enough without Hogle's interference. Adding religion to the mix simply polished the whole mess to a high sheen.

The pastor's only child was one of the girls who'd been killed in the accident—but grief was poor justification for Hogle's actions. How could a man of faith feed his devoted flock such nonsense? Jace shook his head. If the people of Misty Lake revered Hogle half as much as they had trusted Doctor Filmore, they'd blindly opened their mouths like a nest full of baby sparrows and gulped the venom right down.

Jace unlocked the door to the house that served as a physician's office in the front parlor rooms and a dwelling for the live-in physician in the back. Ben Filmore had relinquished the house to Jace after he and his wife moved their belongings to the hotel. The space would be more than adequate, once everything was set to rights. Currently, however, the place was a mess.

On Jace's first night in Misty Lake, a tree limb had crashed through the roof of his new parlor during a nasty storm, delaying the opening of his practice indefinitely. Furniture was piled in the corner. The musty rug still hadn't dried completely from the rain that had poured into the room, and he'd be sweeping up acorns for weeks.

Thanks to his neighbor, Henry Whalen, repairs were almost complete, but the clutter would take many long days to organize. If Jace were half as superstitious as Mrs. Tremont and the others, he'd have taken the unfortunate incident as a sign of ugly things to come.

Jace sidled between the crates and other debris and made his way into his office. A tall cabinet housed drawers full of files on everyone Ben had treated, which Jace assumed included every resident in town. He directed his search to Madeline Sutter's file. Upon retrieving it, he fingered through the contents, bypassing her early history, childhood illnesses and the like, until he found the documents relating to the accident.

Madeline Sutter, age twenty-one, deceased.

That was it? Jace shuffled through the file, searching for more, but no other details followed that final notation. He leaned back, running a hand through his hair. Mrs. Tremont had said Madeline suffered a badly broken leg in the accident, but the file contained no report of that injury either. Jace would have to go to the source. He needed an explanation, a sound voice of reason after all the rubbish he'd heard today, and he needed it now.

Doctor Filmore was still in town but not for long. He'd informed Jace last week that upon finishing up some loose ends with the various committees with which he was involved, he'd be joining his wife in Boston, where their adult children now lived, and his train to the city was departing today. Checking his watch, Jace realized he had only hours to catch Filmore before the old man left town for good.

Jace hurried from the office and walked the short distance to the Lakeview Hotel. The smell of lemon oil and freshly polished furniture greeted him as he walked through the door. The mid-May weather had been particularly mild, and the hotel's staff was busy preparing for the early influx of summer residents.

According to the hiring committee that selected Jace as the town's physician, Misty Lake had recently become a popular retreat destination for affluent urban families. Boating, swimming, and other outdoor recreations tempted droves of city dwellers seeking country amusements. A boon for local business. Prospective patients for Jace.

Jace offered greetings as he breezed through the wood-paneled lobby. Hanging floral arrangements wafted on the crisp breeze sailing in from the row of open windows facing the lake. He made his way upstairs to the doctor's room, then knocked on the door.

"Tell me about Madeline Sutter," he demanded as he stepped into the room.

Doctor Filmore froze. He stared at the open door, looking ready to bolt. "She hasn't been my patient in years," he said, closing the door. "After the accident, she refused my treatment."

"Is it any wonder?"

The insult seemed to spur more shame than anger as Doctor Filmore stared at Jace like a guilty child.

"Mistakes happen, Ben, I understand that," Jace said. "The shock and disbelief over the dead girls, the collective hysteria. The confusion. She was insentient; her pulse was weak. But when she regained consciousness after all those hours, you had to have known she'd been comatose and not dead."

Doctor Filmore averted his eyes.

Jace had received some strange responses to his queries about the accident, but he hadn't expected one from Ben—a physician. Jace suddenly realized he was no longer looking at a doctor. He was looking at a man. A man afflicted with the same grief and misery that plagued the others.

Yet as tragic as this accident was, it was no excuse for what followed. Ben hadn't offered any explanation for Madeline's stunning recovery, so people let their pain form one. The result was cruel and depraved. And despite his oath as a physician, despite his morals as a human being, the good doctor had done nothing to stop it.

"The girl needed your help, Ben." With each silent moment, Jace grew angrier. Denial was the coward's way out, and it was a path for which Jace had no tolerance. He may as well have been speaking to the wall—or his father. "Say something, Goddamn it, Ben."

"I have a train to catch."

Jace shook his head in disgust. "You son of a bitch." He turned on his heel and walked out the door.

Chapter 3

Grandfather called out again, prompting Maddie to quicken her pace down the stairs.

"We have a guest," he announced from the parlor.

The news stopped her in her tracks. They never had guests. She resumed walking toward the sound of voices echoing through the foyer. She entered the parlor to see Jace Merrick standing by the fireplace, his brawny form a stark contrast to Grandfather's frail figure beside him. She stood motionless in the arched doorway as his presence sank in.

"It's a pleasure to see you again, Miss Sutter," Jace said.

His polished appearance caught her off guard. Dressed in a dark coat and trousers, he looked even more impressive than he had four days before. His thick hair was brushed back from his face, which was freshly shaven and deadly handsome. Her nerves knotted inside her, strangling her voice so much that she could only respond with a nod. Whatever was he doing here? Had he somehow discovered her secret and come to give her away?

"Doctor Merrick told me the two of you crossed paths the other day," Grandfather said.

Her heart pounded as her gaze flew to Jace. His blue eyes held hers for what seemed like forever but hinted nothing about what he might say next. She pursed her lips, disliking him immensely for his reserve.

"Thank you again, Miss Sutter, for directing me back to town. If it weren't for you, I might still be lost in those woods."

She exhaled in relief.

"How fortunate she found you." Grandfather turned to Maddie. "I'm surprised you failed to mention your discovery during our discussions of late." A smile trembled on his lips.

"I...uh. It must have slipped my mind," she said, moving into the room.

"Have a seat, Doctor Merrick." Grandfather gestured toward the sofa. "Rhetta will bring tea."

Maddie took a seat in one of the adjacent chairs before the men followed suit.

Grandfather leaned forward on the gold-handled cane between his knees. "So tell me, Doctor Merrick, what brings a big city doctor, like yourself, to Misty Lake?"

"My desire to sleep." Jace smiled. It was a simple little smile that lasted the briefest of moments. Yet it managed to turn her insides to mincemeat.

A less reclusive, less pathetic woman might remain unaffected by the flash of straight teeth, the perfect mouth. But not Maddie. She gave a stiff fluff to her beige skirts, loathing him all the more for his appealing smile and good humor.

"Sleep?" she asked in a desperate attempt to focus on something other than his enticing lips.

"Working night duty in the emergency ward offered little to none. I look forward to building my practice here, where my schedule will be less challenging and my eyes will close more often."

"How's business faring so far?" Grandfather asked.

"I'm busy with house calls, but I've yet to open the office officially. When I arrived last month, I was greeted by a fierce storm and awoken by a tree limb crashing through my roof."

"Oh my," Maddie said.

"That storm was a mean one," Grandfather said. "Hovered over the lake for hours."

Jace nodded. "The damage to my patient waiting room was extensive and forced me to delay opening my practice."

"Unfortunate, indeed," Grandfather said.

"Roof repairs are almost complete, though, and once the mess inside is put to order, I can finally unpack and set up."

"Well, good luck to you!" Grandfather waved his cane with enthusiasm. "And I must say I'm pleased Filmore finally hung up his stethoscope. I'm only sorry I didn't choke him with it while I had the strength."

Maddie pinned him with a scolding glare.

"Grandfather, please."

He waved her away. "You'll find I'm a man who speaks my mind, Doctor Merrick. I haven't the time nor the wind to waste on decorum, so you must forgive my bluntness, even if my granddaughter can't."

Maddie rolled her eyes.

"Of course," Jace said, clearly amused.

Rhetta whisked into the room, depositing a tea tray on the table. Her shy glimpse at their guest quickly prompted another.

Maddie rolled her eyes again. This house had gone far too long without company. "Thank you, Rhetta," she said.

With a nod of her capped head, Rhetta left them to their tea.

"So, you don't miss the excitement of the hospital?" Maddie asked as she poured the tea.

His smile faded. "My memories sustain me. Brutality, disease, starvation. All the worst of human suffering housed under one convenient roof." His expression was casual, but she saw the dismay in his eyes, felt his tension as she handed him the cup. "You have a very fine house, sir," he said, glancing around. "I've passed it often on my house calls."

"We have the best site on the lake." Grandfather puffed his chest. "What started as a summer retreat eventually became home. Maddie oversees the entire estate. Account books and all."

"Is that so?" Jace turned to her with a nod of approval. "Very impressive, Miss Sutter." He regarded her intently, his gaze dropping to her mouth.

"Please, call me Madeline."

Something flickered in his eyes. "Madeline." He spoke her name as though testing the sound, and she'd never heard anything better. Straightening in her seat, she shook off the sudden heat that slivered through her.

"My granddaughter keeps things running smoothly. I rest easy in her capable hands." He released a long sigh. "Speaking of rest. I hope you don't mind, Doctor Merrick, but it's time for my nap." Grandfather endeavored to rise, and Jace stood to help him.

"It was good to meet you, sir."

Grandfather steadied himself with the handshake Jace offered. "And very good to meet you, young man. Please stay and enjoy your tea." He tossed a wink at Maddie, and she lowered her eyes, hoping Jace didn't see it.

"Please don't mind my grandfather, Doctor Merrick. It's been a while since we've had company."

Jace returned to his seat. "Call me Jace." His gaze followed Grandfather's excruciatingly slow departure from the room. "How long has he been ill?"

His observation didn't surprise her. Although he was a doctor, one had only to glance at Grandfather to detect his poor health. To Jace's credit, he'd refrained from humbling Grandfather by mentioning it in front of him.

"Going on four years now," she said.

"Rheumatic fever?"

She nodded. "The after effects are more apparent every day."

"Heart disease progresses at various rates, depending on the patient. There's little that can be done to stop it."

"Yes, I know." She sighed. Even Maddie's miraculous power hadn't checked the forward march of Grandfather's illness.

"I'd be happy to examine him if—"

"Thank you, but there's little that can be done. You said so yourself. Besides, he'd never allow it." She shook her head. "After being examined by a specialist in Albany, he accepted his condition, and now he refuses to be poked and prodded by more doctors."

"His words, I suppose?"

Maddie smiled.

"If he changes his mind…"

"He won't." She took a sip of her tea and tried to relax. "I also owe you thanks for not mentioning the incident with the deer."

"I see no need to worry your grandfather with your recklessness." His brow arched as he pointed his finger in a playful threat. "So long as you don't go repeating such a stunt."

She shook her head, grateful for the reprieve. "No, of course not."

"I never found the deer, by the way."

"No?" she asked, trying to sound sufficiently surprised.

"But I did find something else." He reached into his coat pocket and pulled out Amelia's letter.

Maddie gaped in surprise. In her haste to escape him that day, she hadn't realized she'd lost it.

"I assumed you'd want your letter returned, since it's personal."

She blanched, snatching the folded page from his hand. "But not so personal you refrained from reading it?"

"I had to read it to discern ownership." He leaned forward. "Though I must admit, I was hoping to learn more about you."

For a moment she felt flattered. How could she not? A handsome man was declaring interest in her. The urge to sail off on the sappy emotion was overwhelming. And pathetic. She stiffened, cursing the lilt in her spirit for what it was: a prelude to pain and disappointment. She'd had far more than her fill of both.

"You have merely to ask around town for enlightenment."

"I did that as well."

She stared, startled by his honesty. He'd been as kind to her as he'd been to Grandfather—avoiding any mention of her diseased reputation in the hope of sparing her feelings. But she sensed he'd gotten an earful just the same.

She dropped her gaze to the floor, disappointment prickling under her skin. Why this stranger's opinion of her mattered, she wasn't sure. She knew only that it did, and the revelation filled her with anger. Anger at him for prying and anger at herself for caring that he had.

She waved the letter. "Well, thank you for returning it." She stood. "I'm sure you're still busy settling in, so I'll show you to the door."

Ignoring her abrupt dismissal, he remained seated, staring up at her. "Upon going through Doctor Filmore's files, I came across yours."

She braced herself against a rush of dread. "And?"

"And I'm intrigued. Survivors of trauma often struggle with emotional after-effects, and some are forced to seek treatment for the assault on their mental faculties. Others find ways to cope with the stress. As a doctor, I'd like to know more about your injuries and recovery." His expression stilled. "Would you mind answering a few questions?"

And there it was. The reason for his interest. It wasn't physical attraction to her that had brought him here; it was clinical curiosity, nothing more. She felt like a fool.

"I would very much mind," she huffed.

"But—"

"As I'm sure you can understand, I don't wish to talk about it."

He stood to face her. "But your case is astounding."

"My case?" She glared at him. "This is my life, Doctor Merrick. Please don't reduce the sum of it to the ridiculous things you've learned from that old fool's files."

Absorbing her words, his expression softened. "He made a mistake, Madeline."

"He did more than that." She clenched her teeth to stave off tears. "He let them all believe…" She took a deep breath. "You know what they think of me. That I'm some oddity of nature."

"I can help change that."

She shook her head. "It's too late. After what Doctor Filmore—"

"Filmore was a coward. The man declared you dead, for Christ's sake. Then to cover his mistake, instead of admitting it, he allowed people to think there was some other dark and mysterious force involved."

She swallowed hard. She'd waited for so long for someone to say it that she hadn't realized how badly she'd needed those bittersweet words until Jace uttered them. The desperation in her voice was clear when she pressed him for more. "And you don't believe that?"

He frowned. "Of course not. I'm a doctor. There's a reasonable explanation for everything."

Well, certainly not everything. But she wasn't about to go pointing that out.

"I can help you. I can help the people of Misty Lake understand that you're not some sort of malevolent aberration. Your case is rare; there's no disputing that. But you're not cursed or blessed or any other such nonsense."

The more he talked and the more he tried to convince her he could help, the more furious she became. It was too late for this now. For three years she'd dealt with her overwhelming sorrow alone. She'd shouldered the guilt and the rage. No one would listen when she'd needed to be heard. Not even Grandfather, which hurt the most. She'd literally talked to the walls to spare him the discomfort of consoling her, and she'd be damned if she would admit to this stranger that her solitary recovery had been as traumatic as the accident itself.

Jace's voice softened. "Filmore was a coward, but you're not. You couldn't have recovered if you were." He took a step toward her. "Give me the opportunity to study your case, Madeline."

She had to steel herself against melting in the warmth of his eyes, the sound of her name on his lips. "And what have you to gain from it all?"

"Knowledge. Knowledge that might help others."

And who was there to help me? "I'm sorry, Doctor Merrick. My answer is no."

* * * *

Maddie awoke the next day ill-rested and weary, having spent the wee hours of the evening fretting her twin problems: her confrontation with Jace Merrick and her decision to attend Amelia's wedding. Gathering her exhausted wits about her, she concluded she would make the first step toward reentering society by refreshing her very much outdated wardrobe. She hoped that acquiring some new gowns would armor her for the ordeal ahead, and in that spirit, she presented herself at Mrs. March's dress boutique immediately upon its opening.

After enduring Mrs. March's less-than-enthusiastic reaction to her first patron of the day, Maddie was ushered to a wobbly bench in the far corner of the shop. She sat in the dreary light, poring through book after book of dress patterns, determined to find something dazzling. While she might be forced to attend the wedding and the slew of other prenuptial events alone, she'd be attending in style.

Maddie turned another page in the book. She tried to focus on the patterns, but her mind kept returning to her conversation with Doctor Merrick and his startling request to "study her case," as he'd called it. He wanted to analyze her as he might a rat in a cage, to see how she'd fared since the accident. Why did men of science have to analyze everything? Was it not in their nature to simply let things be? He'd told her he'd wanted knowledge from her that might help others. While Maddie believed this was partially true, she suspected it was his ego—and his desire to be the first person to explain something inexplicable—that drove the doctor's need to delve deeper. Whatever the reason, one thing remained clear. Jace Merrick saw her as the others did, as an oddity. True, he had a medical explanation for her revival after the accident, but he regarded her as a specimen to be studied, nonetheless. How foolish she was for having hoped otherwise. There was something about the man and the way she felt in his presence, as if he'd roused her after years of hibernation. The feeling was both exciting and terrifying. And immensely annoying.

In matters of men, Maddie was accustomed to holding the upper hand. Once upon a time she could have charmed Jace Merrick out of his boots. The Fair Five were the very opposite of wallflowers, and most people had thought Maddie as the boldest of the bunch. Flirtation was a powerful device, and one she'd wielded with skill. How easy it was to entice a man with a smile or a bat of the eyes. Would the good doctor be so easy to seduce? The appealing thought made her flush.

"Anything yet?" Mrs. March called through the bolts of fabric and ribbon.

"Not yet," Maddie replied with a start.

Mrs. March hurried away, frustration echoing in the clipped sound of her footsteps. Although Maddie couldn't see it, she knew the rude woman's mouth was pursed tighter than the gray bun on her head.

Maddie continued to browse the next book, turning page after page, until she saw it. The perfect dress for the rehearsal dinner and dance. She smiled, staring at the pattern. The form-fitting bodice, the cascading layers of silk and lace.

"Good morning, Miss Sutter."

Maddie's spine stiffened in dread as she recognized the pretentious cadence of her former fiancé's voice. Dragging her gaze from the book on her lap, she steadied her nerves, then looked up to face him.

"Daniel."

He stared down at her, his green eyes drinking in the sight of her in the same thirsty way that used to curl her toes. Presently, it made her want to retch. Seeing him after all this time, and here in the dress shop, was surprise enough. It took her several long moments to force her attention to the woman on his arm.

"May I present Miss Lucinda Brewer. My betrothed."

Hearing the news was like taking a slap. But the sting of shock subsided as Maddie absorbed the brunt of it, determined to maintain her composure. She'd had three years to prepare for this. Three long years during which she'd imagined the moment she'd come face to face with her replacement. *A woman more suited to being my wife,* he'd said at their last meeting.

"How do you do?" Maddie whispered through the memory of those crushing words.

"I'm very well, thank you." Even the dismal lighting couldn't shadow Miss Brewer's radiant complexion and glimmering blond curls. "I've heard so much about you." Her kind expression confirmed that she had, indeed, heard plenty, and Maddie shriveled beneath the woman's pensive smile. Miss Brewer's eyes harbored no rancor, no jealousy, just an unmistakable look of compassion that left Maddie breathless. And utterly humiliated.

Daniel silenced his fiancée with a firm pat to her arm. The reprimand sent Miss Brewer's gaze to the floor, along with Maddie's sinking confidence.

"We're in town for Cousin Lester's wedding," he said.

While Maddie had expected Daniel would attend, the wedding was more than three weeks away. She flipped the page of the book.

"You're early," she replied.

"We wished to extend the trip to give Lucinda the chance to get to know everyone."

Maddie glanced up. He smiled, a beaming smile full of perfect teeth and arrogance. She smiled back, acidly.

"How nice."

He abandoned all pretenses for a moment, his smirk vanishing without a trace. The man actually looked disappointed that she hadn't fallen to pieces at his feet, and she congratulated herself for holding her emotions so firmly in check. But the respite was fleeting, and after a beat, Daniel resumed his smug assault with renewed vigor.

"Amelia will, no doubt, miss your presence at her nuptials," he said.

His false regret was too much. The hair on the back of her neck rose with her temper. How dare he assume she would decline the invitation? How dare he assume anything at all?

"I wouldn't dream of disappointing my dearest friend."

His eyes widened. "You plan to attend?"

Even Miss Brewer seemed stunned.

"Certainly," Maddie cooed. "Why ever would you think I wouldn't?"

"I assumed your grandfather wasn't up to escorting you."

"He's not."

Daniel's eyes narrowed in warning. "Consider the impropriety of attending unescorted. People will talk."

Maddie's blood boiled under her skin.

"They always do." She shrugged. "Unlike you, I don't allow mere talk to guide my actions." The barb left him speechless, which suited her fine. "But what makes you think I'll be attending unescorted?"

"I…"

"You've been away a long time."

He studied her, his irises darkening with something unrecognizable. "From what I hear of your situation, little has changed."

Maddie clenched the book in her hands. Tears burned in the back of her throat. After he'd broken her heart and their engagement, she expected his pity, his guilt. Even his usual condescension. What she hadn't expected, though, was spite. At this moment, her former love resembled his uncle, the pinched-faced Pastor Hogle, and Daniel's suddenly triumphant expression made her wonder how she'd ever cared for him at all.

"So, tell me, Madeline. Who is this escort of yours?"

His question filled her ears with the sound of a challenge. The couple stared, awaiting her answer. Maddie wanted to run. Instead, she reacted in the moment. In anger. In defense of her pride.

"Who else but my fiancé?"

He blinked hard but recovered quickly.

"Your fiancé?" His skeptical gaze trapped her in a vise-like grip. "And who might that be?"

He sought to rip away her last shred of dignity, but she refused to let go. Consequences be damned, she simply could not resist.

"Doctor Jace Merrick."

Chapter 4

Oh Lord, what had she done? Maddie held her breath until Daniel and his fiancée departed the shop. She exhaled an audible sigh, heart pounding.

She estimated she had all of an hour, perhaps less, before the shocking news of her engagement spread through town. She shot to her feet, trying to stay calm. Once the drumming pulse at her temples receded to a level where she could actually hear her own thoughts, she contemplated her next move.

She had to get to Jace before anyone else did.

Smoothing her skirts, she glanced into the mirror by the wall. The beige day dress and ancient straw hat she'd chosen that morning made her look mousy and plain. Inconspicuous. Since the accident, she had preferred to fade discreetly into the background of things for obvious reasons. But today she could not afford subtlety.

"Mrs. March," she called. "Mrs. March!"

The sound of the woman's footsteps grew louder. The measuring tape draped around her neck dangled from her hefty bosom as she halted in front of Maddie, hands on hips.

"What is it? Have you finally decided on something?"

Maddie glanced to the forgotten book of patterns on the bench. "No, no," she said, shaking her head. "But I wish to purchase the blue hat in the window."

Mrs. March huffed. "I'll have it wrapped, and you may stop back for it tomorrow." She started away.

"I shall need it immediately."

The woman stopped, her furrowed face resembling a month-old potato.

"If you could please just get it down from the window. I wish to wear it home."

Mrs. March drummed her fingers on her ample hips, contemplating the request.

"Very well." The inconvenience of undressing the window display was apparently worth the sale. Money was money, after all, even if it came from Madeline Sutter's pocket.

Maddie followed on the woman's clipped heels to the front of the shop. Mrs. March climbed onto a stool to retrieve the hat, thrust it toward Maddie, and then stepped aside. Maddie placed the hat on her head, quite pleased by her reflection in the mirror. The color suited her nicely. She adjusted the flouncy brim, admiring the weave and the cluster of silk flowers.

It had been ages since she'd purchased anything so fashionable. She'd abandoned her frivolous pursuit of the latest styles long ago, along with so many of her other favorite amusements.

"Thank you, Mrs. March." Maddie paid for the hat. "I'll return later for the old straw," she said as she hurried from the shop.

She walked toward the doctor's house, playing in her mind how she'd approach the matter. There was no sense trying to guess how Jace would react to hearing the news of his sudden engagement, so she pushed all such distressing speculation from her head. She'd no choice but to proceed.

The only way she could stroll into Amelia's wedding and face Daniel and the others was on the arm of her fiancé. She would simply have to charm Doctor Merrick into playing along. True, winning him over would entail offering to answer his dreaded questions about her recovery, but compared to the humiliation she'd suffer if he failed to escort her, the invasion of her privacy seemed minor.

Fear tightened her chest. Jace's refusal to help would prove disastrous. She was already a pariah, an abomination. Why on earth had she risked adding pathetic liar to the list?

She inhaled a deep breath to summon her courage. As Jace had mentioned, she wasn't a coward. If she had learned anything about herself during her recovery, it was that she possessed real strength. Which meant she'd find some way to turn these unfortunate events to her favor—even if it killed her. First, she'd appeal to Jace's thirst for knowledge. Her case was astounding, hadn't he said so himself? He would not spurn the rare opportunity she presented; she was sure of it. She made a final adjustment to her hat, standing taller. If professional considerations were not enough to sway him, she'd dispatch every flirtatious weapon in her rusty arsenal to win him over. He might be an egotistical doctor, but he was still a man.

Before she knew it, she was standing in front of the doctor's residence. She glanced up toward the sound of hammering above. Henry Whalen, town handyman and former friend, frowned down at her from the rooftop as he pounded away. Apparently, Jace had enlisted Henry's service in repairing his roof.

Shrugging off Henry's snub, Maddie stared at the house to which she'd sworn never to return. The peeling white shutters and neglected flower boxes had the same forlorn look as they had on her last visit, an ominous reminder of the nightmare she'd endured inside these walls. The blinding pain in her leg. The endless interrogation. The stunned faces staring down at her. *Do you remember your name? Do you know where you are?*

Butterflies took flight in her stomach. Closing her eyes to steady her nerves, she charged up to the porch. She blew out a breath and knocked on the door.

Jace answered wearing a wrinkled shirt and a look of surprise. His disheveled appearance and the open book lodged under his arm made it evident she'd interrupted his work. Here stood a man who spent his time wisely. Convincing him to squander it in service of petty lies would be no easy feat.

"Good morning, Jace." She enhanced the chipper greeting with a beaming smile.

His wary expression told her she'd have to tone it down.

"Madeline." He stepped aside as she swept past him into the house.

She scanned the desk tucked in the windowless alcove to the left. A lamp glowed over piles of papers and books. His coat hung from the chair he'd abandoned to answer the door.

"I don't mean to intrude…" She murmured some pleasantries regarding the weather, that it was a fine day for walking. The empty chitchat she'd perfected over the years rolled easily from her tongue. "Grandfather and I were just discussing how pleased we are that you moved to Misty Lake. This town can use a doctor with your experience."

She sashayed to the front room in dramatic style. Maintaining a semblance of grace proved difficult in the room's alarming disarray. Meandering through the clutter, she edged past gaping trunks and crates, skirts swishing.

"You're looking well." He dropped the book to a chair as a sly smile crept onto his face.

"Why, thank you." Puffing her chest, she whirled toward him, assuming a pose that would heighten his view. "I feel wonderfully fit." He regarded her quizzically, as though she'd said something odd. Relaying the state of one's health to a doctor seemed appropriate. The sudden glint in his eyes seemed anything but.

His gaze trailed up and down the length of her, but this was no clinical inspection. Awareness shivered down her spine. His blue eyes caressed her body like a physical touch, leaving gooseflesh in its wake. He moved closer. An air of urgency engulfed her. She'd poked a sleeping bear, faced him in the danger of his own den, and yet she stood unafraid. Quite the opposite, actually.

"New hat?" he asked.

Her confidence soared. She smiled, genuinely pleased by his notice. She gave a few dainty taps to the brim.

"This old thing?"

Grinning, he reached toward her.

The heat of his nearness pulsed through her veins. Breath hitched in her throat.

With a sharp tug, he tore off the price tag.

Maddie cringed. Lowering her eyes, she directed a silent curse to Mrs. March and her intentional oversight. She glanced up at Jace. Despite the sinking feeling, he could see straight through her, she muddled on.

"As I was saying, Grandfather and I are certain your practice here will be very successful."

"Why don't you stop fluffing my feathers, and tell me why you're here?"

She opened her mouth to protest but sighed instead. So much for charming him. Apparently her days as an irresistible belle were behind her, along with the best days of her life. She acknowledged the loss, turning so as not to look directly in Jace's eyes.

"I've had a change of heart." She dragged a gloved finger along the dusty edge of a nearby table, then faced him again. "I've decided to answer your questions about my ordeal."

His brow arched as he considered her in that way he seemed to consider everything. Skeptically.

"Why?"

His surprising lack of enthusiasm deflated her poise. "I…have a favor to ask in return."

"Your grandfather?" Lines of concern framed his eyes; his mouth was drawn tight.

In that briefest of moments she glimpsed who he was. A serious professional utterly devoted to the welfare of others. Her admiration of him was genuine. This man's work had meaning—true value—and suddenly she felt ashamed for involving him in some trivial charade to recover her pride.

"No, Grandfather's fine."

Jace took another step closer. The scent of him wafted toward her, scattering her thoughts. That strange sensation returned, that force of attraction that pulled and tempted her body in a most discomfiting way.

"What is it you need?"

His husky tone held the promise of things she couldn't describe and yet somehow desired. Something so close and yet so far away. All at once the question flew from her lips.

"Would you escort me to a wedding next month?"

"Your friend Amelia's."

She nodded, knowing he'd read all about it in the letter he'd found.

"That could be arranged."

She exhaled in relief; she was halfway there.

"Since you're kind enough to act as escort, I wish to ask a slight something more of you." She gave a demure smile and a coy toss of her hair.

He pursed his lips in return. "Out with it."

She took a quick breath for the courage to proceed. In for a penny, in for a pound.

"I'd like you to attend not only as my escort, but as my fiancé as well."

His eyes bulged, and his arms dropped to his sides.

"It would only be temporary," she assured him. "After the wedding, I will jilt you, of course."

"Jilt *me*?" He coughed.

"Why yes. I can't very well regain my reputation if you jilt me."

"So that's what all this is about." He circled his finger in the air, encompassing her less-than-stellar performance. "Regaining your reputation."

"That's none of your concern."

"Oh, but I think it is—especially if we're to be married." He smiled wolfishly. "And beyond that, it's disappointing. And here I felt flattered."

She bristled at his teasing tone. "I must attend as a properly engaged woman. Propriety is everything to these people."

"And what of my reputation as the jilted party?" His mouth quirked, and she frowned at his joking tone.

"Men don't have reputations. They have prowess," she snapped. "Besides, you're a doctor. The only opinion that matters to you is your own."

This garnered a smile.

"Will you do it?"

His smile faded as he tilted his head. The tender expression overwhelmed her. His eyes shone with compassion. Reluctance. She stared into the blue depths, saw his refusal rising to the surface.

"Madeline—"

"Please, Jace. You must."

Her desperate tone had signaled a warning. She saw it at once. His shoulders stiffened, and the softness fled from his face.

"And why is that?"

She'd prefer to bite off her tongue than proceed, but she'd no choice now other than to tell him the truth.

"Because the damage is done. I've already announced it."

"Announced…" His narrowed eyes flashed wide. "Our engagement?" He shifted his weight against his surprise. "You announced our engagement?"

"I had to. I'm sorry."

He blinked, shook his head, looking addled.

"Allow me to explain."

A vein emerged at his throat. Blood crept up his neck, flooding his face. "You'd damn well better explain."

"Please, calm down."

Planting his feet, he crossed his arms on his chest and glowered down at her.

"By all means, please enlighten me as to the reason for my recent engagement."

She grappled for words. "Amelia is the only friend I have left. I must attend her wedding, but my cousin Marvin is unable to escort me." Jace listened, unaffected. Maddie lowered her eyes, rambling in the shadow of his angry regard. "I had hoped to find another suitable escort, but before I had the opportunity, Daniel and his fiancée cornered me at the dress shop."

"Daniel?"

Attempting to contain her anger at Daniel was fruitless. Bitterness laced every word.

"Daniel Hogle. My former fiancé."

"And the plot thickens."

She scowled at his arrogant tone. As if he had the slightest understanding of what Daniel's desertion had cost her.

"Daniel pretended to express regret that I could not attend the wedding—because he, like everyone else, assumes I'll never find a man foolish enough or desperate enough to serve as my escort." Her anger again gave way to pain. "I can withstand the hatred. But the pity…" She forced a smile over her shame, lowering her eyes. "My pride got the better of me, and I spit out a lie." She glanced up.

"And just how do you propose to substantiate your lie to the good people of Misty Lake?" he asked with a strong dose of doubt. "Considering we've known each other for less than a week?"

"I've already thought about that," she said, encouraged by his question. "You mentioned you go out on house calls each day and have passed my house several times."

He tilted his head. "Go on."

"Everyone knows of Grandfather's failing health. For all they know you could very well have been treating him during house calls this past month since you've arrived in town."

"Are you suggesting I lie?"

She frowned. He looked so genuinely aghast by the prospect, she felt like a criminal for corrupting his virtue. "You wouldn't actually have to lie. You would merely allow people to assume what they will." Maddie tossed her head toward the sound of the incessant hammering above. "One word to Henry would be enough. When it comes to me, the gossip flies faster than the wind through this town. They'll believe it, trust me."

"Seems you've thought of everything," he said.

"I had hoped you'd agree to the ruse in exchange for the opportunity to study my case."

His face was unreadable, cool as a stone. She was doomed.

Several torturous moments passed as Maddie awaited her fate.

"Unfortunately, I've come to realize I haven't the time to study your case. I must prepare for my patients, and as you can see, that felled limb left this office in a state of chaos. Setting things to rights will involve tremendous effort. Not to mention the bookwork that needs to be completed before I can accept new debts." He rubbed his fine chin as a shrewd look crossed his face. "Unless…"

He dangled the word like a carrot, and she couldn't resist. "Unless?"

"Unless I found someone to assist me."

She thinned her lips. This was not going as planned. He was supposed to be so interested in the story of her recovery, he'd agree to anything. Or else so overset by her charm that he'd willingly cede the upper hand. Jace's sly grin gave her the distinct feeling she'd never stood a chance.

"Your grandfather mentioned your skill at maintaining accounts. Perhaps you—"

"You want me to work here? For you?" The suggestion was preposterous for reasons only she understood. To be trapped in this office in the company of sick and wounded people would be a nightmare. She'd be unable to heal patients in Jace's presence and yet watching them suffer wasn't a reasonable option either. The problem was that the man had her over a barrel, and he knew it.

"The arrangement would be only temporary." He smirked. "Just until you jilt me, of course."

A maelstrom of emotions spun through her. Confusion, distress, and relief. She could barely think in the beam of that blasted smile.

"Working here will give credence to the ruse. You'd be helping your fiancé set up housekeeping and his medical practice. It makes perfect sense," he added. "You may begin on Monday. Ten o'clock."

She felt herself nod, although she couldn't be sure. In three short days she'd be working here. Her mind reeled as she turned to leave—there seemed to be nothing left to say.

"As your employer, I'll expect you to be prompt."

She rolled her eyes as she moved toward the door. He followed behind. "Oh, and one more thing."

She stopped, regrets pelting her like hailstones. With a single thoughtless fib, she'd precipitated this whole enormously idiotic arrangement. But there was little she could do to change that now. She turned to face him with a look of surrender. "Yes?"

He pulled her into his arms.

Her mouth fell open, heart racing against the solid wall of his chest. Her senses swirled with the smell of worn linen and the hot flesh beneath. She blinked, met his eyes, feeling drunk. She didn't move. She didn't want to. His grip on her tightened, and she was overcome by a truth she couldn't deny. Whether she'd planned it or not, she'd named him as her fiancé because she'd hoped to land here. In these arms. His eyes locked with hers. The moment stretched to eternity. His gaze dipped to her mouth, and he lowered his head.

Her small gasp dissolved between the warmth of their lips. Her breathless excitement. His mouth slanted on hers, divine pressure, so sweet. Her body hummed. His fluid pace was ardent, possessive, and thoroughly consuming. For the first time since the accident, she felt truly alive. Resurrected.

The world faded around her as he kissed it away. She closed her eyes and let it all disappear. Rising on her toes, she curled her hands in his velvety hair. Heat coiled through her body, a twisting, winding thread of pleasure that caused her to ache. Parting her lips to the brush of his tongue, she heard herself moan. The slick feel of his tongue against hers set her ablaze. She plunged into the taste of him, eager to burn.

He dragged his mouth away, his breath a rush of heat on her cheek. "As your fiancé, I'll expect plenty of that as well."

She stared stunned through her hazy arousal before he turned her toward the door and sent her through it. Maddie stepped outside into the sunlight and wandered along Main Street, her brain still encased in a velvet fog. People passed, trailing whispers, but she paid them no heed. She'd had a productive day. She'd return home with a new job, a fiancé to escort her to Amelia's wedding, and the greatest kiss of her life.

Chapter 5

Jace closed the door behind Maddie, whistling a breath through his teeth. *Damn.* He'd kissed her as punishment for implicating him in her ridiculous lie, and instead, he was the one feeling flogged. Her passion had taken him by surprise. Shaking his head, he smiled at the way she'd come flouncing into his home with the intention of seducing him. Madeline Sutter had flirted her way out of trouble before. That much was clear.

He shook his head to reclaim his senses. He had his hands full with house repairs and preparing the office for patients. The last thing he had time for was playing make believe with the most infamous woman in town. Acting as her fiancé would do nothing to enhance his professional reputation either, but it would take him an age to open the business without additional help. After paying Henry to patch up the roof, Jace hadn't the funds in his budget to hire anyone else.

Still, he almost felt guilty for turning Madeline's ploy to his advantage. Any charms she'd used in the past to beguile men senseless wouldn't work on him. Not entirely, anyway. While he'd agreed to play along with her charade, he would set the rules. Or so he'd thought until that kiss. He licked his lips at the memory of her taste, the feel of her supple body pressing against his.

The jolting pleasure had rocked his control. She was alluring as hell with those simmering eyes and lush mouth, and his accelerated response proved he'd been too long without. The one thing he missed about Pittsburgh Hospital: its ample supply of willing nurses with whom to sate his body's carnal demands.

Maddie was no nurse, but she certainly seemed willing. He couldn't help wondering about her relationship with Daniel Hogle and whether they'd indulged a few urges of their own together. This was not quite the sleepy little town he'd originally judged it to be, and Jace was eager to learn more about its residents and their histories. Nothing intrigued him more, though, than Maddie.

He took a long breath to shake off his lust and strode to his desk. He couldn't dwell on this now. He had too much to do, and he needed to focus. Fortunately, aside from a few minor emergencies, business had been quiet.

Already he felt the perpetual strain of hospital work easing from his bones. Like a tightly wound clock, his body had run on that coil of steady tension—that incessant pressure he'd often released in the company of a woman.

He had definitely been too long without.

He bent over the ledger he'd abandoned for Maddie's visit, and tried to concentrate. The only thing that came close to exciting him more than the all-too-brief interlude with his pretend fiancée was the opportunity to study her case. From the misidentified coma, to her full recovery from an injury Doctor Filmore had diagnosed as permanent, Jace would get a first-person account of everything Maddie had experienced.

Although she wasn't technically a patient, it struck him now that it would be best to treat her as such. Jace was nothing if not ethical. In this particular instance, maintaining his ethics would deny him a repeat taste of the delectable Miss Sutter. But he'd do what was right. Beneath Maddie's provocative façade, he'd glimpsed her fragility. The ordeal she'd survived would leave anyone vulnerable and he knew that, despite their mutual attraction, it would be better for her if he maintained a professional distance.

If he could glean from her just one shred of insight into how to help others suffering from the after-effects of trauma, his restraint would be worth it. His deficiencies in this area of medicine kept him awake at night. No matter how many patients he saved, he could not forget the ones he had lost. He had to know why. Why some physically sound patients failed to get past the mental blockades of their ordeal, while others, like Maddie, moved on with their lives.

He thought about Kathy, and how miserably he'd failed her. His throat constricted with guilt. If only he had understood the depths of her despair, he might have saved her from herself.

More and more Jace found himself treading in his father's shoes. Inch by inch he moved closer to understanding what had led to the once-respected physician's undignified demise. He shook away the icy fear that he might repeat the dead man's mistakes, too. Shrugging on his coat, he stalked outside for some much-needed air. He stood on the porch, letting the crisp breeze fill his lungs. The scent of lilacs drifted from the overgrown shrubs dominating the small yard.

Henry Whalen rounded the corner of the house. Hammer in hand, he wiped his forehead with the back of his fist. Tufts of red hair pointed north as he waved. "Morning, Doc."

Jace tossed him a nod. "How's the roof coming along?"

"Good as new." Henry tossed the hammer to the ground, then headed to join him. The gate that enclosed the front yard creaked open as the gangly young man slipped through it. Sweat beaded on his freckled face, which was blotchy and sun burned. "Was that Madeline Sutter I saw earlier?" he asked, jogging up to the porch.

Now was the moment to put Maddie's plan in motion, so Jace took a breath and smiled suggestively.

"Yes, it was. Daily house calls come with the job, of course—but some are much more pleasant than others."

Henry frowned, shoving his hands into the pockets of his denim overalls. "So what was she doing here?" His nettled tone took Jace aback.

"Well, Henry, that's not any of your business, now is it?"

"No, sir, I suppose not. Just curious, is all." He averted his eyes, glancing out toward the street. "She doesn't come to town often."

"Judging from your reaction, I can understand why."

Henry shrugged. "There's nothing saying she has to stay in Misty Lake." The harsh words lacked any trace of civility.

Jace could hardly believe the difference in the man from only moments before. Why did these decent people simply accept all the rubbish piled around Maddie's feet? "So that's your defense?" Jace asked. "That she should leave town?"

"It would sure be easier on folks if she did." Henry lifted his chin against Jace's stern frown. "That girl was dead."

"She was in a coma. An extended state of unconsciousness."

Henry was shaking his head before Jace had finished, rejecting the explanation like a stubborn child. He may as well have slapped his hands over his ears and chanted la-la-la.

"A coma," Jace repeated.

"Maybe," Henry said. "But either way she was gone." He toed a loose floorboard. "She came back from somewhere," he muttered.

Jace stared, baffled and exasperated. "And where do you suppose that was?"

Henry glanced away.

"Unlike some folks, I don't claim to know. I just know it's strange." He turned back, fixing his eyes on Jace. "She died on her birthday, you know. May twelfth. She came back on Friday the thirteenth."

Jace stiffened against a surge of surprise. Talk about adding fuel to the fire.

"Coincidence."

"You can call it what you want." Henry swatted at a fly. "I'll keep my distance, just the same."

The idea that this homely fellow found Maddie unappealing was so absurd it was laughable. Jace couldn't resist.

"She's pretty, though, huh?"

Henry smiled, looking more like himself. At least his sense of humor was untouched. "Yes, sir, she is." His smile faded. "They all were. The Fair Five, we called them. Those girls had us all smitten... Daniel Hogle was crazy for Madeline in particular. For a while after the accident, I thought he might marry her anyway, but his uncle wouldn't stand for it."

"So she was punished for surviving," Jace said. "For something beyond her control." His anger came through in his tone, but he couldn't help himself. "Narrow minded..."

"This is a small town, Doc. Losing those girls hit us hard. They were my friends." Sorrow clouded Henry's eyes. He steeled his bony shoulders, as if adjusting his stance might combat his grief. "They were daughters and kin of folks we've all known our whole lives. The mere sight of Maddie Sutter adds salt to the wound."

Something inside Jace clicked like a switch. Maddie was more than a scapegoat. She was somehow responsible for what happened. Jace heard it in Henry's voice now as clearly as he had in Mrs. Tremont's last week. He was eager to hear Maddie's account of the accident and wondered if that alone might absolve her—perhaps her neighbors simply needed to hear a true version of the facts.

"You should watch yourself around that one, Doc. Pretty or not, something about her ain't right."

Jace doubted Henry would be so vocal in offering his opinion of Maddie once he knew she was Jace's fiancée. Henry wasn't a cruel man by nature. He was a product of his environment, infected by the nonsense fears of this odd community. Jace was more determined than ever to help Maddie battle the groundless bias against her.

Being engaged wouldn't hurt his practice—but engagement to Maddie might. He didn't care. He would play her fiancé, despite any disapproval. This town needed his services, which meant he had little to lose. And there was a wealth of knowledge to gain. In return, Maddie's engagement to him might help them to see she was a normal woman. A woman worth having.

What harm could it do?

"You'd better get used to seeing more of her, Henry. She'll be helping me here in the office."

Henry's eyes bulged.

"She's a bright woman, and I can use the assistance."

"People won't like that."

"Then I suggest they brace themselves." Jace took a deep breath, unable to resist. "Because during the short time I've known Madeline, our casual acquaintance has fast become something more."

* * * *

Maddie walked toward home, consumed by a jumble of thoughts she was struggling to sort. It had been a long day. Strangely, the shock of seeing Daniel and hearing the news of his engagement had dissipated. As had the pinching feeling in her chest borne of their encounter in the dress shop.

She currently had more pressing concerns. Namely, Jace Merrick and his unforgettable kiss. She sighed, thinking of little beyond her own desire as she ambled along. She inhaled deeply, letting the fragrance of wildflowers and pine fill her lungs. Releasing the breath brought her back down to earth, where she landed with a thud in the middle of reality.

She'd entangled herself with a man who could destroy her. A man with a scientific mind and keen perception. What was more, she'd invited him to probe into her life, the darkest days of her existence. If he somehow discovered her gift in the course of his inquiries... Well, Maddie didn't want to think about the consequences of that. Jace would not treat such information lightly, and if exposed, she might find herself confined to an asylum or worse.

She wandered into the house as if lost in some dream. After removing her new hat, she peeled off her gloves, then tossed the garments atop the table in the hall. She supposed she had to inform Grandfather of what she'd done before he heard it from Rhetta or Gil. The two made frequent trips to town and were bound to hear the news of her engagement sooner or later. She felt a fresh wave of dread as she realized she'd have to enlist their help, as well as Grandfather's, in supporting the premise that Jace had been treating Grandfather all along.

She walked through the foyer and down the long hall, checking each room that she passed. The echo of her footsteps on the marble floor waned as she padded across the carpet in the solarium. Through the wall of windows facing the lake, she saw Grandfather outside on the patio, enjoying his afternoon port in the sun. A thick afghan covered his legs from the constant chill he suffered despite the warm weather. Staring out at the water, he looked so at peace, so resigned to his fate. So ready to go.

She stopped in the arched doorway. Leaning on the doorjamb, she watched, trying to etch the picture of him in her mind. Staring at Grandfather's regal profile, she felt—once again—deeply ashamed of what she'd become. A liar. A woman willing to use a man she barely knew for her own selfish purposes. Swallowing back her guilt, she pushed herself from the doorjamb and plastered on a cheery smile.

"Hello, Grandfather." She sank into the wicker chair at his side.

"How was the shopping trip?"

"Eventful," she said for lack of anything else.

He turned toward her, brows arched like a pair of furry gray caterpillars as he waited for her to elaborate.

"I ran into Daniel and his fiancée at the dress shop."

He frowned at the mention of the man he'd once liked but had grown to despise. "Tell me that you gave him hell."

"I can only tell you that the meeting drove me to do something foolish. When he assumed I would not attend the wedding for lack of a suitable escort, I invented one." She fidgeted with her hands on her lap. "I told him that I was attending with my fiancé."

Grandfather coughed, nearly spilling his port. "Good lord, Maddie! I'm curious to hear how you plan to dig yourself out of that one," he said as he set down the glass.

"I already have."

His eyes flashed wide.

"Doctor Merrick has agreed to act as my fiancé until after the wedding."

"And why on earth would he agree to such a thing?"

He seemed less stunned by her lie than Jace's agreement to participate in it. It stung to know she was so repellant. That even Grandfather realized no man would touch her with a ten-foot pole.

"He's a doctor. I'm a curiosity."

He frowned. "You're no such thing."

"Perhaps you can speak to Rhetta and Gil?" she asked, changing the subject. "If anyone questions them about the engagement, they can simply mention that Doctor Merrick made house calls here."

His eyes dimmed as he nodded. "They're loyal to a fault," he said. "No worries there." He took another sip of port and stared back toward the lake. "After your parents died, I made a promise at their graves to protect you."

"None of this is your fault. You must know that."

"Perhaps. But it changes nothing. Men should be lined up to court you, the way they used to be. You should be engaged to a man who loves you, planning to start a family of your own, not clinging to the fading shreds of the one you have." His icy hand reached for hers. "I only wish you'd reconsider leaving—"

"You'll not get rid of me so easily," she said, fighting back tears. "And neither will they."

He stared at her, his eyes so sad.

"This is my home," she uttered.

"But after I'm gone…?"

"That won't be for ages, old man." She forced a teasing smile. "In the meanwhile, I must do this. And as frightening as it is to face them, it's time I rejoin the world."

With surprising strength, his bony fingers gripped hers in the paper thinness of his hand.

"You're a strong girl. You'll be fine."

Whether the reassurance was for her benefit or his, she felt better.

"I've missed Amelia terribly. A part of me is actually looking forward to the wedding."

"Of course. And you and Doctor Merrick will make a very handsome couple." His tired eyes sparkled. "I'm a fine judge of character. He'll help you get what you want." He slid his hand from hers and turned back toward the water. He seemed pleased by the idea of her and Jace. Too pleased. She could hear it in the tune he began to hum. This practical, no-nonsense man was so deeply worried about Maddie's future he was willing to pin his hopes on an illusion.

Maddie stood, staring down at him.

"It's a ruse, Grandfather. Please keep that in mind."

He glanced up with a trembling smile.

"I will, if you will, girl," he said with a wink.

Chapter 6

Maddie didn't know where to begin. Standing amid the clutter in the alcove that made up Jace's office, she was struck by the feeling she would be more housemaid here than office assistant.

"I've made some progress," Jace said.

She glanced out to the patient waiting area, trying to see where. Beneath the newly patched ceiling, several of the larger trunks had been shoved to the outermost corners of the room, but there were piles and crates of books and miscellaneous items everywhere else.

"Are those potatoes?" she asked.

He nodded, gazing at the heaping crate by the sofa.

"One peck to be exact. Payment for lancing a boil."

"Of course," she said, suppressing a smile.

"I've also earned five pounds of fresh dressed deer meat and a sack of feed for my horse. And the office has yet to open officially."

"I assume your wages in Pittsburgh fit more easily into your pocket?"

He shrugged, grinning.

"Such exchanges are customary in the country, I'm told. I'm literally earning my supper, but I appreciate compensation in all forms." He maneuvered through the clutter. "Once you're done shelving the books, you can start unpacking the trunks." He pointed to a pile of items on the floor. "Put those things in one of the empty crates, and I'll donate them to the clinic in Troy." He turned back to the task of dragging a crate of books across the floor.

It was as if their kiss had never happened. She didn't know what she'd expected, but he didn't seem the least bit awkward in her presence. He didn't seem anything at all. She knew she should feel relieved, but his indifference bothered her. A lot.

Her attraction to him was not so easy to dismiss. Neither was her urge to explore it. Everything she'd missed during the past three years of her stalled life—all her buried passion for living—was now bubbling to the surface. She could practically feel her desire for this man escaping through her pores.

From the corner of her eye she watched as he searched through the crate. His sleeves were rolled up to his elbows, exposing his forearms. His hair hung over his face. Maddie wasn't sure which aspect of him she preferred—the rugged, disheveled man with the flexing muscles she saw now, or the distinguished, finely attired gentleman who'd visited over tea at the house. He was two opposing sides of a coin with no losing toss.

Less than ten minutes alone with him and all she could think of was his lips on hers. Pathetic. Well, she'd made her own bed, she supposed.

Carrying a pile of books, he gestured with his chin toward the tall bookcase.

"I'll relocate those books to a lower shelf so you can arrange them with these." He set the books on the desk.

The cramped corner allowed her little space for maneuvering and even less space for two. From behind her, he reached for the hefty volumes on the shelf above. Her senses peaked. His chest brushed her shoulder, sending a rush of heat through her veins. Her body all but crackled with the tension of his nearness, the delicious smell of his neck. He glanced downward, acknowledging the contact. His eyes met hers in a flash of awareness that stilled her breath.

He felt it, too.

His gaze dropped to her mouth, and her lips parted in response as she waited, urging him with her eyes to move closer, to touch her, to forget about these dusty books and simply kiss her. *Please.*

As if hearing her silent appeal, he shifted toward her. Her heart pounded. He licked his lips, his blue eyes darkening in the way they had before. She hung suspended on the edge of that look—that look that told her something wonderful was about to happen. He drew in a long breath. Grumbling a curse, he pulled the books from the shelf, then sidled in the opposite direction. The books landed with a thud on the desk he passed as he strode away. She stared after him, perplexed and disappointed. Closing her eyes, she released a frustrated sigh.

She'd missed her chance with Daniel. Back then, she'd assumed she had all the time in the world to explore physical desire. To discover what all the fuss was about. The accident changed everything. She knew now that there were no certainties in life, no guaranties or promises of tomorrow. There was only today, and she'd lost so much already. The secret ability she'd acquired in the aftermath would cost her more still.

Truth and honesty, the bonds of trust that formed true love, an enduring marriage. These sacred things were forever out of her reach, so why not snatch up what passion she could?

Plus, it was clear that the girlish curiosity she'd felt for Daniel was a pale, paltry shadow when held against the powerful attraction she felt for Jace. Perhaps it was the force of her loneliness that drew her toward a man from whom she should be running. Or maybe the danger was part of the appeal. Either way, she might never have another chance to experience the bliss of so deep a craving. And if anyone found out? She was already a pariah, what did it matter if she ruined herself?

The more she justified the exciting prospect and the more she looked at Jace now, the more convinced she became that the risk to her heart would be worth it. Perhaps she could keep him so distracted with pleasant entertainments that he would conveniently forget his interest in her medical history. The sound of his voice pulled her out of her thoughts.

"I have to leave for an hour to check on Mrs. Tremont. Before I go, I wish to clear the air between us," he said. "Regarding…what occurred the other day."

Jace didn't strike her as a man who minced words, and his repressive tone dismayed her.

"The kiss?"

"Yes, Madeline, the kiss. I shouldn't have taken such liberties with you. You have my assurance that it will not happen again."

Her heart sank to her knees. "May I ask why?"

He stared, stone-faced. "I'm a doctor."

"You're not my doctor."

He blinked. "No. But you're…"

"A grown woman," she answered as he searched for words. "A fact you seem to have noticed."

He conceded with a nod, his lips curving into a smile that stilled her breath.

"Yes, I've noticed, Maddie." Any trace of humor melted as his sultry eyes moved down the length of her and back again.

A shiver snaked up her spine. Heat coiled in her belly. He wanted her. Despite her tattered reputation, he wanted her. His reluctance to act on his desire stemmed from something else entirely, and whatever it was, she was determined to conquer it.

She moved toward him, her steps slow and deliberate.

"Before the accident, I was quite sought after."

"Undoubtedly." His tone conveyed his amusement.

Not exactly the response she'd sought. Was he truly so dense?

"I had many suitors."

His demeanor turned rigid as he regarded her closely.

"Meaning?"

"Meaning I've been kissed before." She lifted her chin. "And more than once."

His wide eyes narrowed.

"Nevertheless, you've committed to sharing information about your recovery with me, and I intend to use it for a serious professional purpose. That means I will conduct myself properly for the duration of our bargain." He reached for the medical bag at his feet. "I'll be back in an hour." Dismissing her with a nod, he left for his house call.

His sudden change in attitude vexed her. The good doctor had obviously caught a stubborn case of the moralities. Surely she could nudge him through this useless ethical dilemma. She had never been one to back down from a challenge, and she refused to start now.

"We'll see about that," she muttered as she rolled up her sleeves and went back to work.

She made her way to the front window in the waiting room, then pushed open the shutters. Dust motes danced in the flood of light filtering through the dingy panes. The mess looked worse in the brighter light. She began unpacking the nearest trunk. She had no idea what she was removing, as everything inside was meticulously wrapped in thick paper to prevent damage during shipping.

As instructed, she moved item after bulky item to a shelf in the examination room. She stooped to browse the various drugs and herbs housed behind the glass doors of the nearby cupboard. Along with a metal pill shaper, rows of jars filled with laudanum, burdock, elecampane, jimson weed, and pleurisy root lined the crowded shelf.

From this cache of medicines, Jace would prepare poultices, liniments, and pills for his patients. She considered all the time and energy expended on applying remedies, the results of which were often ineffective. All the needless suffering…

The sound of a wailing child in the distance poured through the open window. Maddie bolted upright, and rushed to the parlor just as the door burst open.

"Doc!" The little boy Mr. Cleary carried kicked his foot beneath the bloody cloth that covered it. "Doc!"

Mrs. Cleary rushed in behind them, tears streaming down her cheeks.

"Doctor Merrick!"

Maddie's heart pounded. "He's not here," she said. "He's gone to see Mrs. Tremont. What's happened?"

"Our boy here jumped from a hay bale onto a nail in the floorboard. It's bad."

"He's barely four years old. We can't lose him, too." Mrs. Cleary wiped at her tears. "Dear Lord, James, what do we do?"

The child yelled louder, his fear feeding on that of his frantic parents. The blood malady that afflicted all of the Cleary children had already proved fatal for the other Cleary sons, and Maddie had never seen the staunch couple so out of sorts. She resolved to do what she could to help, consequences be damned.

"Give him here," Maddie said.

They stared, horrified, as if she were Satan personified demanding their child.

"Give. Him. Here." Maddie wrenched the screaming child from his father's arms. "Go send someone for Doctor Merrick," she instructed Mr. Cleary. "Mrs. Cleary, you wait here." She started for the examination room. "What's his name?"

Mrs. Cleary blinked. "Joseph," she said. "Joey."

Maddie rushed the boy to the examination room. She kicked shut the door, leaving a gaping Mrs. Cleary outside. Maddie sat on a chair, wrestling the squirming child on her lap. "Keep still now," she said more harshly than she'd intended. She'd always lacked patience with children, but she had to keep the boy calm. "Shh. It's all right, Joey, shh."

The boy settled against her as she peeked beneath the saturated cloth to assess the situation. Blood spurted from the small hole in his foot with surprising force. It showed no sign of stopping. Joey was in trouble, and he needed help immediately.

Maddie tossed the sopping cloth aside, and it hit the floor with a splat. Her hands shook. There was so much blood, and the child was so small. Excluding herself, Maddie had healed only one other human being. But the stove burn to Rhetta's palm had been no life-threatening injury. This surely was. She had to try.

Situating the boy firmly on her lap, Maddie used her free hand to clasp Joey's foot. Blood filled her palm, oozing through her trembling fingers. Over Joey's whimpers, Maddie hummed to the boy, squeezing his foot softly at first until she could get an adequate grip over the injury. Maddie closed her eyes and squeezed harder. Joey whimpered and squirmed in her lap. Bouncing her knees gently to soothe him, Maddie concentrated on the beat of the rhythm, nothing else. A surge of heat consumed her; hot tears stung her eyes. The heat from Maddie's hand intensified.

Joey stiffened at the strange sensation, whimpering some more. The heat poured freely now with little effort.

"Shh. Don't be afraid," Maddie cooed. "It's all right." And somehow she knew that it was.

The sound of frantic voices carried from the outer room. Mrs. Cleary sounded wild.

"She took Joey in there!" Heavy footsteps echoed through the door, growing louder as they neared. The door flew open, and Jace charged inside. Mr. Cleary followed on his heels.

"He's a bleeder, Doc."

"Hemophilia?"

"Yes, sir. We've lost two boys already. The nail went straight through his shoe. John Baldwin is hitching the wagon so we can take him to Troy."

"That won't be necessary," Maddie said. "He's—"

"Get him up on the table," Jace ordered as he washed his hands in a basin of water.

"He's all right. He's—"

"Now," he said, spinning around. He dried his hands, then prepared a fresh compress.

Maddie set Joey gently on the table.

"Lie back, son," Jace said, nudging Maddie away. Joey's eyes widened in fear, and he started to cry. Ignoring the child's protests, Jace lowered him to his back. "Let's have a look," he said as he examined the injury with competent efficiency.

Jace dabbed at the blood, his moves deliberate and swift, as though his body was one step ahead of his brain. Unlike Maddie's trembling hands, his were steady and strong.

Maddie wrung her bloodied hands on her skirts and watched. Jace furrowed his brow, then leaned in for a closer look. His grim expression worried her. Would the blood come gushing? Had Maddie been too quick to deem Joey healed?

"It's slowing," Jace said, reaching for the compress.

The Clearys huddled closer, responding in unison. "Slowing?"

"So it appears," Jace answered, dabbing at Joey's foot.

"How?" Mrs. Cleary spun to Maddie. "What did you do?" She swiveled back to Jace. "What did she do?"

"She did nothing," Jace snapped. "The blood is clotting." Releasing Joey's foot, he straightened to face the Clearys. "The puncture was deep enough to sever important vessels, but the blood appears to be clotting now." He turned to Joey. "How do you feel, son?"

The boy averted his teary eyes, lips quivering.

Maddie couldn't blame the child. The intensity in Jace's expression would frighten a wildcat.

"Answer the doctor now, Joey," she said. Sidling to the table, she patted Joey's knee. "How do you feel?"

"I want to go home," sniffed the tiny boy.

"Of course you do, sweetheart," Maddie cooed with a smile. She turned to Jace. "May I help him up?"

"No, you may not." He turned, preparing a fresh basin of water. "Punctures are prone to infection. The wound must be cleaned."

Maddie soothed the boy as Jace carefully cleaned and bandaged the small foot.

"Get him to Troy," Jace told the Clearys. "With his condition it's possible the bleeding may resume."

Maddie shook her head. "I don't think—"

"Keep his foot raised, and keep him as still as possible during the trip. You're taking a spring wagon?" he asked as he hefted the boy from the table and deposited him in his father's arms.

"Yes, sir."

"Good. We'll give him a bit of laudanum to ease his nerves. Cushion him in the wagon so he's not bouncing around."

Mrs. Cleary nodded furiously. "Thank you, Doctor Merrick." She brushed past Maddie, then stopped, turning slowly to face her. The woman's reproachful attitude toward Maddie hadn't changed much since she'd last seen her, but the harsh line of her mouth softened a bit now, and her cool eyes seemed warmer. "Thank you," she uttered softly in Maddie's direction before she hurried after her husband.

Jace escorted the trio to the waiting wagon outside. Maddie watched through the dingy window as he helped load Joey inside. Wringing her balled fists, Maddie tried to relax. Her simple healing efforts were not always successful. Her failure to cure Grandfather had proved it. But this attempt had been a resounding victory, and she knew, with sudden clarity, that she could no longer stand idly by as her neighbors bled and suffered—even if it meant that they would soon despise and fear her more than they already did. She would be careful to avoid exposure, of course. But she would not squander her gift.

Exhaling her pent-up tension, she began to calm. A few minutes later the wagon ambled down the street.

Jace strode into the house and closed the door firmly behind him. "What the hell do you think you're doing?"

She blinked. "Pardon me?"

"I'm the doctor here, Madeline, not you."

"Oh, for goodness sakes."

"I strongly suggest you remember that."

"I was merely attempting to soothe the child. And I thought I might apply an herbal poultice that Rhetta sometimes uses for household cuts. But it was unnecessary in the end…"

"An herbal poultice? For bleeding?" He glared. "These are my patients. Do not ever undermine me again. There will be no simple country remedies or backwoods mumbo-jumbo in this office."

"The boy was frightened out of his wits. I had to do something."

"The boy could have bled out on my table! Had that puncture been a fraction deeper, he very well might have!"

"I—"

"You're not qualified to treat patients! That's not why you're here!"

Maybe not, but she was here. And she'd saved Joey's life. She snapped shut her lips, biting back a retort that would turn his world on its side.

"Well, I don't even wish to be here!" she spat instead. "And I certainly don't wish to be a nurse. Or a housekeeper."

"And I didn't wish to be your fiancé. So we're even on that score." He strode toward the examination room. "Come wash your hands," he called over his shoulder.

Maddie followed, then proceeded to wash her hands in the basin of water he'd prepared. He fumbled through his medical supplies. "For someone who doesn't wish to be a nurse, you certainly spend a good amount of time with your hands soaked in blood."

She frowned, scrubbing harder, but had no response.

"Your unsterilized hands, no less," he muttered. "Even a minor infection can turn deadly." He tossed her a towel. "These are people, Madeline, not wounded deer."

She dried her hands, then forced herself to face him.

His voice softened as he collected himself. "I understand the instinct to help, but your interference could have hindered my treatment. Or made matters worse."

She opened her mouth to protest, but his scowl warned her against it.

"You will stick to the tasks of organizing the office and patient records. Nothing more. Is that understood?"

His condescending tone was infuriating. She nodded, simply to appease him. If nothing else, this incident had taught her one thing about Doctor Jace Merrick. Even if she performed a miracle right under his nose, he would likely never believe it.

Chapter 7

Jace spent the next morning on another house call, where he remained for several hours treating a man with a fractured arm. Another of the region's sudden storms struck shortly after he departed from the secluded clapboard house in the woods, making for a slow trip down the mountain. On the outskirts of town, several cabins and cottages surrounded the numerous lakes in the area. Jace hoped he would soon have a better understanding of the roads and pony paths leading to these more remote locations.

House calls comprised a good portion of country practice, so it was imperative to maintain the buggy in prime condition. Traveling to treat patients in the winter months would be daunting, not to mention precarious in the dark. A few summer rain storms, and already the route was a mess.

The buggy trudged and slid in the mucky ruts, and rain battered the top. The long trips usually provided Jace with time to reflect on his patients and budding practice. Today, though, his thoughts seemed to wander to Maddie. During the trip up the mountain, and all last night, he had remained furious with her about what happened with Joey Cleary. She had no business challenging his orders when it came to his patients—it was dangerous on every level. And yet he couldn't help but admire the way she argued her own cause after the fact. The woman was infuriating. Maddening. And far too distracting.

He'd come very close to kissing her again yesterday. So close, in fact, that he'd been tempted to send her home right then and there—to put an end to this ridiculous scheme of hers before it truly began. But he'd agreed to play her fiancé, and after feeding Henry the bait to set the charade in full motion, he was now bound to see it through.

If he was being honest, part of him wanted to continue with her. He wished he could claim true indifference, but how could he? Even now, his brain was busy worrying about her, fearing she might be caught walking home in the midst of this downpour. Trees swayed with the force of the wind. The damage to his roof proved how quickly storms in this area could intensify. If Maddie weren't still at the office when he arrived, he'd go back out to find her.

By the time he reached the office it was late afternoon, and the storm had turned fierce. Maddie stood at the window, as if awaiting his return. While he could justify his relief at finding her safely sheltered, the sudden vitality in his weary steps as he unrigged the buggy told him something else. He was happy to see her.

Christ Almighty.

He snatched up his bag, then dashed for the door. He ducked inside, shaking off the rain. Maddie greeted him with a towel and took his bag.

"I'm glad you're still here," he said into the towel as he dried his face.

"You are?" Her pensive smile warmed the chill from his bones.

"This storm is a mean one."

Her smile fell.

"I thought it best to wait it out," she said as she reached for the towel. She hung it on a peg by the door, then followed him down the hall. "The mountain road can be a challenge in bad weather. I was beginning to worry."

He couldn't remember the last time anyone worried for him, and her concern caught him off guard.

"The trip was unpleasant, but no broken wheels." He glanced around, surprised by what he saw. She'd cleaned and arranged the patient waiting room. He could actually see the braided carpet beneath the large center table and the chairs lining the walls.

"It was damp in here," she said to explain the fire crackling in the hearth.

Flames flickered, setting the room in a golden glow. The vase of lilacs on the mantel scented the once-musty air. In one day, her hard work and subtle touches had transformed the room from dreary disarray to a cozy, comfortable place for his patients.

"You've done a fine job with the room."

She smiled, and he welcomed the jolt of energy that coursed through his veins. Her dark hair was pinned up, but the twined knot had loosened considerably during her chores. A few wisps brushed her temples and coiled along her neck. The unfettered look stirred his senses. As did the open buttons at her delicate throat. He took a deep breath to ward off his arousal. The smell of onions drifting from the kitchen made his stomach growl.

"Mariah Whitby stopped by with a nice roast beef," she said. "Compliments of her mother for your help yesterday morning."

"Is that what smells so good?"

"I've cooked supper. Henry told me you were on the mountain for a house call until almost midnight. Since you were out so early this morning, I thought you might be hungry."

Jace was unused to this kind of attention—he'd been on his own for so long. Her concern for his welfare was as discomfiting as it was pleasing.

"I'm famished," he admitted. But not solely for food. Coming home to a woman certainly had its advantages, and he'd never considered them as thoroughly as he did right now. He pushed away his base longings as he peeled off his wet coat.

"It's still pouring out there," she said. "Perhaps I'll join you for supper." She tilted her head, lips quirking. "Unless you fear dining with me would threaten propriety."

She was incorrigible. And as alluring as hell.

"I can't very well send you out in the rain."

She grinned like a cat that had cornered a mouse. "Rhetta does most of the cooking at home, but I can manage a simple pot roast. It should be ready soon. Some coffee in the meanwhile will warm you up."

After removing his boots and changing his clothes, he met her in the kitchen. She'd tidied here, too. The linoleum floor shined, as did the white tiled walls. A jar of flowers sat between two place settings. The room fairly breathed with her presence. Pots steamed on the stove. He sat, watching as she darted about, serving the coffee and checking the doneness of the roast and potatoes. The checkered apron tied around her small waist accentuated the tantalizing curve of her hips. The plainness of her beige dress did nothing to camouflage the shapely figure beneath, and her confident flirting told him she knew it. She turned suddenly from the stove.

"I'm sorry about yesterday," she said. "I'm not one to stand idle during emergencies."

"So I'm discovering."

She smiled, reaching for her market basket by the sink. She pulled out something wrapped in newspaper, then placed it on the table next to his steaming coffee.

"What's this?" he asked.

"A peace offering."

What was she up to now? He eyed her warily, but she seemed quite sincere. He opened the newspaper, uncovering the item inside. The wooden box was the size of a brick, but much lighter. The forest scenery carved into the lid was exquisite. Jace turned it from side to side, inspecting the well-crafted piece. He opened and closed it, his eyes honing in on the small, engraved initials on the bottom corner. *M.S.* He glanced up. "Did you make this?"

"Along with sixteen others," she said. "I chose that one for you because of the deer in the trees." She pointed. "See?"

He stared at the tiny deer nestled among the pines. Madeline Sutter was an artist. Her talent for such intricate work surprised him. "I'm impressed."

She shrugged. "It keeps me busy."

He contemplated his response. While he hated to spoil the pleasant moment and their upcoming supper, he had to broach the subject sometime. It was the crux of their involvement and the reason she was here, despite how easy she made it to forget.

"Is that how you coped? By keeping busy?"

She stiffened, backing away. "I started carving because it was something I could do from my bed while my leg healed. Grandfather had taught me how years earlier, but back then I was too consumed with social activities to squander time on solitary ones." She smiled at the irony. "After the accident, Grandfather felt I needed something to occupy my mind."

"To help you forget?"

She nodded, her gaze drifting away.

"He's a smart man, your grandfather. I, too, have prescribed hobbies and other pursuits to distract patients from dwelling on their pain."

Her eyes flew to his. "Did that help them?"

He wasn't prepared for the question, and it took him aback. He thought of Kathy and the night she was pulled from the river.

"No."

Maddie didn't seem surprised, and her complacency stung.

"While craftwork helped fill the hours of confinement as I recovered, it did nothing to help me forget. I came to realize that, although I might wish to erase the past, denying the pain of what happened was not the solution."

"It's more harmful to dwell on the trauma," he countered.

"Perhaps. But having lived through the experience, I can assure you that ignoring it is harmful as well. At first I tried to obliterate the memory. I tried to push out all thoughts of it. I tried desperately."

He nodded, hating the distress in her eyes. "You were distraught."

"I was angry." Her sharp tone softened. "I was hurt and afraid. Confused. The emotions raged inside me like some rabid beast. Though I tried to lock it away, a thing so furious can't be caged."

"But over time—"

"No." She shook her head. "It finds a way to torment, to manifest, if not in the light of your waking hours, then in the darkness of your nightmares. It will free itself somehow. And the more you try to ignore it, the more powerful it becomes. Until you face it down."

He listened intently, more fascinated by this young woman's words than any he'd read in the textbooks or heard in the lectures at medical school.

"How?"

"By not pretending this terrible thing never occurred. By accepting that it happened." She lifted her chin. "I forced myself to not only recall the accident, but to memorize it."

"Memorize it?"

She nodded. "Every horrific detail of it."

He stared.

"Then I wrote it all down. Everything. I described the fear, the terrified faces of my friends as we clung to each other, the piercing screams." Her voice dipped so low he barely heard her. "The crush of their bodies slamming into mine."

He swallowed hard. "What possessed you to torture yourself that way?"

"I had to. Only by ingesting it, could I purge it. Does that make any sense?"

His thoughts whirled in his head. He'd based his treatment of Kathy on exactly the opposite. But Kathy was so fragile. So broken. So unlike Maddie, who harbored a strength beneath her delicate appearance. An instinct to fight back.

"That must have been very difficult, Maddie."

"I thought it might kill me." She forced a small smile. "Not that I cared at the time. For months I could barely function. I couldn't eat. I couldn't sleep. The only thing I did was cry. And carve those boxes."

With his thumbs, he caressed the smooth surface of the box in his hands. He imagined a good amount of her tears had varnished the wood, and the treasure was made more precious in the knowledge of all that went into it.

"Once I'd written down every last detail I could remember, I forced myself to read what I'd written. Over and over. Every day I read, until the accident was no longer this monstrous, fearful thing I couldn't control, but an event in my life that I'd survived. It became a part of me—not I a part of it. Eventually the nightmares began to subside."

Suppressing a request to read her journal, he absorbed her words like a sponge. His thoughts grew heavy with the weight of all she had learned and all she'd done to heal. The woman was brilliant. Courageous. Beautiful.

"So you conquered the beast."

"Tamed it," she corrected. "I still struggle with occasional nightmares, and I still can't bring myself to board a wagon. But I'm moving on with my life." She motioned with her eyes toward the window. "Now if only they would allow it."

She smiled then, and he'd never admired anyone more. He stood, drawn to her by a force he no longer wished to fight.

"To hell with them." He stepped closer. Her eyes told him that she knew what was coming. She leaned back against the sink, waiting for him, inviting him with a look, and a brief lick of her lips. "To hell with it all," he murmured as he took her in his arms.

Capturing her lips, he opened his mouth to the eager thrust of her tongue. She wrapped her arms around his neck. The fierce response drove him wild. He plunged deeper into the sweet depths of her mouth, tasting, probing. The sounds of their moans melded in the pleasure and slow slick of their tongues.

He gripped her hips tightly as she pressed her body to his. The brush of her breasts teased his chest, the light pressure against his ribs building with the rhythm of the kiss. Dragging his mouth across her cheek, he kissed the satiny skin of her neck. Her head tilted to the side as he trailed his lips down her throat and then up again. Burying his face in her hair, he inhaled the floral scent of her, the faint smell of lilacs and summer and freshly fallen rain.

She clutched his shoulders. Soft sounds of pleasure spilled from her lips as she pressed light kisses to his jaw.

"Oh, Jace," she murmured against his neck. The arousal in her voice was too much. He cupped her luscious bottom, pulling her to his hardness.

She gasped into his ear, her hot breath firing a shot of desire straight down to his shaft. Her hands ran down his back, his sides, exploring with the perfect touch of palm and fingertips. Like liquid heat, sensations drizzled down his spine. He marveled at the passion in that touch, those small hands.

The same hands that had crafted the wooden box...

He froze amid a gust of sobering thoughts. What the devil was he doing? He drew back, setting her away. Her half-closed eyes flashed open, and her lips parted in surprise. Her breathless passion stilled his heart. He could barely speak. Forcing the words from his dry throat, he said, "We must stop this before we are carried away."

"But I want to be carried away." She reached for him, but he took a step back.

"I can't do this," he said.

"Of course you can." She reached toward him again.

He shook his head. "Madeline..."

She grimaced, looking stricken. "Don't you want me?" The tremble of uncertainty in her voice stunned him. Did she truly not comprehend the extent of his lust? Her sudden self-consciousness made it harder to resist showing her exactly how much he wanted her. How much he wanted to show her the pleasure she craved. Deserved. How he wanted to toss her onto the table and show her it all.

He inhaled a long breath. "Whether or not I want you doesn't matter."

"It matters to me." She stared up at him with a look that clenched his heart. Disappointment swam in her eyes. She seemed so fragile, so vulnerable. She'd been cast aside by her former fiancé, by the whole damn town. To reject her now...

But he had to be sensible.

She'd been through too much, and she'd come too far. He couldn't risk hurting her. She had trusted him by sharing the details of her painful recovery, and for this, he was grateful. Her remarkable progress would teach him a lot. The knowledge she offered was enough; he could not take advantage of her by taking more. He would not use her that way.

"You've set a plan to regain your reputation. If you hope to achieve that goal, we must maintain decorum, especially when we're alone."

She frowned, rolling her eyes.

"You do wish to continue with the charade, don't you?"

"Of course," she snapped. "But we're engaged. It would—"

"We are not engaged."

"I know that. I'm simply pointing out that as far as everyone else is concerned, we are. Why not enjoy it while we can?"

He steeled himself against her offer, tempting as it was. "Let's not risk doing anything either of us might regret."

She lifted her chin. "I will not shatter like broken glass, if that is your fear."

But he was not so certain of that, and he refused to take her word for it. Maddie was a strong woman, but she was a woman, nonetheless. Physical intimacy provided fertile ground for flourishing emotions, and women tended to form quick attachments. Maddie was angry now, but she would be grateful for his good judgment later on.

"We shall stick to the plan."

She straightened, planting her hands on her hips. "Must you always be so sensible, Jace Merrick?" Her question was laced with disdain. Her defiant stance resembled the one she'd taken the first time he'd seen her when she'd ordered him off her property. "Have you never once been tempted to toss caution to the wind?"

"Never." He ground out the lie and bit back the terrible, frustrating truth. *Not until I met you.*

Chapter 8

Jace's rejection hurt more than Maddie could have imagined. As she walked to his office the following morning, she replayed the humiliating scene in her head. She'd all but begged him to take her, right there in his kitchen, offering herself to him as casually as she'd served up the gravy. *Would you like a bit of me with your pot roast?*

Her face flushed with the memory of his polite refusal and the awkwardly silent supper that had followed. Despite her burning embarrassment, she tightened her shawl against the damp chill of the morning. Sunlight winked through the treetops along the deserted trail, but it would be hours before everything dried following yesterday's storm. Although she'd made this trip to town by herself hundreds of times before, she'd never felt as alone as she walked the soggy path.

This latest spoilt tangle with Jace had forced Maddie to face facts. The doctor would not be seduced, and she must abandon her hope of a brief affair. Her disappointment was palpable, but she would try to look to the bright side. Thanks to Jace, she would attend Amelia's wedding on the arm of a handsome man. She'd been greedy to wish for more. Resigned to the circumstances, she lifted her chin and stepped up to the porch. The door was ajar, so she pushed it open, then stepped inside. She stopped, recognizing a voice from inside the parlor.

Pastor Hogle.

Her stomach lurched. What on earth did he want? Dreadful thoughts raced through her head. She hadn't come this close to the charlatan since she'd attended church three years ago, where he delivered a vile sermon crafted to ensure she'd never return.

She trembled at the memory of sitting alone on the long pew. Not a soul had rejoiced at her recovery. As Pastor Hogle preached venom and lies, she had realized how thoroughly he despised her. And in the resounding silence of the congregation, she'd heard what they'd all wanted to say.

That she should have died, too.

Swallowing hard, she forced her feet to move. She inched down the hall past the umbrella stand and hat rack to listen. The floorboards creaked beneath her weight, and she cringed, knowing her presence had been detected. She had no other choice but to show herself. Mustering her strength, she rounded the corner, then stepped into the room.

"Good morning," she said stiffly.

A frown of disgust crossed Pastor Hogle's face before he pulled his eyes from the sight of her. His frosty dismissal made her feel sick. She wanted to run.

He resumed the conversation as if she didn't exist. "As I was saying, Doctor Merrick, my nephew has informed me of the disturbing news that you intend to marry this woman."

Maddie gasped as her eyes flew to Jace.

He stood calmly, but a vein bulged at this throat. His balled fists remained at his sides, emotions tightly locked inside the steady hands of a seasoned physician.

"And why would news of our engagement disturb you?"

"Why don't you ask her?"

"I'm asking you."

Jace towered a full ten inches over the stout man. Undaunted by the disadvantage, Pastor Hogle gave a stiff tug to the lapels of his pastoral coat and took a step forward. What he lacked in height, he possessed in self-importance. He drummed his fingers on the hat in his pudgy hands.

"Manners prohibit me from maligning her in your presence."

"And yet you have no trouble doing so from your pulpit."

Jace had obviously heard of the incident. Her face burned as she realized that he'd known all along of her public disgrace. His defense of her only shamed her more; standing up for her would hurt him as well. No one did anything in Misty Lake unless Pastor Hogle sanctioned it. Her broken engagement to Daniel was proof. The pastor was the most powerful man in this town, and crossing him would have consequences for Jace.

Pastor Hogle's lips tightened.

"This town needs a doctor. And if you wish to have a successful practice, you need this town." Hogle spoke with the mesmerizing vitality that had kept his congregants in his thrall for as long as she could remember. "Your association with her will only hinder that success. Misty Lake has accepted you as its physician, despite your young age and unsettled status. Had I any indication you'd attach yourself to this…woman…I'd have insisted that your request to practice here be denied."

"Whom I marry is none of anyone's concern. My competence as a doctor does not hinge on that choice."

"Does it hinge on your parentage?"

Jace's face went taut, save the twitch in his jaw.

"You'd be wise not to speak of my father."

Maddie was baffled by the conversation's sudden turn, but from Jace's enraged reaction, she hoped the Pastor heeded the warning.

"And what of the Cleary boy?" Pastor Hogle asked.

Maddie's heart pounded.

"What of him?" Jace asked, obviously confused by the second rapid-fire change in the pastor's focus.

"I've spoken in length with the Clearys about what occurred here."

"The boy was treated and is doing well. The details of his case are confidential. Doctor Reed is nine miles away, sir. If you have misgivings regarding my medical abilities, feel free to take your business to him."

Pastor Hogle blinked. No one spoke to him as Jace did now. Maddie's heart raced faster as the tension between the two men increased.

"You won't be losing my business alone, Doctor. All of my parishioners—"

"We're done here," Jace said.

"Don't be a fool, Doctor Merrick. Appearances can be deceiving, and she's not as she appears." His chest puffed with a swell of righteous indignation. "You're new in town, but it's my duty as a man of God to warn you that this woman is an abomination."

Jace's brows shot up in surprise. His blue eyes darkened to black as his face turned to steel.

"Miss Sutter has a name. And you've no right to speak of her this way."

Pastor Hogle's face gnarled in a scowl that sent chills down her spine.

"I earned that right, Doctor." He shoved his hat on his head. "On the day she murdered my daughter."

* * * *

The impact of the pastor's words struck so hard that Jace saw stars. His surprise veered quickly to anger, but he couldn't move. Even after Hogle stormed from the house, the man's shocking speech reverberated through the room, keeping Jace rooted where he stood.

Jace turned to Maddie, cursing under his breath as he took in the sight of her. She sagged against the wall, her face alarmingly white. Tears welled in her eyes. He charged toward her.

"Are you all right?"

Her moan of anguish tore at his heart. She turned her head, closing her eyes.

"Madeline," he said, stepping closer.

"I'm fine," she croaked.

But she wasn't fine. She was far from fine. His anger at Pastor Hogle burned like a scalding fury inside him, but he had to stay calm.

"Look at me," he said softly.

She turned her face to the wall as if hoping to vanish inside it.

He grasped her shoulders. "Look at me."

She recoiled from his grip. "I'm fine." She struggled to move, but her knees buckled beneath her. She sank, blue skirts crumpling around her, as Jace caught her in his arms.

"Come sit down with me."

She shook her head furiously, regaining her footing. "I don't want to sit down." She wrenched from his grasp, clutching the wall.

Jace touched her back. "They're just words, Maddie. Words."

"But he's right!" She spun toward him, her eyes glazed and wild. "I killed them. It was my birthday, my foolish idea to picnic in the most remote spot on the mountain." She swiped at her tears. "It was my fault, don't you see?"

What he saw was the same survivor's guilt that had plagued Kathy. The same desperation he'd been too busy, too arrogant—too heartless— to see.

"It was an accident. You have to move on."

"I don't have to do anything." She lifted her chin. "I'm not going to the wedding."

The pain in her voice told him she meant it. In one morning, she'd been set back three years. His anger at Pastor Hogle returned full force. "Maddie—"

"Leave me alone!" With that she shoved herself from the wall and fled the house.

* * * *

Jace had every intention of chasing after Maddie following her dramatic exit. Unfortunately, a medical emergency prevented him from getting any farther than the sidewalk, where he had been summoned directly to the Caldwell home.

Broken bones took precedence over Maddie's emotional crisis, and by the time Jace had returned from riding up to Taborton to set Asa Caldwell's ankle, it was well after midnight.

Maddie didn't come to work the next morning either. Convincing himself she needed some time alone, he'd taken the coward's way out and simply hoped for the best. The day after that, Jace's practice opened officially. A steady stream of patients had kept his thoughts of Maddie at bay, but he'd decided that if she didn't show up by day's end, he'd ride out to check on her.

Mrs. Cleary had brought Joey to the office that morning for the first of the weekly visits Jace had suggested they institute in the wake of his accident. Jace sat at his desk, scribbling notes in Joey's file. Fortunately, the bleeding hadn't resumed during the trip to Troy and the clot had held nicely afterward. The boy was luckier still that no infection had formed. Nail punctures—to the foot especially—often infected the tissues.

According to Mrs. Cleary, Pastor Hogle had questioned the family about Joey's treatment and his interaction with Maddie especially. Pastor Hogle might still blame Maddie for the wagon accident, but did the man actually believe she would attempt to harm an innocent child?

The pastor's grief for his daughter had poisoned his mind against Maddie. Whether the rift could ever be repaired, Jace couldn't guess. He knew only that he would never allow Hogle to hurt Maddie again.

This fiercely protective sentiment took him by surprise. He closed the file, leaning back in the chair. Somehow this woman had penetrated the barriers he'd placed between himself and his patients. Detachment allowed him to do his job. But the rules he'd lived by did not apply when it came to Maddie. Although he didn't know how or why it had happened, he had to accept that it had.

And he had to see her.

Jace arrived at the Sutter house just before sunset. The housekeeper, Rhetta, led him to the parlor, where Maddie's grandfather sat by the fire, reading the papers. The room was stiflingly hot. The old man was ill, but seemed to be holding his own. A glass of port kept him company. After a brief exchange of pleasantries, Jace said, "I'd like to speak with Madeline."

"That makes two of us." Mr. Sutter adjusted the worn afghan on his lap. "I'm glad you're here, doctor. I was considering sending for you tomorrow."

"What's happened? Is she all right?"

"My granddaughter has locked herself in her room and hasn't left it in two days. She told me she's not going to Amelia's wedding, and I'd like to know what happened between the two of you that changed her mind."

Jace sighed. "Pastor Hogle stopped by my office the other day."

"That son of a—" He broke into a rattling cough that left him breathless.

The man could barely vocalize his anger, let alone act on it. As Mr. Sutter caught his breath, Jace was struck again by how defenseless a target Maddie truly was. Her only ally in Misty Lake was a homebound invalid.

Jace handed Sutter the glass of port on the nearby table.

"I'd be happy to examine you sometime," he said as the man drank.

He waved Jace away. "Save your concern for my granddaughter."

"I see where she gets her stubbornness," Jace muttered. "It's none of my business, but in light of what I've seen, I'm compelled to ask. Have you never considered sending her away?"

"Every day." Mr. Sutter's eyes dimmed. "I damn near insisted," he said. "When she wouldn't leave me, I decided we would go together. Two years ago we were all set to depart for Boston." He shook his head and gave a solid rap to his chest. "This damn ticker of mine had other ideas. Now I'm unable to travel any farther than the porch." He shook his head. "And she refuses to leave me."

Maddie's commitment to the ill man was commendable. Jace swallowed as he thought of his father. Perhaps if Jace had remained at home and not gone off to study in Philadelphia, he could have prevented the man's eventual ruin.

"May I speak with her, sir?" Jace asked.

"You can try." He pointed a bony finger to the ceiling. "Her room is the third one on the right. Forgive me for not showing you the way."

Jace gave a quick nod before heading up the wide staircase. The upper level was as impressive as the rest of the house. Each fine piece of furniture adorning the hall gleamed with freshly applied polish, as did the cherry wood floor.

He knocked on the door to Maddie's room. The sound echoed through the hollow silence of the long hall, but no answer. A prickle of fear crawled up his spine, a spike of panic he couldn't control. He knocked harder.

"I'm not hungry, Rhetta," Maddie called from inside.

He exhaled in relief, recovering quickly from his momentary lapse.

"Open the door, Madeline."

"Jace?" The surprise in her voice was evident.

He turned the door handle to no avail. "Yes, it's me. Open up."

"Go away."

"I'm not going anywhere, so open the goddamn door."

The bolt sounded before she flung open the door. Her appearance startled him. Her disheveled hair hung around her gaunt face. Her eyes were puffy and red against her pale skin.

"What do you want?" Her hostility took him aback.

"I want you to be sensible."

"Of course you do."

He ignored her sarcasm. "Are you finished feeling sorry for yourself?"

"Go to hell." She moved to slam the door, but he wedged it open with his foot. With an exasperated sigh, she turned in surrender, then stomped across the room.

Jace followed her inside. Gazing around, he saw clearly the carefree girl she'd been before the accident interrupted her life. Floral walls and pink curtains matched the frilly pillows adorning the brass bed and window seat. Above the stenciled dresser hung a framed painting of three kittens in a basket. He glanced at the untouched food tray on the small worktable in the corner.

"When was the last time you ate?"

"Why do you care?"

He stared.

"Honestly, Jace." She shifted her weight, hands on hips. "Why are you here? I've promised already to let you study my case."

He frowned, alarmed by this side of her.

"My astounding case, I believe you called it." She spun toward the dresser and yanked open the drawer. "Here. This is what you want. Let's not pretend otherwise."

He stared down at the journal she'd tossed to the bed. For a moment, he was tempted to take it and go. He could learn so much from the hell in those pages. A study inside the mind of not only a trauma victim but a sole survivor, as well.

She shook her head as if reading his thoughts. "You see me as they do, no differently."

"That's not true, and you know it."

"I know no such thing. I all but threw myself at you, and you—"

"I am trying to do the right thing!"

"For whom?" She glared at him, chest heaving. Narrowing her eyes, she tilted her head. "Tell me about your father," she demanded.

He frowned. "We are talking about you."

"We're always talking about me!" She threw up her hands. "Everyone talks about me!" Her voice broke on a sob as she turned away. "I'm so tired of it all," she muttered. "So tired of shouldering all the blame." She shook her head. "Every morning I open my eyes and, for that one brief moment between waking and remembering, I am happy. Then the memory returns before my feet hit the floor. I trudge through the days weighted by the burden of my own skin." Her defeated slump conveyed her hopelessness. "I can't go to the wedding," she whispered.

He stared at her back and the chaotic spill of knotted hair tumbling over her shoulders. He struggled to think of a useful response.

"You're stronger than you realize, Maddie," he said finally. "I've dealt with soldiers who couldn't cope with their traumas as well as you have. Besides, you can't hide away in this room forever. You've come too far. Amelia is your friend. Think of her."

She turned to face him. "Think of her?" She gave a bitter laugh. "Perhaps if Amelia had given a thought to me, I wouldn't be in this position."

Jace stared, surprised by her tone.

"She was one of the Fair Five, just like me. Only she was fortunate to have left for England before the accident." Maddie's voice dipped as she lowered her head. "But she was still one of us."

"She never returned?"

She shook her head. "They will all welcome her with open arms when she visits." She lifted her chin. "A part of me hates her for that."

Her honesty was unnerving. As was her pain. The way in which she punished herself was too familiar for comfort.

"You don't hate her, Maddie. You miss her."

Maddie's troubled eyes welled with tears. "I needed her." Her voice broke on a sob, but she swallowed it back. "She left me here—alone—while she traveled the world. While she went on with her life. She's getting married, and she'll quickly disappear again." A tear slid down her cheek. "She's the only friend I have left."

"That's not true," he said, taking her hand. "You have me, too."

She glanced up. A soft blush crossed her pale cheeks as she met his eyes.

"If only you were my doctor back then." A small smile trembled on her lips. "You would have made them see that I'm not an abomination. That I'm the same person I was before the accident."

"Only you can do that."

"How?" Heart-rending desperation filled her eyes. "How do I make them forgive me?"

She stared up at him, pleading for answers he didn't have. Tears glistened on her dark lashes. He felt so damn useless, so helpless, he could barely breathe.

"I don't know," he said, moving closer. He stepped into the subtle scent of her. Lilacs and rain. He pushed a lock of hair from her face. "But I think you must start by forgiving yourself."

Chapter 9

Maddie appeared at Jace's office the next morning to finish the book work she'd started before Pastor Hogle had paid his visit. Jace was filled with relief at the sight of her. When she strode to the desk and got down to business as if the incident with Hogle had never happened, he felt more than relief. He was proud of her. This woman never ceased to surprise him. She was vulnerable but resilient. And Jace admired the hell out of her.

In a yellow dress and matching hat, she filled the room like sunshine. The light of her presence touched everything around her, illuminating every nook and corner inside the dreary room. Inside him.

Christ Almighty.

He was so full of nonsense he didn't even recognize himself. He was obligated to maintain a polite distance from colleagues and patients so that he could make clinical decisions objectively—and without the personal feelings that might cloud a physician's judgment. He was not heartless, but random emotions had no place in his profession, which meant they had no place in him.

With a shake of his head, Jace forced his emotional control to click back into place, and with it, his reasoning. He suspected his failure with Kathy was the direct and only cause of this silly infatuation with Maddie. As soon as he helped Maddie reclaim her old life, his desire for her would fall away naturally. If only the people of Misty Lake weren't making his job so damn difficult.

The wedding was fast approaching and the upcoming weeks would be challenging, no doubt, but he was determined to succeed. For his sake as much as Maddie's.

Shaking his head again, Jace retired to the examination room without a word to prepare a headache snuff he'd promised to Mr. Linton. A short while later, Jace made his way back to the office, with both the snuff and

Mr. Linton's file in hand. Maddie looked up from the books when he entered.

"Here's another file." He dropped the papers onto the desk, then turned to leave.

"Jace."

He stopped and turned to face her.

"I wanted to thank you for coming to see me last evening."

His chest tightened against the sincerity in her dark eyes.

"Don't mention it."

She frowned at his dismissal. "Of course not, Doctor Merrick."

His brow rose at her nettled tone. "Is there something else you wish to say, Madeline?"

"There was," she snapped. "But it's obvious my gratitude makes you uneasy."

"That's because it's unnecessary."

"Nevertheless, I wanted to thank you for going out of your way to help."

"I'm a doctor. It's what I do."

She lowered her eyes. "Yesterday, you claimed to be my friend." She met his gaze, tilting her head. "Or was that claim merely a white lie to make me feel better?"

She looked more embarrassed than angry, and he felt like a cad.

"I am your friend," he said quietly.

"Then please stop acting like we just met at a train station! You can be both a person and a doctor at the same time, can't you? Many other physicians manage it. And most people accept thanks when it has been offered to them. Some even enjoy saying 'you're welcome.'"

He couldn't help smiling in the face of this little speech.

"You're welcome," he said, holding his hands in front of him. "And in addition, I formally surrender."

She nodded triumphantly.

"Now, may I get back to work, madam?"

"Yes, doctor," she teased.

He shook his head, chuckling in spite of himself.

"I'm going across the street to take this to Mr. Linton," he told her.

She glanced at the clock on the mantel. "But it's almost ten o'clock."

"That's why I must hurry. If any patients arrive before I return, please have them wait." He shrugged on his coat. "I know Mrs. Elden is coming in this morning, just make her comfortable until I get back."

"Would you like me to deliver the snuff for you?" she asked.

The unexpected offer pleased him. And not solely because it would save him some time. Maddie rarely ventured outside the office while in town. Another small step on her road to self-guided redemption.

"I'd appreciate that," he said. "Tell him to take no more than an occasional pinch. On second thought, I'll write it down for him. His memory has been slipping."

She stood, waiting as he scribbled down the dosing instructions. Her subtle scent was annoyingly distracting. He handed her the note. Her slender fingers grazed his, the brief contact sending a pulse of heat through his veins. She offered a small smile before leaving him alone with his lust.

Jace ran a hand through his hair as he strode to the kitchen for a quick cup of coffee. He sipped his breakfast, wondering how much longer he could go on like this, but soon thoughts of Maddie were chased off by the sound of footsteps in the hall.

"Hello," someone called from the parlor.

Jace rose to greet the petite young woman standing in the patient waiting area.

After six weeks in Misty Lake, Jace now recognized most of the town's residents. This stylish woman was no local and more likely a summer visitor. "Good morning. You're my first patient today. Have a seat, and I'll be with you in a moment."

"Oh, I'm not a patient, Doctor Merrick." She shook her head, red curls bouncing around her freckled face. "I'm Amelia Strope. Madeline's friend."

"Ah, the lovely bride to be. Do come in, Miss Strope."

"Amelia, please." Dimples graced her cordial smile as she glanced around. "Is Maddie here?"

"She's making a delivery to a patient across the street, but she should be back soon."

Amelia stepped toward him, lips trembling, her owlish eyes brimming with tears.

"Oh, Doctor Merrick," she sobbed. "I...I..."

Jace wasn't sure what was happening.

"Are you all right—?"

"Congratulations!" the girl cried. She threw her arms around him.

He somehow managed to maintain his footing against the sudden weight clinging to his neck.

"I heard the news of your engagement. Forgive my dramatics, but I'm just so happy for Madeline." She hugged him tighter.

Aside from the curse he bit back, he didn't know what to say. It was up to Maddie to set her friend straight about their charade. Rolling his eyes, he patted Amelia's back in silence and waited for the uncomfortable moment to pass.

"So happy." She sniffed.

Jace sighed. Other than a few mumbled acknowledgements, this was the first genuine offer of congratulations he'd received on their engagement, and it was a lulu.

"She's a wonderful girl, as you've obviously discovered, despite all the gossip." Amelia released Jace and wiped at her eyes. "I'm a good judge of character, Doctor Merrick. Maddie is lucky to have you."

Jace swallowed hard.

"So… Your wedding is soon," he said in his desperation to change the subject.

Crisis averted. Her tear-stained face filled with excitement. "Two weeks from Sunday." She prattled on about the wedding with enthusiasm until the cheery tone of her voice faded. "I know Maddie had reservations about attending."

"Sound reservations."

She lowered her eyes. "Unfortunately that's true. But I honestly believe it will be good for Maddie to be there. My fiancé, Lester, agrees."

"I'm guessing that convincing his family proved more difficult?"

"They blame Maddie for the accident. She was driving the wagon that day—and she was skilled at it—but she and the girls were traveling a difficult path. Anyone could have lost control of those horses in the rain and on such steep ground. Sadly, Lester's uncle has more grief than reason when it comes to this subject. Elizabeth was his greatest joy, you see, and he had long ago deemed Maddie a bad influence on the rest of us."

Jace narrowed his eyes. "And why was that?"

"From the time we were little, it was always the same thing: Pastor Hogle would accuse Maddie's grandfather of allowing her too many freedoms and the two men would have angry words. Later on, the pastor thought Mads was fresh—and too familiar with men. And while she was certainly the most flirtatious of the Fair Five, she was always a good and decent girl underneath. No one knows that better than I do." Amelia shrugged. "So, in the end, I just threatened to elope if the Hogles didn't comply with my demands."

"I see," Jace said.

"Of course, this caused quite the family ruckus. I'd never tell Mads about it, though I've a feeling she suspects as much."

Jace had to agree. "After meeting Pastor Hogle, I admire your fortitude."

"The man can be intimidating, but he doesn't frighten me. Some of his parishioners, however... Well, they are another story." She shook her head. "Pastor Hogle's influence has had a terrifying effect on a few of them, I'm afraid. I'm just glad you are man enough to stand up to him and the rest." She frowned. "Unlike Daniel who—" Her hand shot to her mouth. "Forgive me."

"Maddie spoke of their broken engagement."

"Yes. That coward abandoned her when she needed him most." She lowered her eyes. "As did I, I suppose."

"You were in England?"

"Yes. I wanted to return when we received news of the accident, but my father thought it best we remain abroad." She shook her head sadly. "I will always regret deserting Maddie that way."

"But you've remained her friend, despite the distance." Jace soothed.

"Despite anything. Always." She smiled. "Attending the wedding is a big step for her. Of course, not as big a step as becoming engaged, but she needs to face these fools just the same." Her smile faded. "She was the belle of the ball before the accident. Everyone loved her. It's all so unfair." She blinked away her thoughts of the past. "No matter. Brighter days are ahead! She has you now, and I'm so thankful for that."

The door opened, and Maddie stepped into the room.

"Surprise!" Amelia shouted.

Maddie's eyes flashed wide. "Amelia?"

Amelia flung herself into Maddie's arms, embracing her tightly. Jace watched the emotional reunion of what remained of the town's Fair Five. Jace had no true friends to speak of, certainly none he had known since childhood. Colleagues, patients, and random lovers. Over the years, he hadn't thought he had either time or desire for more. He now realized he may have been wrong, and a hollow void opened inside him as he stood there watching the two women hold each other. Maddie had lost some of her dearest companions, but he'd never had any at all.

Chapter 10

Amelia hugged Maddie so tight she could barely breathe. The familiar strawberry scent of her hair hadn't changed.

"Enough, Amelia." Laughing, she broke free of Amelia's embrace.

"But I'm so happy to see you, Mads." Tears shone in her big blue eyes.

Maddie swallowed hard, feeling guilty for the way she'd spoken of her friend to Jace just yesterday.

"I'm happy, too."

"I've met your Doctor Merrick," Amelia said, winking at Jace. "And I must say, he works awfully fast. I'm so pleased for you both. Not to mention utterly stunned. The first thing I heard when I stepped from the carriage was that you're engaged to the town's new doctor. How did this happen?"

"Very suddenly," Jace tossed in.

Maddie frowned, feeling guilty for having withheld the truth from her friend. But she couldn't chance disclosing the sham to Amelia in a letter. A matter such as this required a face-to-face confession. And the sooner the better.

"Amelia, I must speak with you regarding our engagement."

"Well, of course you must. I want to know everything."

Maddie glanced to Jace, who shrugged in return. It was obvious he'd be no help.

Amelia took Maddie by the hand. "You can tell me all about it on the way to the dress shop. The other girls are meeting us there."

"Now?" Maddie asked.

"I'm sorry for the lack of notice. I went to your house first. But the dresses have arrived earlier than anticipated, and Mrs. March wants to fit them right away. She's set aside the entire morning for us." She turned to Jace. "You don't mind, do you?"

"Not at all. I'm sure you two have a lot to talk about."

Maddie ignored his veiled remark. Summoning the courage to confess her lie, she left the office with Amelia, and they walked toward the dress shop. "There are four of you in the bridal party. Lester's sisters, Gertrude and Dolly, of course, and my friend Caroline."

"I look forward to meeting Caroline," Maddie offered truthfully. But she felt nothing but dread at the thought of reuniting with Gertrude and Dolly, whom she'd known for years.

"And Cousin Philip and Cousin David have arrived from Boston. They're in the bridal party, too. Philip will be so happy to see you." She nudged Maddie's shoulder. "You remember how smitten he was with you when we were girls?"

Maddie laughed. "Yes, I remember."

"Poor Philip. He was so disappointed to hear you're spoken for."

"Amelia—"

"So, how did you and Doctor Merrick meet, anyway?"

"Quite by chance," Maddie answered. "And in the nick of time."

"Oh?"

"Amelia, I must tell you something, and you must promise to keep my secret."

Amelia tilted her head, regarding her closely. "Of course."

"Jace and I are not engaged." Maddie released the breath she'd been holding.

Amelia stopped in her tracks. "I don't understand."

"It's a ruse. I met Daniel and Miss Brewer by chance a few weeks ago. Oh Amelia, he was so smug and awful to me, I couldn't bear it—he all but snickered into his elbow when he confronted me about finding an escort for the wedding. So I had to tell him that I was engaged. And since I had no fiancé at the time, I made one up. In the form of Jace Merrick."

Amelia considered this for a long moment, during which Maddie wanted to shrivel into her shoes.

"And Doctor Merrick agreed?"

"Yes." Maddie nodded.

The glow in Amelia's cheeks dimmed like an expended candle. Her disappointment made Maddie feel ill.

"Oh, Mads," she said quietly. "I don't think I quite realized how miserable things have been for you." She shook her head. "I suppose I wouldn't allow myself to think too deeply on it."

"So you understand my reasons for the lie?"

Amelia nodded. "Yes."

"I'm so relieved. But you must promise to keep the secret. You mustn't even tell Lester."

"I owe you my silence." Amelia's small smile warmed Maddie's heart. "I'm so sorry I wasn't here for you."

Maddie swallowed hard, feeling guilty again for the way she'd spoken of Amelia to Jace.

"I've missed you, Amelia."

"I've missed you, too." Tears welled in her eyes. "I miss them, Mads."

"So do I." She and Amelia had written little of the accident and their lost friends in their letters to one another. Given the physical distance between them, it was natural to maintain a superficial tone in correspondence. But now that they were together again, there were many more intimate things Maddie wanted to say. Today, however, was not the day for depressing talk. It was a day for celebration.

"Enough of this now," she said with a fluff of her skirts. "We have shopping to do."

They chatted all the way to the dress shop. The miles they'd spent apart closed quickly, and it felt like old times. The young man seated on the bench outside the door stood as they approached.

"Miss Strope," he said with a tip of his hat.

Amelia's cordial reply lacked her usual warmth.

"Matthew." She extended her arm. "This is my good friend Madeline Sutter."

His thin mouth tightened as he turned to Maddie. The chill of his icy eyes ran up and down the length of her.

"I know who she is." He pulled his gaze from Maddie. "The girls are waiting inside," he said, returning to his seat.

Amelia led her up the few stairs toward the door. "Don't mind him."

The directive was easier said than done. Maddie was used to receiving rude treatment, but there'd been something hinging on sinister in the way Matthew had looked at her. "I've seen him before," Maddie said. "Who is he?"

Amelia led Maddie to a secluded spot behind a tall display of spooled ribbons.

"Matthew Webster. Faithful parishioner to Pastor Hogle. He drifted into town a few years ago, penniless and heartbroken after being jilted by his girlfriend in Albany. Pastor took him under his wing. He resides in a room behind the church now."

The pastor's treatment of Maddie made it difficult to conceive of his capacity to extend such charity to anyone.

"I see," she said. But she did not.

"Since then Matthew has formed quite a fondness for Dolly."

Maddie blinked.

"Dolly? But she's only, what, fifteen years old?"

"Sixteen," Amelia said. "Matthew is a good seven years older, but I'm told Pastor Hogle approves. Dolly's appearance matters not a whit to Matthew, and because of this, I'm trying hard to warm up to him. However, his behavior is...somewhat unsettling."

"Unsettling?"

"He escorts Dolly everywhere. Barely lets her out of his sight. Honestly, I don't know how she can tolerate it."

Maddie agreed this sounded a bit odd.

"The pastor is grooming him to be a man of the church." Amelia sighed.

Maddie glanced back at the man perched like a stone gargoyle outside the door. For some reason, this news bothered her most. She shook off thoughts of Matthew as she and Amelia approached the Hogle sisters. Gertrude frowned at Maddie before whispering something in her younger sister's ear.

Mrs. March bubbled with smiles and small talk, catering to Amelia and her bridesmaids as though she were fitting gowns for the Queen of England. With the exception of Maddie, of course, she bent over backward to accommodate the wedding party. Maddie was used to brusque treatment from the dressmaker, so she paid little heed to the woman's obvious slights.

Dodging Gertrude's palpable contempt proved more difficult. Lester's eldest sister was not pleased to be in Maddie's company and was not afraid to telegraph her displeasure at every opportunity. In contrast, Lester's younger sister, Dolly, didn't even offer a glance in Maddie's direction. The child was so focused on hiding the large birthmark on her cheek that she nearly disappeared into the wallpaper.

Maddie hadn't seen Dolly in ages, but the wine-colored stain on the girl's face hadn't faded with time. Dolly had grown in years and in self-consciousness. She kept her head low, her hair like a curtain, hanging over her cheek.

Thankfully, Amelia's friend, Caroline Weiss, provided real solace in what might have been an awkward afternoon. Her pleasing demeanor and good humor made her easy to like. Caroline resided in Albany and seemed unaware of the gossip surrounding Maddie's past. Maddie hoped to befriend the girl while she could. Pathetic, yes. But it was worth a try.

It had been a long time since Maddie had been in the company of other young women, and despite Gertrude's sour attitude, she found herself enjoying the familiar chatter. Meanwhile, Mrs. March fitted them all with great efficiency. Each white dress would arrive the morning of the wedding, complete with the white slippers and gloves Amelia had selected. Instead of a garland of flowers, each bridesmaid would wear an elaborate white hat with a short veil and silk orange blossoms attached to the crown.

"You will be certain to remove the price tags from the hats before delivering them, won't you, Mrs. March?" Maddie asked, unable to resist.

The woman's mortified expression quickly turned defiant. "Of course," she snapped.

Maddie gave the lady a syrupy smile before turning back to the mirror. After admiring her own reflection for a few moments, Maddie looked around at the progress the other girls were making. Dolly stood on a riser, while Mrs. March inserted pins at her hem. The dress fit like a glove to the young girl's svelte figure.

"Lovely," Maddie uttered.

"Oh, yes," Caroline agreed.

Amelia nodded. "What do you think, Dolly?"

The girl glanced up in surprise.

"She knows nothing of fashion, Amelia." Gertrude tugged the fabric at Dolly's hips. "All those johnnycakes you eat are taking their toll." Gertrude frowned, stepping back. "Your figure is all you have going for you, Dolly. You'd better take care to keep it."

Dolly lowered her eyes.

"Her figure is perfection," Maddie snapped.

Gertrude glared at her. Grumbling under her breath, she turned to admire a nearby display of bonnets, but it was Dolly's small smile that affected Maddie more.

When their fittings were complete, Amelia suggested tea at her parents' summer home on the lake. Dolly's eyes sparked in favor of the idea. She glanced to her sister, but Gertrude was quick to refuse the invitation, stomping out that tiny flame. Dolly had no choice in the matter but to follow Gertrude to the door, where Matthew waited to usher them home.

"Are you certain you won't join us?" Amelia asked Gertrude.

"The girls must get home," Matthew interjected before Gertrude could respond.

"Very well, then," Amelia uttered. She turned to Maddie and Caroline, and they started on their way.

Thankfully, Amelia's parents were out visiting friends in Albany when the girls arrived. Maddie would have to face them eventually, but dealing with Gertrude and Dolly had been enough for one day. Entering the foyer of the large house, Maddie felt as if she were stepping back in time. The memories returned in a rush. The Fair Five fluttering through the house like birds let loose, the parties and teas, all the wonderful times they'd spent here together. She released a bittersweet sigh, glancing around. Evidence of the upcoming wedding was everywhere.

Large trestle tables held piles of beautifully wrapped wedding gifts. Outside, the gardeners were busy trimming hedges and readying the lush lawn for the pre-wedding festivities. The entire atmosphere was filled with anticipation of the joyous occasion—the wedding of the season.

A pang of sadness arced through her. Maddie would never experience the thrill of being a bride. The secret she kept was too great, too substantial to keep from a husband. The weight of it would be too much to carry through marriage.

Amelia led them to the patio. "Now remember, ladies, the picnic is one week from tomorrow," she said. "I hope the weather holds out."

"You worry too much," Caroline said. "The weather will be glorious for the picnic next week and for the wedding the following weekend."

"From your lips to God's ear," Amelia said. "There will be a large tent for the lakeside ceremony at the hotel, just in case. It will be such fun! We've arranged rooms at the hotel for everyone."

"Even the locals?" Maddie asked.

"Certainly. I want the entire bridal party at my disposal, day or night, all weekend long." Amelia laughed. "Oh, Philip, there you are." She waved her cousin into the room. "Come see Maddie."

The tall man strode toward them, nodding to Caroline before stopping in front of Maddie.

"How good to see you again, Miss Sutter." He beamed, gazing down at her with an intensity that spurred a blush to her cheeks.

"Philip is a banker in Boston now. Cousin David is here as well, though I'm not sure where."

"He'll be down soon," Philip said. He turned back to Maddie. "You do remember me, don't you, Miss Sutter?"

"Yes, of course. But you've changed considerably since we last met all those years ago." She smiled.

Philip smiled too.

He had, indeed, grown considerably from the clumsy boy who had spent summers here. This man was well spoken and confident with warm brown eyes. He stood at Jace's height, but was leaner, less muscular.

Philip had often served as an entertaining diversion in the absence of Daniel and the other local boys, who'd spent many of those long hot days hunting and fishing. Maddie had toyed with Philip's affections back then, but it seemed he didn't hold her girlish behavior against her.

"You're even prettier than I remember," he said.

Maddie would have laughed, but the sincerity in his compliment stopped her.

"I've thought of you often through the years." He released her hand. "Your fiancé is a lucky man."

"And you're still a charmer." She tossed her hair, enjoying the subtle flirtation. She'd never made an effort to know Philip years ago. He'd merely been a device to alleviate boredom, nothing more. Now her prickle of regret turned to shame. They'd all changed with the years, but Maddie had never felt it as much as she did these past weeks.

Philip's brother, David, joined them for tea in the sunroom overlooking the lake. Maddie fell comfortably into the lively conversation and laughter, and the remainder of the afternoon passed as quickly as a breeze.

It dawned on her how easy life could be in the company of strangers. Her confidence grew stronger as the afternoon progressed. She'd survived the dress fitting, and tea at the Strope house had been a delight.

Perhaps she could leave Misty Lake someday after Grandfather was gone. She pushed away the sad thought of losing Grandfather, then was struck by another. If she left Misty Lake, she would lose Jace too. His friendship had come to mean so much to her. She'd told him things she'd never told anyone, and she realized suddenly that she had come to depend on him. She didn't know what the upcoming weeks of wedding festivities held in store for her. But with Jace at her side, she felt ready to face it all.

Chapter 11

It was just past two o'clock the following Monday when Jace's final patient of the day left the office. The remainder of the afternoon was reserved for house calls, which Jace squeezed into his schedule two days a week. As had become their ritual, Maddie set up a tray of coffee, then headed to the parlor where they would enjoy a break before Jace set off in his buggy.

These brief respites were the best part of her day. Over coffee, Jace would assign her tasks, report on the status of supplies to be ordered, and discuss his schedule. When new patients summoned him, she'd offer Jace driving directions and insight into what to expect when he arrived, anything that might aid in his house calls.

She walked down the hall, slowing her pace as she glanced into the small alcove that served as an office. In the lull of his hectic afternoon, Jace sat, hunched over his desk, scribbling notes in patient files and attending to paperwork. Muted lamplight draped his wide shoulders and tense profile as he worked.

The sight of him filled her with admiration. Jace was a fine doctor, and she felt grateful to have had this opportunity to get to know him. The small contribution she was making to his growing practice had drawn her from isolation. It felt good to be doing something constructive. Something real.

A twinge of shame coursed through her. Jace was far too busy with more pressing tasks to partake in the scheme she'd concocted. But she needed him. She could not do it alone. She proceeded to the parlor, resigned to this truth. Less than two weeks remained until the wedding rehearsal dance. She placed the tray on the table. Coffee sloshed in the rattling cups, alerting her to her trembling hands. Nerves knotted in her stomach every time she envisioned spending an entire weekend with Pastor Hogle and the others who despised her.

In for a penny, in for a pound…

Maddie set up the coffee as Jace entered the parlor. Tossing his coat over the back of a chair, he released a long breath and took a seat on the sofa.

"I've another stack of patient files for you to organize," he said, reaching for the cup she offered.

She nodded. "How was Mr. Linton this morning?"

"He's doing remarkably well. Hasn't suffered any more headaches and is getting out more as a result."

Maddie smiled. "I'm so glad to hear it," she said, though she'd suspected as much.

"He mentioned you were kind enough to prepare an herbal compress for him."

Despite Jace's casual tone, she stiffened in dread of his censure for interfering with his patient.

"And he said that you heated it thoroughly before helping him apply it."

"It seemed to give him some relief," she uttered.

"While I'd prefer you refrain from treating my patients, in this instance, I think your heated compress may have helped calm his nerves. Combined with the snuff I prescribed, he's feeling much better," he said. "Well done, Maddie."

Her relief gave way to guilt as she shifted nervously in her seat. She'd cured Mr. Linton behind Jace's back, and he was applauding her for it. Although she didn't regret her actions, she felt the weight of her deception.

"The poor man was in such pain. It was the least I could do."

"He asked me to extend his thanks."

"He did?" she asked, truly surprised. The gruff man had barely acknowledged her presence in his home. An interesting development.

"I trust you set things straight with Amelia the other day?"

"Yes," she said. "I confessed that we weren't engaged. She was disappointed but understanding."

"Good."

"It was so wonderful to see her," Maddie said. "And the dress fitting went well." She omitted the rude treatment she'd received from Gertrude and Mrs. March, which would come as no surprise, anyway. "It was fun hearing about Amelia's plans. The wedding promises to be quite the affair." She stared down at the cup in her hands. "They've hired a ten-piece orchestra to perform at the rehearsal dinner dance."

"So why the glum face?" he teased. "I thought all women enjoyed dancing." He grew serious again, and she saw the physician in him surface. "Is it your leg?"

"No, my leg's fine." She leaned back in her seat. "But I haven't danced in three years." She glanced up at Jace to see his reaction. "I may be rusty."

Jace eyed her, pursing his lips. He placed his cup on the table, then stood at her side.

"Let's see." He held out his hand. "May I have this dance, Miss Sutter?"

She stared up at him warily. "There's no music playing."

"Use your imagination." He wiggled his fingers, urging her to take his hand. "I have a reputation to uphold," he said. "I can't be seen dancing in public with a woman who can't follow my lead."

Laughing at his quip, she grasped his hand.

"Then perhaps you'll simply have to follow mine."

Jace's lively grin warmed her as he pulled her to her feet. She relished these rare glimpses of his easy humor, the way he always made her feel better. For a man who could be so somber, Jace had a lighter side, too. She felt honored that he shared it with her.

With a long graceful stride, he led her to the middle of the room. The braided carpet beneath their feet absorbed the sound of their steps as they moved slowly around the furniture.

Jace glanced down at her feet. "You haven't missed a step."

"I'm not certain you'd notice if I had," she teased, although his dancing was surprisingly practiced.

He laughed. "Insulting my ballroom skills?"

"Not at all. You're as light as air on your feet, Doctor Merrick."

"Blame my boots," he said. "But this exercise is to assess your dancing ability, not mine."

She nodded with mock solemnity. "Yes, of course," she said as he whirled her around.

He pulled her closer, and the heat of his body engulfed her. She leaned against his shoulder, closing her eyes. Though she'd not dare dance so improperly in public, she couldn't help herself now. Jace moved, and she vibrated with each movement, each muscle flexing beneath his shirt. In his strong arms she felt so safe. Special.

"This is nice," she murmured. Had she spoken that aloud? She fought for something less dreamy to say. "Where did you learn to dance?"

"My mother taught me," he said. "Out of sheer boredom, I suppose. We'd dance for hours while my father saw to his patients."

This peek into his past made her yearn for more. Aside from the ugly confrontation with Pastor Hogle, this was his first mention of his family. Jace kept the door to his personal life tightly closed, and she slipped carefully through the narrow opening he'd drawn.

"Your father was a doctor, too?"

"Yes. For over twenty years."

"So you're following in his footsteps."

She felt him stiffen in her arms.

"Not if I can help it," he said.

She stopped, staring up at him. He averted his eyes. Resuming the dance, he stared over her shoulder.

"What happened with your father, Jace?"

They moved through the deafening silence for several long moments before he spoke again.

"It seems like a lifetime ago," he said softly. "After I decided to become a doctor, my father and I dedicated two evenings a week together to discuss various cases and treatments." He shook his head. "Even back then I could sense his frustration."

"Frustration?"

"My father was unable to distance himself from his patients. Their pain became his, their suffering his. And he hated the limitations of medicine. His limitations. He became increasingly unhappy over the years. With each patient he lost, he lost a bit of himself, too. He became a different person."

"What do you mean?"

"His failures afflicted him like a disease, and his confidence in medicine dwindled to nothing. To combat his inconsolable sense of defeat, he turned to alternate forms of healing."

Maddie's breath caught.

"Alternate forms of healing? What does that mean?"

Jace frowned, and Maddie swallowed hard at his look of disgust.

"Ridiculous, illogical practices involving faith healers and witchdoctors. The occult." Jace's shoulders tensed with restrained emotion as he spoke. "He buried himself in case studies of this nonsense, applying it in his practice. The man he was—the competent physician he'd always been— disappeared, and his patients were talking. Naturally, their trust in him began to dissipate. As did mine."

Jace's obvious revulsion for these alternative therapies made Maddie shiver. She shuddered again as she imagined his response should he ever discover her secret.

"In his desperation for results, he abandoned traditional medicine—his life's work—for hocus-pocus."

Maddie shook off a shudder of fear. "What happened?"

Jace shrugged, as if he wasn't quite sure. "By the time I returned home from school for the Christmas break, it was too late. His practice was already suffering. He'd lost a young patient that week, and the boy's distraught parents blamed him for not saving their son. Talk of a lawsuit spread like wildfire through town. My father refused to discuss his treatment of the boy with me, though I suspect it involved more quackery than medicine. He holed up in his office, looking more hopeless than I'd ever seen him. After promising he'd get some sleep, he insisted I return to the house ahead of him." Jace's voice dropped so low Maddie barely heard it. "I found him at his desk the next morning. He was dead."

Maddie cringed in surprise. "Oh, Jace, I'm so sorry."

"An empty syringe lie on the desk in front of him." Jace lowered his eyes. "Cause of death was attributed to cardiac arrest, but I've no doubt he died from opiates. What I'll never know for certain was if the overdose was intentional."

The pain in Jace's eyes echoed through Maddie's core. She would never have guessed he'd endured such a trial, and she couldn't help wondering how Pastor Hogle had known of it. Jace had risked much by making an enemy of the pastor. And he'd done it for her.

"All those years as a doctor, he helped so many people." He shook his head sadly. "Medicine was his life until he'd lost any sense of meaning in it."

"As you did in Pittsburgh?"

He glanced down at her, surprised that she'd suspected this.

"Yes. It happened to me, too."

Maddie lowered her gaze. She knew Jace well enough to know he rarely spoke of these events, and she felt flattered and gratified that he'd confided in her. Sill, a heavy uneasiness formed in her chest. She forced herself to look up at him.

"What about your mother?"

His face hardened over his distress. "She was used to his absence," he said bluntly. "Even before he died. The years of staring at his vacant chair at the dinner table, the empty space beside her in bed, had primed her well, I suppose."

"She must have been a strong woman," Maddie said.

"Oh, she bore it as best she could. She was a truly wonderful mother—attentive, clever, and unfailingly kind. But there was always a shadow of sadness in her. And in the end, she wasn't so very strong. After my father passed, people looked at us differently. To escape the scandal of his death, she moved to Ohio to be with my aunt. She died a year later."

"I'm sorry," she uttered.

They moved slowly over the carpet. She rested her head on his shoulder. She felt his intake of breath, as though inhaling the contact.

"Life is so fragile. So short," she began. By rote, her fingers splayed, caressing his tense shoulders. Her body melted as the stiff muscles beneath her hands began to relax.

He shook his head. "Maddie…"

She gazed into his eyes.

"Let's say we live for today. For the moment."

He stilled, absorbing her words. Conflicting desires marred his handsome face. Surrender, resistance, a combination of both…

His voice came out hoarse. "What is it you want from me?"

Nothing. Everything. She truly did not know.

"I want you to escort me to the wedding," she uttered softly. "I want you to be my friend." She licked her lips. "I want you to kiss me."

He drew in a breath, then slowly exhaled. The whisk of warm air on her cheek fluttered through her. Her legs turned to jelly. He stared down at her, his blue eyes filled with such feeling, such substance that it made her afraid. The sudden shift inside her own center frightened her even more.

This thing that they shared went far deeper than lust or loneliness. She felt it in the root of her being, felt it down to her bones.

Lowering his head, he pressed his lips to her forehead. She closed her eyes, accepting the tender gesture, not for the bittersweet refusal it was— but for what she must let it become.

A safeguard against losing her heart.

Chapter 12

"I have to go check on Mrs. Mead," Jace said, releasing Maddie from his arms. He raked a hand through his hair and fought for control. It wasn't merely lust now. He cared for her.

"Yes, of course." She fluffed her skirts awkwardly and took two steps back.

The rattled look on her flush face wrenched in his gut. He hated to leave her this way. Emotion collided with reason.

"Want to ride along?" he asked before he could stop himself.

She snapped up her head in surprise.

He had never before invited her to join him on a house call. He was clearly sunk. Spending less time with her seemed the better solution to his brewing dilemma, but as always, her presence blurred the boundaries of good sense.

"I can drop you off after I see to Mrs. Mead," he offered, by way of explanation.

"All right," she said. "Just give me a moment to gather my things."

Jace shrugged on his coat, qualms multiplying as he snatched up his bag. He stepped out to the porch. The smell of the petunias she'd planted wafted from the window boxes. He inhaled the scented breeze, soothed by the homespun simplicity of the fragrant aroma. Jace had deemed the flowers unnecessary, until Maddie had pointed out that, despite the modest signboard identifying his medical practice, the neglected boxes made the weathered house appear vacant. Colorful blooms now welcomed his patients with an air of permanence—a hallmark of a reliable physician.

Presenting this impression was especially important, as Jace was unmarried and, therefore, considered unsettled. Soon after Maddie had planted the flowers, Jace had relocated four wicker chairs from the shed to the porch. Her influence was subtle but sure. It was an intrusion he minded less every day.

This alarming fact shrieked through his brain, alerting him to imminent danger. After reflecting on his past and his parents' one-sided marriage—after that dance with Maddie in the parlor—he needed the earsplitting warning.

Maddie hurried from the house, fastening the ties to her bonnet. Her demure smile was unnerving. Settling next to her in the buggy unsettled him even more. Her skirts filled the tight space between them, brushing his thigh. His senses devoured her nearness, her arousing lilac scent, her heat. Jace snapped the reins. The buggy jerked to a start, but he couldn't escape the building tension—or the peripheral view of her breasts.

He drove through town in frustrated silence. The mild weather drew people outside to their porches and gardens. Recognizing Jace's buggy, they waved, quickly retracting their greetings as they recognized the passenger seated at his side.

If Maddie noticed their disrespect, she made no mention of it. But then again, what could she say?

He had to give her credit for facing them instead of cowering. He admired her dogged resolve to reclaim some semblance of her former life—and certainly Maddie would have to agree that these weeks of office work leading up to Amelia's wedding had been good for her regardless of whether she achieved her goal. The two of them made a fine team and were getting on well.

Too well, in point of fact. Jace had lately become a master of resistance. Evasion.

Or so he'd thought until that dance. Until he'd held her in his arms and felt her body pressed to his. Until he'd confided in her the story of his father.

Until that sobering moment when he'd looked down into her eyes and felt himself falling.

* * * *

Maddie sat beside Jace, trying to weave what she'd learned of Jace's past into something she could use to her advantage. But the result of this effort was disheartening. Try as she might to spin a happy outcome, Maddie kept returning to the uncomfortable truth: Jace condemned his father for exploring the very type of alternative healing that Maddie herself performed. There was no conceivable way around that small detail.

This knowledge made Maddie feel more isolated than ever before. And more fearful. If Jace somehow discovered that she'd been treating his patients…no. She would not—could not—let him find out. But nor would she quit ministering to the men and women of Misty Lake on the sly.

She was helping people as surely as Jace was, and by doing so, she was helping herself.

Maddie's ability to ease the suffering of others had lately given birth to something else inside of her—a new compassion and regard for her neighbors. Before the accident, Maddie had been shamefully self-centered and cared mostly for shallow amusements. But her gift had taught her to look beyond her own pleasure for the first time, and she was satisfied with the person she had recently become.

"The road has dried out well," Jace said woodenly.

He'd remained strangely quiet since their dance, but if the state of road conditions was to be the extent of their conversation, she was in for a long trip. He tipped his hat to a laundress hanging out her wash. After one glance at Maddie, the woman's sweet smile quickly soured.

Combating the snub with a lift of her chin, Maddie turned to Jace. "Do you think you will be happy here in Misty Lake?" she asked.

"I like it fine. Despite the delay in opening, my practice is progressing nicely."

She sighed. Jace's impersonal doctor mask was firmly back in place. "What about the people?" she prodded. "Do you like the people?"

He shrugged. "People here are set in their ways. Traditional." He shook his head. "And they're hard pressed to trust me."

"Your association with me doesn't help."

"It's my age," he countered. "Although I'm educated in more advanced medical practices, they're reluctant to trust someone so young. Not a day goes by when a patient doesn't mention Doctor Filmore." He shook his head. "Ironic, isn't it? Their blind faith in that bastard?"

It was more than ironic, she thought, as she slumped farther down in her seat.

"Treating wary patients is difficult. They don't heed my advice, even as their health suffers for it. As an outsider, I can see the advantage to living among people you've known all your life. But as a doctor, the insular nature of this community is often maddening."

She shrugged off the hard truths in his assessment of her neighbors.

"They'll learn to trust you eventually," she said. "As I have." She offered him a smile. "Quite a feather in your cap, that, since my belief in doctors was shattered to pieces by your predecessor."

His profile softened as he turned to face her again.

"You're a fine doctor, Jace, and it's only a matter of time before they see this, too."

His humble expression took her aback. Jace was not a modest man. A certain degree of arrogance was inherent to his profession—his personality. That she'd managed to flatter him with her candor was a charming surprise.

"I hope you're right. Some lives might depend on it. Not to mention the success of my practice."

Jace turned the buggy onto the dirt road that led to the woods. He gestured with a jut of his chin. "Speaking of stubborn patients…"

The Mead house came into view. The rustic house sat nestled in a small clearing in the woods at the top of the hill. The trail was narrow and steep. Maddie held tight as the buggy trudged along, until they stopped in the drive in front of the house.

"Mrs. Mead can be difficult," Jace said. "During my last visit she threatened to clunk me with a rolling pin when I attempted to listen to her lungs."

Maddie chuckled, picturing the scene. "Shall I wait here?" she asked.

Jace shook his head. "It may be a lengthy visit. Come inside with me." He pointed a finger. "But stay out of the way."

She nodded but promised nothing. She'd had enough of staying out of the way.

He helped her from the buggy, and they walked to the porch. Mrs. Mead's son, Carter, opened the door before Jace had a chance to knock.

"Go on in, Doc," Carter said. "I'll be out in the garden if you need me." He acknowledged Maddie with a cool nod as he ushered them inside.

The air was permeated with the delicious aroma of Mrs. Mead's famous buttermilk tea cakes. Heaping plates of freshly baked cakes lined the large working table in the center of the kitchen. Mrs. Mead sat beside the table, a wet towel covering her foot, which was raised on a chair.

Maddie stood with her back to the sink as Jace saw to his patient. Craning her neck, she watched as he lifted the towel, unveiling Mrs. Mead's swollen foot. He frowned at the beads of fluid seeping through the blistered skin of her toes.

"You haven't been following my directions, have you, Mrs. Mead?"

The large woman waved him away. "I'm much too busy to rest my feet every time they start aching."

"And what about the diet?"

She grimaced, as though she smelled something vile.

Jace glanced around the kitchen. "You're still baking these cakes every day?"

"Of course," she snapped. "It's my living."

The discord between doctor and patient was obvious. Maddie sensed where this was going, and it wouldn't go well. She considered returning to the buggy to avoid the uncomfortable scene unfolding, but curiosity—and the urge to help make peace—kept her glued at the sink.

Jace opened his bag. "And as you're baking all these sugar-and-lard-stuffed cakes, are you sampling them?"

Mrs. Mead narrowed her eyes.

"What are you getting at?"

"Oh, I think you know, Mrs. Mead. I'll ask you again, are you tasting the cakes as you bake them?"

"I must sample each batch."

"Uh-huh." He slipped his stethoscope beneath her bibbed apron and proceeded to listen to her heart.

To Maddie's relief the woman made no move for the rolling pin.

"And how many batches do you bake each day?" he inquired as he checked her pulse.

She lifted her chin.

"At least eight," she grumbled, tugging her wrist from his grasp.

Jace frowned.

"As I've mentioned before, this foot problem is a result of poor diet. You must lose some weight. Thirty pounds at least."

Mrs. Mead's jaw dropped with the force of an anvil.

"You must cease this baking and eating so much."

"Well, I never..." The older woman's cheeks blazed with fire.

"And that's why your feet are the size of tree stumps," Jace said.

Mrs. Mead gasped, and Maddie gasped along with her. She had to say something to defuse the situation before Jace went too far.

"Baking is her livelihood, Doctor Merrick. The local hotels depend on her to supply these cakes for their guests."

"That's right," Mrs. Mead chimed in. "The summer season is now underway. I have orders to fill and a family to support. You can't expect me to quit baking."

"No one expects that," Maddie assured her. She glanced to Jace, then wished she hadn't.

His face was like steel. A vein emerged at his throat. Maddie turned to Mrs. Mead before he erupted.

"But perhaps it's unnecessary to taste every batch, ma'am."

"I—"

"You've been baking these cakes day after day for well over ten years. No doubt you follow the same family recipe."

"Well, of course."

"Then you don't really need to test them, do you?" prodded Maddie. "You know your formula consistently yields a wonderful product."

"Perhaps. But my grammy always said the key to our tea cakes is the light and fluffy crumb. I must ensure that's what I deliver to my customers every single time."

"That's ridiculous." Jace snorted.

Mrs. Mead glared at him.

Maddie did too. Jace's coarse bedside manner would win him neither friends nor patients. No wonder people were reluctant to take his advice.

"Mrs. Mead, Doctor Merrick is only concerned for your health."

"And you, of all people, are here to defend him?"

"He needs no defending," Maddie shot back. "He's here to help you. He can't do that if you refuse to do as he says."

The stubborn woman clamped her lips.

Maddie took a quick breath to summon her patience. "You're an exceptional baker, Mrs. Mead. I suggest you trust in that ability and taste only once per day. I'm certain the quality of your cakes will not suffer. And I believe your health will improve, too."

The woman slumped back in the chair, considering this.

"I suppose I could try."

"Wise decision," Jace said as he examined her foot more closely. "I'm going to increase the dosage of your medication." He pointed a finger. "And I advise you to follow my directions. Because if you don't, we might be forced to amputate that foot."

Her eyes flashed wide with fear.

"All right," she snapped, but more in defeat than anger.

"Very good." Jace pulled his ledger from his bag and scribbled something in his notes.

"But remember, Doctor Merrick, I'm blaming you if my cakes aren't up to par. Imagine selling them without tasting them first," she muttered.

"I'll accept full responsibility," he said as he wrote.

"The cakes will be delicious," Maddie promised. "They've always been my favorite treat of the summer."

The compliment seemed to appease Mrs. Mead.

"I suppose you may as well take some then. I always bake extra." She leaned to the table and filled a basket with golden loaves. Maddie accepted the hard-earned reward with a smile of relief that the visit was over.

"I'll be back to check on you at the end of the week," Jace told the woman as he packed up his bag.

"Yes, yes, good-bye." The woman waved them out the door.

The fresh air felt wonderful as they walked the stone path to the buggy. With each step, Maddie awaited Jace's censure for her interference, preparing her defense. Had he used one iota of tact with Mrs. Mead, Maddie would not have been driven to meddle.

"That went better than expected," he said finally.

Maddie stared agape.

"You're not serious?" She tilted her head as she realized he was. "Jace, have you never heard the expression about catching more flies with honey than with vinegar?"

He frowned. "People need to use common sense. They must follow their doctor's instructions. It's as simple as that."

"From what I witnessed in there, it's not always that simple."

"My patients are my responsibility, Maddie."

"I understand that, but I—"

"You're not a physician."

His lofty tone only served to provoke her. "And you're not in Pittsburgh anymore. People here are set in their ways, you said so yourself. These patients are your neighbors. Neighbors you have to face every day."

"It's my job to save my patients, not befriend them. I won't risk their health by tiptoeing on eggshells to spare their feelings."

"I'm not suggesting you do. I'm merely suggesting you don't insult them. That you soften the manner in which you present your advice."

"So much for staying out of the way," he muttered.

"I had to do something. For goodness sakes, you all but told the woman she was fat."

"It got her attention."

"But not her cooperation. And isn't that more important?"

He stared in silent annoyance.

Maddie sighed. "You're a fine doctor, but your treatments will do no good if patients refuse them. I'm only trying to help—"

"I don't need your help." The stern look in his eyes proved he didn't think he did.

She shook her head, seething. "No, of course you don't." Her sarcasm infused each word. "An accomplished big-city doctor like yourself wouldn't need help from an under-educated society girl like me."

He glared at her, his jaw twitching. "Then we are agreed."

He said nothing more as they boarded the buggy and started toward town. He sat silently, clenching the reins.

She sat stiffly beside him, clenching her teeth, her hands, and every clenchable muscle in her body. They rode for miles without a word until Maddie spied the glimmer of the lake in the distance. It was a welcome relief. Another few uncomfortable minutes and she'd be home.

"Perhaps it wouldn't hurt to be more flexible," Jace offered suddenly, clearing his throat.

She blinked, turning to face him. He stared straight ahead as he drove. "I need their trust."

Maddie nodded at the simple concession before turning away from him, determined to hide her tiny—but admittedly triumphant—smile. As absurd as it was, Jace also needed Madeline Sutter, the town pariah, to help win over the very people who shunned her.

Chapter 13

As Caroline had predicted, the weather was glorious for the picnic the following weekend. A mild breeze cooled Maddie's flush of anxiety as guests assembled on the freshly manicured lawns of the Strope house. Following light refreshments, the party would journey the short distance to the picnic grove at noon.

Maddie's grip on Jace's arm tightened as more guests arrived. Amelia hurried off to greet Abigail and Jim Pike. Behind them Daniel arrived, escorting the pretty Lucinda and his cousins, Gertrude and Dolly. Matthew Webster lagged closely behind. Henry Whalen and Bitsy Wager stood nearby, nibbling on cookies and chatting together like the life-long friends they were.

Maddie sipped her lemonade, summoning her strength to face these people who'd rather not face her. She turned her focus to the conversation between Jace and Lester until Amelia returned.

"Everyone has arrived, so we'll depart as soon as the food hampers and linens are packed in the wagon," Amelia said.

Maddie scanned the group of twenty or so mulling about the property. "Is this really everyone, Amelia? Somehow I thought there would be more guests today."

Amelia looked around.

"No, Mads, this is it…and then some." She frowned in the direction of Matthew Webster. "Matthew wasn't officially invited, of course, but I should have expected he'd follow Dolly regardless." She shrugged off her obvious displeasure. "In any event, we're a small party today."

"A young party," Lester chimed in. "No one over the age of thirty is allowed to join us."

Amelia patted his arm with patient indulgence. "Making wedding arrangements with our parents has been a bit of a trial."

"A nightmare," Lester corrected.

"We decided a picnic with our peers would be more relaxing."

Lester raised his mug of beer. "And more fun."

Maddie smiled, relieved by the temporary reprieve from the company of Pastor Hogle and the other more hostile residents of the town. Exhaling a breath, she allowed the tension to drain from her shoulders. A comfortable calmness settled in its place.

When she and Jace had arrived earlier, she'd been a tangle of nerves. Jace had led her up the stone staircase and into the wolves' den with his hand planted firmly on hers. He'd given her fingers a squeeze and said, "I'll be the doting fiancé. You relax and try to have fun."

So far, he'd been true to his word. The only time he'd left her side was when he'd fetched her lemonade. She clung to him like an extra appendage as they strolled amid the unfriendly faces and whispers. Maddie's greeting to the passing Hogle sisters was soundly snubbed. Embarrassment heated her cheeks. Ignoring the slight, Jace engaged her in meaningless chitchat meant to put her at ease. While she appreciated the effort, she couldn't help feeling ashamed. Jace's association with her could damage his career, whether he chose to admit it or not.

He had risked his reputation by playing her fiancé, and in doing so, he had made a fool's bargain. He trusted Maddie to give him information that might help others. But all the while she had intended to keep the real truth of her recovery to herself.

Strangely, if ever she had the courage to tell someone her secret, she supposed that someone would be Jace—the one person, aside from herself, for whom the disclosure would cause the most damage. Jace based his life on proven scientific theory, and Maddie's gift defied everything he believed in.

If only things could be different.

Her sideways glance lingered as she studied his profile. His hair curled at his collar, needing a trim, but the effortless style enhanced his appeal. The fitted tweed coat complemented the wide breadth of his shoulders. Muscle flexed in the arm she held. The memory of his touch, the press of his hard body against hers, roused a desire she couldn't ignore. His heat penetrated her glove, seeping through her fingers and weakening her knees.

This mad attraction consumed her mind and body. Even when she was angry at him, she wanted him. She nestled into the spicy scent of him. Despite all evidence to the contrary, she suddenly felt like the luckiest woman there.

Amelia and Lester mingled with them in between attending to their duties as party hosts. Other than that, Maddie and Jace kept to themselves, which was where everyone seemed content to leave them. Oddly, she didn't mind. She wasn't alone, and she relished the difference it made to have someone at her side.

"Good morning, Maddie!" Caroline waved from the porch. Philip and David exited the house behind her. "You're just in time to sign up for this afternoon's scavenger hunt," she said as they approached.

Relieved by the trio of friendly faces, Maddie offered quick introductions to Jace.

"Scavenger hunt?" Jace asked.

"We're breaking into teams of two." Caroline grinned slyly at David. "Each couple is given a list of items to hunt." She handed the list to Jace. "There's a prize for the winners."

Jace held the list so that he and Maddie could read it together. "One acorn cap," she read aloud, "a pinecone, a twig no longer than your thumb..." She rolled her eyes.

"Quite a challenge, I know," Caroline said with a giggle. "I've a feeling the men devised this pitiful game to get us women alone with them in the woods."

"Of course we did," Lester declared as he joined them. "What better scenario in which to steal a kiss." He slapped Jace on the shoulder. "Am I right?"

"Say no more, friend, just tell me where to sign up!"

Everyone laughed, and in that moment it struck Maddie how charming Jace was when he remembered to be. Something else struck her, as well. If any kiss stealing occurred between them today, she would likely be the thief. His eyes caught hers, and her body ached with longings far from platonic. She decided at once that if given the chance to pilfer a caress or two, she would rob the man blind.

The party departed in four wagons, but as previously arranged, Jace drove Maddie in his buggy. While her fear of boarding a wagon was one she vowed to overcome, she wasn't quite brave enough to attempt it yet. Instead, she enjoyed the ride in the buggy, and the serene view of the mountains. Fluffy clouds drifted above, and her mind drifted with them, returning to the day of the accident. A day that had begun just as this one.

"The mountain trail is that way," she said, pointing.

Jace glanced to the dirt road that led into the woods. "Where the accident happened?"

She nodded.

"Do you want to tell me about it?"

She shifted uneasily in her seat. No one had ever asked her to speak of it. Even when she so desperately needed to. While she was uncertain she wanted to speak of it now, she felt she owed it to Jace to oblige his interest.

She took a long breath. "We were having such a wonderful time. The storm rumbled in quickly. We thought we could make it back to town, but by the time we packed up our picnic and headed down the mountain it was pouring. We were soaking wet and laughing as we drove down the trail. Then a bolt of lightning struck very close. The horse tore off, and the reins went flying. We were headed straight for the tree. There was no way to stop. No time to jump. It all happened so fast."

"What's the last thing you recall?"

"Lying in the mud. The paralyzing pain in my leg." Her voice cracked with emotion. "The silence beneath the pounding rain. I knew they were dead. I closed my eyes to die, too."

Jace reached for her hand and gave it a squeeze.

Staring down at her fingers cradled in his, she felt so safe, so shielded from the horrors of the past. "It was my fault," she said simply. She didn't cry or shed a tear. She merely spoke the words, opening her soul to voice what she'd never voiced to anyone, never voiced out loud. "Pastor Hogle never allowed Elizabeth to drive. He claimed it was man's work and an unseemly pursuit for a lady. We all thought it was nonsense of course. So I didn't refuse her when she asked if I would let her drive the wagon that day. I knew she had virtually no experience guiding horses, but I didn't give it a second thought. In fact, I spent more time worrying about whether someone would see Lizzie in the driver's seat and land me in trouble with the pastor. How utterly stupid I was—I never should have given over the reins."

"Elizabeth was driving?"

"Yes."

"Does anyone know this?"

She narrowed her eyes. "What does it matter?"

"They blame you because they think you were driving. Maddie, has it never occurred to you that, perhaps, if they'd known… If you'd told—"

"I couldn't tell." A lump of despair rose in her throat, and she swallowed it down.

Jace stared, perplexed. "Why not?"

"Because I am alive and she's dead." She blinked against a prickle of tears and raw grief. "Nothing remains of Elizabeth but her memory, and I'll not tarnish all that's left of her by placing blame on her, too."

He shook his head. "You weren't driving, Maddie."

"But I should have been. I tried to get her to give over the reins, but I should have tried harder. Perhaps I could have restrained the horse from panicking."

"And prevented the lightning from striking, as well?"

She bowed her head sadly. "It doesn't matter. They're all gone now. The damage is done." She sighed. "I only wish I understood why I survived and they didn't."

"There are dozens of explanations. You landed just right. Or on softer ground."

Jace was always thinking logically. She knew there had to be a reason more than her body physically enduring her injuries. "That's not what I mean." Guilt clogged in her throat. "Why did I survive?"

"No one can answer that question. But you did survive. And you've made great strides to overcome the trauma," he said. "It doesn't matter why your life was spared. What matters is that you get on with it."

He turned his focus to driving and left it at that. And strangely, it was enough.

The sound of laughter spilled from the crammed wagon up ahead. Ribbons streamed from pretty bonnets in the breeze. Despite the solemn tenor of their conversation, Maddie couldn't help smiling.

"Is there some poultice or salve that can treat birth marks?" she asked, eager to change the subject.

"Birthmarks like Dolly Hogle's?"

"Yes."

"If there is, I haven't learned of it. I know some of the grandma cures have claimed to lighten the appearance of the red pigment, but I've never seen any first-hand evidence to it." He shook his head. "Raising the girl's hopes with flimsy promises would do more harm than good."

"She seems so sad."

Jace blinked. "Not too sad to snub you."

"Elizabeth was her cousin. Like Pastor Hogle and the rest of her family, she blames me." She gave a small smile. "All except Lester."

"I like Lester," Jace said. "And it's obvious he likes you."

"He's the only Hogle who still speaks to me. Whether that's due to Amelia or not, I don't know, but he's always been kind. I couldn't wish for a better husband for her."

"They seem well matched."

"Why haven't you married?" The question popped out before she could stop it, and she clapped her hand over her mouth in surprise. Jace laughed heartily before responding.

"That was the first thing the hiring committee asked when I applied to practice here," he said with a smirk. "Were you feeding them lines from behind a curtain?"

"No, I was not," Maddie huffed. "And don't think I haven't noticed that you just neatly sidestepped the question."

"I told the committee I'd been too busy to find a woman who could tolerate how busy I'd been."

She regarded him warily. "Is that the truth?"

"One version of it." He smiled.

She smiled too. "What's the other?"

"Marriage wouldn't suit me."

"Why ever not?"

"I live for my work. Outside of my patients, I've never been responsible for anyone other than myself."

"But you could change that if—"

"I've no wish to change."

While his commitment to his work came as no surprise, his firm commitment to bachelorhood did.

His profile was rigid, but his harsh tone softened. "I started reading medicine with my father when I was sixteen years old. Not because it was his wish, but at my mother's urging. The field fascinated me, and I was eager for the chance. But my mother seized on the idea early on in my adolescence because she knew it was my only hope of forming any sort of relationship with the esteemed Doctor Merrick, Senior."

Although he spoke the words matter-of-factly, she could hear the sorrow born of his father's neglect.

"Oh, Jace."

"Being a physician takes commitment. Unwavering devotion. My father told me once that a man can be a good husband or a good doctor, but not both. In the end, he wasn't much of a success at either." Jace paused, hesitating. "And I won't make the same mistake."

"But don't you ever get lonely?"

He shook his head, averting his eyes. "I have plenty to occupy my time."

She blinked, shaking her head. "There's a difference between boredom and loneliness."

He turned to face her. "Not to me."

He focused on driving, closing the subject, but his words lingered in her head—her heart. She brushed off her baseless disappointment. Marriage was not an option for Maddie. So, why did Jace's aversion to it bother her so? She had no answer. She knew only that she could never have him, and she supposed a part of her felt pacified that no other woman could either.

Once they arrived at the sprawling picnic grove on the hill overlooking the shimmering lake, the two servants catering the luncheon began unpacking the food. Meanwhile, the guests settled about like weary cattle on their blankets.

Maddie and Jace claimed a shady spot beneath a tall oak tree. Abigail and Bitsy sat nearby, sketching the scenery. Gertrude spared Maddie from her scowls by meandering off to collect flowers with Lucinda and Dolly. Matthew wandered behind them, amusing himself with a walking stick he'd found along the way.

Maddie watched as Matthew marched up to Dolly, then positioned her arm, adjusting the small parasol she held to better block the sun. Attentive didn't begin to describe this behavior. It was simply controlling—as if the girl was incapable of discerning her own tolerance to the heat.

With a frown, Maddie turned her attention to Jace, settling into the blanket and the pleasant surroundings. Mugs of beer and claret were served, and it wasn't long before the men began setting up to play horseshoes.

Daniel paced off the distance between the stakes that Henry and Lester hammered into the ground. Then strode purposefully toward Maddie and Jace.

"We need another man for horseshoes, Doctor Merrick."

Jace glanced to Maddie for guidance.

"That is, if you can tear yourself away." Daniel's note of humor fell flat on his challenging tone. "I'm sure Madeline won't mind a whit." Planting his feet, he crossed his arms smugly and stared down at Jace as he waited.

Jace didn't belong in Daniel's shadow, and Maddie was only too pleased to let him prove as much to the entire assembled party. She smiled widely and turned to her sham fiancé.

"Go ahead, my darling," she said with an exaggerated squeeze of his arm. "I'll watch from here."

Jace played along beautifully. Clasping her hand, he said, "I won't be long."

She smiled in gratitude, enjoying the charade much more than she ought. Daniel's cheeks heated as he watched their tender exchange, and she swelled with satisfaction. Then Jace shifted toward her instead of away, and to her surprise, he drew her hand to his lips. His gaze held hers as he kissed her glove—a deliberate, measured kiss that sent tingles down her spine. Thoughts of Daniel and vindication faded away. In Jace's blue eyes she was lost, consumed by desire.

Jace stood, releasing her hand. He shrugged off his coat, then dropped it on the blanket next to her. She sighed, watching him. With commanding confidence, he brushed past Daniel as he strode through the grass. Henry and Lester waited, horseshoes in one hand, mugs of beer in the other.

"These two can't handle their beer, Doc, so we've got an advantage," Henry called with a smile.

Since Jace wasn't indulging with the others, Maddie was apt to agree.

"Beer only improves my game," Lester countered, lifting his mug high.

Maddie rolled her eyes at Lester's insatiable thirst today. At this rate, he wouldn't last until luncheon.

Henry chuckled. "We'll just see about that."

Several people gathered to watch. Caroline spread a blanket next to Maddie's, and Philip and David were quick to join her. Maddie hoped the friendly company would distract her from Abigail and Bitsy, who sat nearby, whispering fiercely about her from behind their sketch pads.

Maddie and the two girls had never been close, but before the accident she'd never spared either of them a kind word or a second thought. Back then, she had eyes only for the Fair Five and barely noticed any of the plainer debutantes. Abigail and Bitsy had been regularly excluded. As had Gertrude. Perhaps their dislike for Maddie was justified.

The ugly memories of the past sprouted around Maddie like so many weeds. Shame colored her cheeks as she straightened on the blanket and tried to focus on watching the game.

Jace scored a ringer with his first toss. The clank of his triumphant shot echoed amid the applause. Jace flashed Maddie a wink, and she smiled back, all aflutter.

"Your fiancé is a fine player," Philip said with a look that told her it pained him to say it.

Maddie offered Philip a kind smile and replied, "I had no idea he was so skilled." She sat straighter, anticipating a fierce competition and hoping that Jace's surprising ability would help wipe the smug expression from Daniel's face once and for all.

Chapter 14

Jace scored once again with another dead ringer. The unbridled happiness on Maddie's face stilled his heart. His throat went bone dry. Without breathing or blinking, he held the rare moment for as long as he could.

She glowed in a deep lilac dress, knees folded casually at her side on the blanket. The dark curls beneath her straw hat glistened in the sun blinking through the treetops. Everything about her aroused him. Her wit, her courage, even her infuriating, but oftentimes practical, advice regarding his patients.

Perhaps he was simply lonely, as Maddie had said. But he'd told her the truth. In the past, any feelings of isolation he experienced would dissolve painlessly in the distraction of treating patients and reading case studies. Since he'd met Maddie, he found that it wasn't as easy to lose himself in work anymore.

He drew his gaze from the pleasing sight of her, discovering he wasn't the only one enjoying the view. Daniel's furtive glances at Maddie were beginning to irritate him. Lucinda strolled beneath her large, yellow parasol in the distance, and Daniel was taking full advantage of her absence to ogle Maddie—the woman whom he'd abandoned when she'd needed him most. If the fool harbored any regrets for what he'd given up, Jace hoped like hell he was choking good and hard on them now.

Jace also noticed the scene unfolding on the sideline. Philip had edged into Jace's spot next to Maddie, refilling her claret glass and honeying up to her like a lovesick schoolboy. Throughout the afternoon, Jace had observed Philip and his strategic proximity, always at a distance, yet always close by. If Jace were a jealous man—which, of course, he was not!—he'd be greener than the grass beneath his boots.

Shaking off his sudden tension, he glanced to Maddie. Trapped by her smile, his angry pulse slowed to an even rhythm. Henry scored his first point, and she clapped and cheered with the others. She seemed different suddenly. Amid the friendly group she seemed more confident, more at ease as the game advanced. Jace was seeing her now as she might have been then. One of the Fair Five.

He should be pleased.

The point of their charade was so that Maddie might reclaim her reputation. Some semblance of it, at least. Jace was merely a means to that end. Judging from the male attention she was receiving, her re-entry into society was progressing better than expected. Why then, did he feel less than enthused?

Jace took a deep breath, trying to concentrate on the game. To his chagrin, Daniel glanced at Maddie yet again and was distracted enough by what he saw to miss his next shot. Jace felt his hands curl into fists as Daniel exhaled another muffled curse.

Jace stepped up for his turn and scored another point. Daniel took an angry swig of beer, then tossed his horseshoe. Close, but not close enough. Lester, on the other hand, missed by a mile but was taking their imminent loss in stride. Swilling his lager next to Jace, he cracked jokes, undaunted by his partner's increasing agitation. Each toss Lester made became more aimless, more reckless, while Daniel's pitches grew more and more precise.

The sound of Maddie's laughter caught Jace's attention, as did the intimate pose of Philip, reclining next to her on the blanket. As the game drew to its conclusion, Jace was glaring at Philip, Daniel was glaring at Jace, and Lester was three sheets to the wind.

Lester's next toss flew high. Too high. And straight toward Daniel, who was so engrossed in ogling Maddie, he didn't see it coming, until it struck him in the head.

"Daniel!" Lester shouted.

Daniel hit the ground like a sack of rocks.

Jace ran with the others to the unconscious man, then knelt at his side.

"Tell me I didn't kill him, Doc." Lester's plea sounded deathly sober above him.

Jace checked Daniel's pulse and breathing. Both were normal and strong. "He's alive," Jace assured him. "I need some ice," he called out.

They all remained planted, gaping down at Daniel like a herd of startled deer.

"Ice!"

Maddie moved first. Hiking up her skirts, she ran—a blur of lilac— toward the table that held the pitchers of beer and lemonade. Grateful for her quick response, Jace proceeded to open Daniel's eyelids and check his pupils. Maddie returned, forging through the crowd. She handed Jace an ice-filled glove.

Impressed by her resourcefulness, he placed the ice on Daniel's head, where a lump the size of an egg had already formed.

Maddie hovered over Jace, clearly distressed. "I'll get your bag." She started away.

"Wait." Jace considered the steep hill to the buggy and the tight nook behind the seat into which he'd stowed the bag for safekeeping. "I'll go. I'll be quicker. Hold the ice like this, and don't let him move."

Maddie nodded, taking over for Jace as he dashed up the hill toward his buggy. In the distance, he glimpsed Lucinda and Gertrude running toward the huddle around Daniel. Jace was confident Daniel had a concussion, and the longer he remained unconscious, the more grave the prognosis. The impact of the blow Daniel had sustained could prove fatal. Jace reached the buggy and pulled out his bag. Barely catching his breath, he turned and ran back down the hill toward the still unconscious son-of-a-bitch on the ground.

* * * *

"Daniel, can you hear me?" Maddie's heart pounded. Over the last three years, she'd built a mountain of resentment toward Daniel, but even at her angriest, she'd never wished him ill. "Daniel?"

He remained dead to the world, his face alarmingly white. She had to do something. Slipping her fingers under the ice-filled glove, she lowered her head beneath the brim of her hat and closed her eyes. Even against the chill of the ice, she felt the heat radiating from the hand she pressed to the large lump on his head.

"Daniel!"

Behind her, Gertrude had arrived on the scene. The shrill sound of her voice made it difficult for Maddie to focus.

"What happened?" Gertrude screeched. "What did she do to him?"

"She did nothing," Amelia snapped. "He was hit with a horseshoe."

"Why is she, of all people—"

"Hush, Gertrude!" Amelia's censure did little to calm Gertrude's hysterics.

"What's she doing?"

"She's applying ice per the doctor's instructions. Now calm yourself, and help tend to Lucinda. She's about ready to swoon."

Maddie closed her eyes tighter. The voices around her began to fade. Gertrude's ranting faded, too. Maddie's hands grew hotter. Ice thawed to water, seeping through the glove.

Daniel stirred. His eyes fluttered open.

Maddie drew a quick breath of relief. "Daniel, can you hear me?"

He blinked hard several times, staring up at her, dazed. "Madeline?" His eyes flashed wide with recognition or fear or both. She hoped the stunned look on his face was due to his injury and not her actions. Could he somehow know what she'd done?

"Oh, Daniel, thank God." Gertrude crouched over Maddie's shoulder. "Let him be, Madeline. He doesn't want your—"

"Stand back." Jace had his stethoscope out and ready to go. "Continue with the ice, Maddie," he said as he maneuvered past Gertrude. "The rest of you, give him some air." The circle around them expanded as Jace knelt at Daniel's side. "Welcome back," he said as he checked Daniel's pulse. He peered into Daniel's eyes, first one, then the other. "Can you tell me your name?"

"Daniel Hogle."

"Do you know where you are?"

"Cousin Lester's wedding picnic."

"Very good." Jace helped him sit up. "Any dizziness?"

"No."

Jace held up a finger and instructed Daniel to follow his movements with his eyes. "How do you feel?"

"I feel…" He glanced at Maddie, and something in his eyes made her stomach lurch. "I feel fine." He reached for the ice Maddie held to his head. "But the ice burns like hell."

"We need it for the swelling. You've got quite a bump under there."

Daniel pushed away Maddie's hand. "It's too hot."

Maddie drew back, her heart pounding. Fear trapped in her chest, and she could barely breathe.

Jace examined Daniel's head. Beneath the wet curls, the egg had shrunk to a bump that was barely visible. Jace's brows narrowed as he leaned closer, manipulating the area with his thumbs. "The ice has helped. You've got a hard head."

Maddie exhaled in relief.

"He should get extra points for taking a shot to the noggin," Henry called out.

Everyone laughed.

"He should stop looking at the ladies when there are horseshoes flying," Jace snapped.

Daniel averted his eyes. It was clear that Jace had noticed Daniel taking surprising interest in Maddie during the game. But for all his earlier attention, Daniel suddenly couldn't stand to look her way. This did not bode well, she thought, as Jace carefully helped Daniel to his feet, listing instructions for him to follow.

Without so much as a thank you to Jace, Daniel turned toward Gertrude and Lucinda, disappearing inside their frantic embraces.

"Remember, Daniel," Jace called. "No more beer or horseshoes for the day. Continue with the ice and keep still."

Daniel stepped from the clinch of weeping women. He slapped Maddie's soggy glove into Jace's hand. "I'll keep still, Doctor Merrick." He jerked his chin toward Maddie without meeting her eyes. "As long as you promise to keep that woman the hell away from me."

Chapter 15

"Daniel!" Amelia gasped.

Maddie's heart pounded.

"He's right, Amelia," Gertrude cried. "That woman is cursed, and everyone knows it. I warned Lester that inviting her would be bad luck—"

"That's enough!" Jace's voice boomed over the throng of startled faces. He took a deep breath, unfurling his fists. With a shocking degree of calm, he said, "Miss Hogle, you're clearly distressed and concerned for your cousin. As a physician—and Miss Sutter's fiancé—I strongly suggest you take both him and your hysterics home."

Gertrude gaped in silence. Seeking support, her gaze flew to Lester.

"I agree, Gert," Lester said, sounding more sober than he had all day. "Matthew, take Daniel and the girls home. Aunt Sally will see to him."

Matthew's derisive glare fixed on Maddie for an endless moment before he grasped Dolly's elbow and ushered her away. Gertrude huffed, but to Maddie's relief, she followed the group to the wagon, where they readied to take Daniel home.

Maddie's erratic pulse calmed amid the air of awkward silence around her. Amelia gave a sharp clap of her hands. "All right, now, everybody, the day is still young. Let's get back to enjoying it. Luncheon will be ready soon."

Everyone ambled off in different directions. Philip ambled straight toward Maddie. He handed her the glove she'd discarded when she'd stuffed the other one with ice. "Are you all right, Miss Sutter?"

The concern in Philip's soft brown eyes earned him a smile. Whatever he'd heard of her past, the dear man remained unaffected. "I'm fine, Philip. Thank you."

Jace placed his hand on the small of her back. "Let's put the unfortunate incident behind us, shall we?"

"Of course," Philip agreed with a nod.

Jace led Maddie back to their spot beneath the tree. Her mind raced as she reviewed her actions. The fear that Daniel might suspect what she'd done—that Jace would find her out—tightened like a noose around her neck. Had Jace seemed surprised by how quickly the lump on Daniel's head had shrunk? She hoped that, due to the ice, such progression was plausible.

Maddie wrenched the stray glove in her hand as they sat quietly. Too quietly. Jace's lingering silence heightened her dread. She'd been lucky so far, but she was taking more chances. Yesterday, while Jace was treating patients in his examination room, she'd been particularly daring with two patients in the waiting area. Under the guise of applying her trusty "warm herbal compress" she'd relieved the severe pain in Mrs. Canfield's arthritic knee, and then she'd silenced the chronic ringing in Mr. Schyler's ears.

Maddie was drawn from the memory by Bitsy and Henry, who were spinning in front of her, trying to capture an elusive butterfly. She watched, entranced by the fluttering thing as it darted around the young couple. Henry finally managed to scoop it into his flailing net, and Bitsy let out a cheer.

Maddie sighed, sympathizing with the poor creature's plight. This business of healing in public was risky. It was only a matter of time before she was caught, too. She inhaled a deep breath, breaking the unbearable stillness.

"Thank you for intervening with Gertrude, Jace."

"It was a pleasure," Jace deadpanned. "That woman is a complete and utter nuisance."

"Pastor Hogle is her uncle. The trait runs in the family."

"Ah, that would explain it." Jace smiled warmly, and all at once, Maddie's fears fell away.

"Luncheon is served!" With a sweeping wave, Amelia herded her guests toward the trestle table where the food was laid out.

Everyone crowded around the banquet, helping themselves to bountiful platters of smoked salmon and ham. Amelia had outdone herself with the bill of fare. In addition to scrumptious sandwiches smeared with caviar, trays of baked beans and tomato salad sat beside a souse of pigs' feet and a variety of relishes.

A hodgepodge of tempting aromas drifted from their plates as they returned to their blanket to eat. Maddie swallowed a bite of her chicken sandwich. "Will Daniel be all right?"

"I'll stop in to check on him later," Jace said. "He sustained a concussion, but so long as he displays no symptoms of dizziness or vomiting, he should be fine." He glanced up. "Thanks to you."

She swallowed hard, nearly choking on an olive.

"The ice was instrumental in controlling the swelling." His eyes sparkled with amusement. "Pity you had to ruin your glove to get it."

"Not to mention a full jar of lemonade," she deflected.

"In all seriousness, Maddie, you've a knack for keeping your head during emergencies. You'd make a fine nurse."

She glanced to the departing wagon descending the hill in the distance. Her mood dimmed beneath clouds of doubt. She couldn't shake that look on Daniel's face... "Not many would agree."

"Ignorant fools. Every last one," Jace assured her with a squeeze to the shoulder.

Guilt twisted in Maddie's gut. Jace was always so quick to defend her. She did her best to shake off her shame.

"Daniel's outburst stemmed from jealousy," Jace said. "And embarrassment for getting clunked in the head while distracted by you."

Maddie stirred uneasily on the blanket. "Oh, I don't think he's—"

"Trust me, Maddie," he said. "You were his fiancée."

"But he didn't want me."

"That doesn't mean he wants someone else to have you."

Maddie considered this, realizing Jace might be right. Had her fear of discovery led her imagination astray? Perhaps it was Daniel's jealousy, not his suspicion of her, that had caused his odd behavior. Men tended to be territorial, and Daniel had spent most of the day staring at her from behind Lucinda's back. Didn't Maddie, in her own selfishness, harbor the same possessive feelings for Jace?

They returned to their meal, sampling one delicious item after another. A plate piled high with currant tarts and apple turnovers made the rounds, not to mention more claret and beer.

Philip approached, this time to serve Maddie a plate of Saratoga chips. "I recall that these were your favorite."

Maddie stared at the chips, stunned he'd remembered this from so long ago. Her heart warmed at his kindness. "They are." She accepted the thoughtful offering with a genuine smile. "Thank you, Philip."

"My pleasure." With a cursory nod to Jace, he strode away.

"He's smitten with you," Jace said, watching Philip's departure.

"Don't be silly," she said. "Gentlemen always cater to the ladies during picnics." She repressed a grin. "Besides, he's well over the crush he had on me when we were young."

Jace's brow rose in surprise. "So you admit he had a crush on you?"

She couldn't resist. "I admit that lots of boys had crushes on me."

"No doubt," he muttered.

With a teasing grin, she nudged him with her elbow. "If I didn't know better, Doctor Merrick, I'd think you were jealous."

"If I didn't know better, Miss Sutter, I'd think you might enjoy that."

She laughed, and he shook his head, lips quirking.

"Come on, everyone," Caroline called. "The scavenger hunt is about to begin. Ladies grab your baskets and your hunting partners. We'll all meet back here in one hour to determine the winning team!"

Jace and Maddie joined the others, following one of the many trails into the woods. The air was cooler in the shade of the trees and thick with the scent of pine and sap. Jace unfolded the list of twenty items as they walked a path of scattered pine needles and cones. The distant sound of the other couples faded as they forged deeper into the woods.

The mere fact that they were alone roused excitement within her. Jace bent to pluck a mushroom from the bark of a felled tree, and Maddie tilted her head for a better view of his appealing backside. He placed the mushroom in the basket she held.

"Only three items to go," he said, though she could not care less.

Searching for the remaining items on the list, they continued along the deserted trail until they came to a small clearing. Maddie's leg ached, and she was relieved when Jace suggested they sit for a while.

Adjusting her skirts, she wrapped her knees to one side, settling nicely on the lush blanket of moss.

"Does it bother you much?" Jace asked, sitting next to her. "Your leg?"

She glanced to the knee she hadn't realized she was rubbing. "During lengthy walks," she said.

"I can prescribe something for the pain."

She shook her head. "No, thank you."

"You prefer to face it head on." He smiled and his blue eyes sparked bluer in the open sunlight.

"Believe me, I've taken my fair share of pain remedies."

His smile faded. "Tell me about the injury."

While she'd rather avoid the subject of her recovery entirely, she couldn't dodge his questions forever. Disclosing a detailed account of her case was part of their bargain, and she had to remember that. After all Jace had done for her today, she owed him. "Doctor Filmore said my leg was badly broken. He set it as best he could, then warned me I'd walk with a terrible limp and the assistance of a cane for the rest of my life. In the worst case scenario, I would be confined to a wheelchair."

"You just had to prove him wrong, didn't you?"

"You're starting to sound like Grandfather," she said with a smile.

"I'm starting to know you better."

She laughed, enjoying his playful and easy demeanor.

He sat with his elbow resting casually on his bent knee, his other leg stretched out before him. "How did you treat it?"

"I depended on a constant dose of pain remedies at first. But after a month or so, I decided to stop." She chose her words carefully. "I used wraps soaked in hot water to combat the pain. Then I'd massage my leg for hours. Each day the pain lessened a bit." She eyed him nervously, awaiting his reaction.

"Heat and massage can be effective in stimulating blood flow to the muscles."

"Most effective," she said with an overeager nod. "After forcing my weight on it daily, I was finally able to take a step without falling. Quite an achievement, since I'd become rather intimate with the floorboards during previous attempts." She smiled. "But I managed that first step. That gave me faith."

"Faith," he muttered. He all but rolled his eyes at the word.

"You don't believe in the concept?"

"My patients' spiritual beliefs don't concern me." His arrogance shot to the surface, piercing each word.

"They should."

He frowned. "I'm a doctor. I treat bodies, not souls."

"And faith has no place in it?"

"I put my faith in science."

Maddie knew Jace's rigid worldview was the direct result of his disappointment with his father. She couldn't blame him for that, but she did feel profoundly sorry for him. A person might find a great deal of comfort in the idea that there were some things reason alone could not account for—that there were other possibilities, earthly or divine, which could offer us hope. Jace allowed his profession to limit his spirit. To smother it. A pang of sadness crept through her. "That sustains you?"

"It has to," he snapped. His profile tensed. Crossing his feet stiffly, he stared into the trees. "It used to."

The surprising vulnerability in his admission touched a place deep inside her. She could only imagine the horrors he'd endured at Pittsburgh Hospital. The despair. The need to comfort him, as he'd comforted her, rose in her chest as naturally as a breath. "It must have been difficult working in the emergency ward."

He stared at his boots, as though weighing his answer. "One day a man was brought in who'd been crushed between two train cars."

Maddie did her best not to grimace.

"I'd seen a lot of fatal injuries during the early months of my residency, but nothing like this." He shook his head. "His torso and legs were pulverized, but he was alive. I moved by rote, attempting to treat untreatable injuries, and all the while I wanted him to die. To stop suffering, and die." His voice sank in remorse. "That was the first time I wanted to give up on a patient."

"You never give up on your patients?"

"No, I do not. First, I do everything medically possible to save them. And if I can't do that, then I do everything in my power to ease their pain until it is ended."

Her thoughts turned to Doctor Filmore and how easily he'd given up on her. Even after he'd realized his mistake in pronouncing her dead. She admired Jace so much. "You're a dedicated doctor."

"I believe I could be, under the right circumstances. At the hospital everything happens so fast. We're trained to treat and release patients as quickly as possible. Some we never see again, others we see over and over. Pathetic addicts, starving and beaten children."

"It sounds horrible."

"It was my job. And I did it well." He averted his eyes. "Or so I'd thought until Kathy Fitzsimmons." He turned back to Maddie, answering before she could ask. "Kathy was a young woman who was dragged by a carriage when her skirt got caught in the door."

Maddie cringed, picturing the horror of the poor woman's ordeal.

"Her fiancé was run over and killed while trying to save her, but Kathy survived. During her weeks in the hospital, she complained of feeling guilt and terrible fear. Since I was more concerned with her healing bones, I insisted she put the accident behind her, reminding her that she was lucky to be alive. A month after being released, she was brought in after slitting her wrists."

"Oh, Jace."

"She begged me to let her bleed, to walk away, to just let her go." He shook his head. "I stitched her up good as new, then sent her home with her parents. But not before I suggested she find a hobby to occupy her mind." He ran his hand through his hair. "Three days later, they pulled her body from the Alleghany River." He lowered his eyes. "She couldn't overcome the trauma of the accident. She was physically recovered, and yet that accident killed her."

Maddie swallowed hard. "Now I understand your interest in me."

"A part of it, yes," he said. "At first."

Her aching heart skipped a beat. "And that's when you left the hospital?"

"Losing Kathy… I needed to understand why."

"She didn't have a reason to hope," Maddie whispered.

"She didn't have a doctor who knew how to save her." He shook off his obvious frustration. "It's the profession I chose, but my inadequacies haunt me." He lowered his eyes. "I'm my father's son."

"But you're not your father." Jace's anguished expression tore her to pieces. "You're only human, Jace," she continued.

"I'm a doctor."

"You're a man." She reached to his cheek, tracing the tense line of his jaw. "A good man."

His lips parted, and he drew a long breath, his chest swelling with restraint and everything that was wound so tightly inside him. Everything she wanted him to release. She stared into his eyes, lured by all that she saw there, all that he was. She drew his face closer, lifting her mouth gently to his.

He stiffened at the contact, his lips wooden and still against hers. His hesitation filled her with dread. She drew back a fraction, steeling her will. Ignoring the reluctance in his troubled blue eyes, she cradled his face in her hands and kissed him again, with a desperate insistence she wouldn't let him deny.

As he exhaled a groan of surrender, his tense lips finally softened. She parted her lips, kissing him with all she was worth.

And to her utter delight and surprise, he didn't resist.

Chapter 16

Jace slicked his tongue against Maddie's, driving into the warmth of her mouth. Wrapping her arms around his neck, she welcomed him with a lingering sigh. His pulse lurched madly. He grasped her waist, pulling her toward him. The crush of her breasts against his chest made the confinement of his bulging erection in his trousers almost too much to bear. His tongue stroked hers, delving deeper.

Since the first time he'd seen her, and every time since, he'd fought this relentless attraction. But today, when he'd watched her on the sideline of the horseshoe game, his resolve had shattered beyond repair. The sound of her laughter, the allure of her smile, the way she looked in this dress...

Kissing her deeply, he cupped the firm roundness of her bottom, then lifted her to his lap. She heaved up her skirts, straddling him, and he feared he might spill on the spot. He pulled her against his hardness. The contact, the blazing heat between her legs, stilled his breath.

She arched her hips closer. Drawing her mouth from his, she gasped for air, tossing back her head. Her parted lips glistened, eyes half closed beneath the fringe of her lashes. Sunlight poured through the treetops, dancing across her flush face. Golden rays framed her features, creating a dreamlike image of a woman's pleasure. Lovely. Her breasts jutted toward him, inviting his touch.

Running his hands up her sides, he skimmed the silky fabric of her dress, tracing the curve of her waist, the swell of her ribs. He inched his trembling fingers higher. The weight of her breasts filled his palms to perfection. She moaned, arching her back as he cupped and kneaded. Blood spiked in his veins.

Her body's response drove him wild. Lowering his head to her breast, he nipped through the fabric, lifting her into his mouth. She raked one hand through his hair, clutching his shoulder with the other. Spreading her legs farther, she ground her hips against him. "Mmm, Jace," she murmured.

His name carried on that breath, filling his ear with a sound he'd dreamt so often of hearing. Sweet Maddie. A brush of guilt stirred his conscience, but he shrugged it away. As Maddie had declared, she was a grown woman. A woman with the guts and fortitude to get what she wanted.

He felt lucky as hell that she wanted him.

He pulled her face toward his and kissed her again. The sweet taste of claret, of her, flooded his senses. Reason flowed away. The feel of her parted thighs flanking his waist, the heat of her pressed to his rock-hard erection pulsed through him as his tongue meshed with hers.

The unwelcome sound of the others in the distance echoed through the woods.

Maddie stilled, pulling back, eyes wide. "They're heading this way."

He ground out a curse as she swung her leg over his, shifting off him. She plopped next to him on the moss, her skirts a tangled heap around her thighs. Straightening the layers over her legs, she adjusted the bodice of her dress into place, then scampered to her feet.

Jace remained seated, spewing a succession of curses and trying to get his bearings. He was still in a state of slightly dazed arousal.

"We mustn't dawdle too long, or people will talk," she said, breathlessly. He choked out a rumbling laugh in response.

"I believe you misunderstand the definition of 'dawdling' if you think that's the activity we were just engaged in," he said with a cheeky grin as he shoved to his feet. He received a playful shove in response.

"How do I look?" she asked, adjusting the slant of her hat.

With surprisingly little effort she'd managed to pull herself together quite neatly. Jace was impressed and a tad wary of her efficiency. Just how practiced was she in escaping compromising positions? Her cheeks were still flush with desire, her lips moist with his kiss. Blowing out a long breath, he resisted the urge to wrestle her back down on the moss and finish what they'd started. "Beautiful," he answered, honestly.

Rising on her toes, she planted a quick kiss on his cheek.

She scooped up her basket, and they headed back toward the others. They all returned to the picnic grove, where Jim and Abigail collected their prize for winning the scavenger hunt. After settling back on their blankets, the guests enjoyed more claret accompanied by watermelon and strawberries.

Jace couldn't think about eating. He could think of nothing, save the lust burning inside him. Every glance at Maddie enflamed his desire and tightened the knot in the pit of his stomach.

He watched enthralled while she ate from her plate of fruit. Placing a plump strawberry between her lips, she bit, sucking slowly before finally slipping the juicy morsel into her mouth. He couldn't take his eyes off her.

She glanced at him, then swept her tongue across her lips, smiling as she chewed. By the time tea was served, Jace was beyond want. This was madness. He had to have her. He waited until she finished her tea, then said, "Since I have to check on Daniel later, we'd better head back now."

"May we stop at your office before you drive me home? I believe I left my shawl there the other day." Glancing up from her plate, she said, "Grandfather won't be expecting me until well after dark." She smiled, a wicked smile that sparked through his blood like a wildfire. "It won't matter much if we must dawdle a bit in town…"

Jace smiled like a fool. He stood, extending his hand to her. She took it, and he pulled her to her feet, practically dragging her along. She laughed behind him as they hurried toward their hosts. They made their excruciatingly long good-byes to Amelia and Lester, waving farewells to Caroline, David, and a forlorn-looking Philip, before finally boarding the buggy and heading down the road toward Misty Lake.

The ride for Jace seemed endless as he sat next to Maddie. The buggy rolled along at an even pace, but it would take another thirty minutes at least before they arrived at his office. The setting sun glowed on the horizon, draping the mountains in a blanket of pink. With each descending inch of the sun, Jace's sensibilities rose higher.

"It would be better if I drove you home," he said, solely because he felt he should.

She regarded him skeptically. "Better for whom?"

He frowned at her veiled challenge. "Maddie, think about it—"

"I have thought about it," she said, shifting in her seat. "And I'm tired of merely thinking about it." She placed a hand on his knee. "Aren't you?"

He stared down at her fingers caressing his thigh and conceded defeat. "And I have nothing to add to this discussion?"

Her brown eyes gleamed with determination. Desire. "Nothing I care to hear."

He smiled in spite of himself. She was beguiling in her honesty. And her touch on his thigh was intoxicating. The hell with chivalry, ethics, and everything else. She'd rendered him powerless.

When they reached the office, Jace parked the buggy in the drive instead of leaving it on the street where the neighbors would spot it. "Go on in through the back door while I see to the horse," he said.

With a nod, she disappeared inside.

Jace stabled and fed the horse quickly, then hurried into the house. The floorboards creaked as he walked down the hall through the moonlight and shadows. Maddie sat in the parlor wrapped in a blanket. Her dress lay sprawled on the sofa beside her. Her ploy to ensure he'd not change his mind was more than effective.

The thrill of anticipation paralyzed him. He swallowed hard as she stood. "Are you sure?" he whispered through the thick air of longing between them.

Without a word, she released the blanket, and it slipped slowly to the floor. She stood in the moonlight, dressed only in her chemise and stockings. He drew in a sharp breath. Her simmering gaze held his as she stepped from the pool of wool at her feet, and he had his answer.

* * * *

In one swift move, Jace scooped her into his arms and carried her through the house. She floated in his strong arms as they moved toward the bed. Her heart pounded. Thoughts breezed through her head, her life as it was, as it had been since the accident, as it would be forever. No guilt, no doubts marred the moment, for she'd allow nothing to hinder her bliss. Instead, she would take what she could. She would cling to this night and this man—this man who'd made her forget how hopeless and lonely she'd been.

Jace placed her gently on the pillows, staring down at her. Her chest heaved with excitement. He peeled off his coat, then tossed it aside.

The mattress slumped with his weight as he joined her on the bed. She reached for him with such need it frightened her. It felt as if she'd waited a lifetime for this—for him. She couldn't stop herself now if she wanted to; but, oh, she didn't want to. She might never again have this chance.

His mouth found hers in the dimness of the room, setting her ablaze. He pulled her over his body. His hardness against her thigh set her flesh tingling. With an arch of her hips, she centered herself on that pulsing hardness.

Groaning, he deepened the kiss. His tongue slid against hers, rousing pleasure in every direction. The sound of his raspy desire filled her ears as he rolled her to her side, then covered her body with his.

She squirmed beneath the weight and the heat of him, heart pounding. She felt his hand on her trembling knee, his fingers sliding under her chemise. Cool air kissed her skin before the scorch of his hand. She closed her eyes, writhing at his touch, the heat, the pressure. His hand trailed higher, taking the fabric with it. He sat back, drawing her upright. He lifted the garment over her hips, and she raised her arms with a shiver as he slipped it over her head, then tossed it aside.

His eyes settled on hers, stilling her heart. She could barely breathe in the warmth and intensity searing her soul. Something passed between them, something she'd never felt nor could describe—something fateful, and more intimate than sitting naked in his bed. She closed her eyes to blink the feeling away, to blink back her tears.

She felt his hands on her breasts, and she tossed back her head, lost in pleasure once again. "Jace," she whispered into the darkness. His hot mouth covered her breast, and she all but screamed. Biting her lip, she raked her hand through his hair, arching her back as his tongue circled and teased.

Drawing away, Jace sat back on his haunches to remove his shirt. She rose up to help, working the buttons in a frantic pace. She tugged the shirt from his trousers, and he tossed it aside. She stared, excited beyond reason at his glorious chest. She reached to touch him, and he drew in a breath. Each movement of her hands on his warm flesh, the soft patch of curls between his nipples, incited her ardor. Her touch incited his, too. She felt the rising need in his rigid pose, saw it on his handsome face.

Lowering her focus, she unfastened his trousers. Within moments he was naked and on top of her. Her flesh burned against his, the contact blazing through her body. He rained hot kisses down her neck and throat. Tension wound from the pit of her stomach, stretching through her limbs. She tossed her head from side to side as pleasure pulled her toward something unknown, something waiting. The tingle between her thighs grew stronger, and she parted her legs in response.

Jace shifted between her damp thighs, spreading her legs. His hardness pressed against her, stirring sensations that were too good to bear. Her bottom rose toward him, her hips writhing for more. He eased inside her, and she flinched, startled by the pain. Grumbling a curse, he drew back. He inhaled a long breath, as if struggling for control. The warmth of his breath fanned her cheek as he pressed a soft kiss to her temple. The sweet gesture, his tender regard for her comfort, relaxed her tense limbs, and the pain began to subside. She ran her hands down his back, over his firm buttocks, urging him on.

Biting her lip, she waited, anticipating more pain. He pushed forward again. Slowly. So slowly that discomfort was minor. Moving gently, he inched deeper and deeper until the pain disappeared and the pleasure returned.

She wrapped her legs tightly around him. He stilled, staring into her eyes. His strained expression softened to a look of relief. He kissed her, a long, lingering kiss that freed his reluctance and sent her reeling.

His hips moved faster. She moaned, arching to meet each thrust, eager to ease the unbearable tension. Her body spun in the wonderful chaos. His soft lips on her neck, his hot breath in her ear. His hard shaft sliding in and out of her. He lifted her bottom, driving deeper. A gust of pleasure overtook her, sent her hurtling over the edge. Clutching his shoulders, she shuddered, panting wildly as the sensations pulsed through her.

With a groan, Jace withdrew from her body, his own trembling with pleasure. His labored breath filled her ear as he pressed ragged kisses to her temple. The warmth of his release on her thigh reminded her of the risk they had taken. Maddie knew enough about such matters to know that precision was imperative in avoiding pregnancy. Her fleeting qualms faded. Jace was nothing, if not precise.

Several long moments passed as they lay there, naked bodies entwined. Pressing her cheek to his neck, she closed her misty eyes, inhaling the scent of him. This moment. And then she heard it. Rising through the haze of her bliss, ringing beneath the pounding pulse in her ears, one lone thought resounded in her head.

She loved him.

* * * *

Jace nestled Maddie against his chest. Stroking her silky hair, he stared at the ceiling, his heart thundering, his thoughts a bouncing jumble in his head. Despite his euphoria, he couldn't help feeling he'd taken advantage of the situation. Of her.

"Don't have regrets, Jace," she said, as if reading his mind. Shifting to her side, she rose on her elbow. Her fingers roamed the hair on his chest, and his breath hitched in response. "I couldn't bear that."

Her honesty never ceased to amaze him. *She* never ceased to amaze him. He brushed a curl from her beautiful face.

"You've done nothing unethical here. We are not doctor and patient," she said.

While this was true, he was having trouble determining just what exactly they were to each other. He'd taken her virginity, for Christ's sake. Something no other man could claim. Why was a part of him gratified by this? Despite his confusion, he was sure of one thing. "I regret nothing," he said quietly. "Not for myself, at least."

"You took nothing I was unwilling to give. I will never marry anyway."

"You don't know that. One day you may—"

"No." She shook her head firmly. "To echo your sentiment of this morning, marriage wouldn't suit me." She touched his face, tracing a path to his jaw. "Rest easy, Jace, please. I expect nothing from you except what you've promised. To help make these people accept me again." She smiled. "Thank you for today, by the way," she said, nudging him playfully.

He smiled too. "Thank you for tonight."

She laughed as he pressed a kiss to her temple.

"You're a good friend," she said. "And I want you to know that no matter what happens at Amelia's wedding, no matter the outcome of our charade, success or failure, I will remember your kindness—and this night—for as long as I live."

The words touched a place deep in his core, stirring a response he was too cowardly to voice. *So will I.*

Chapter 17

Jace took Maddie home, then drove back toward town. Moonlight provided excellent visibility as the buggy rolled along, but he was too distracted by other thoughts to appreciate the favorable traveling conditions.

It was well past ten, and Jace hoped Maddie was correct about her grandfather's intention to retire early. The idea of Maddie having to face the gallant old man now—tonight—gripped Jace in guilt.

But even the possibility of an awkward encounter between Mr. Sutter and his granddaughter wasn't enough to tear Jace away from reliving the evening's passion in his imagination. The more Jace tried to concentrate on the road, the more his mind's eye flashed to images of Maddie's silken skin, the feel of her thighs wrapped around his waist, the warmth deep inside her...

He'd never spent such a night with a woman—never shared such a connection with anyone. Physically, he desired her, but Maddie's intelligence and perceptive sympathy were equally seductive to him. It was this latter discovery that surprised him most.

Each moment in her presence was another tug at his tightly knit resolve, another yank that threatened the integrity of who he was. As much as he feared unraveling as his father had, he felt himself longing for something outside the realm of his work.

Jace had confided in her today, told her things he'd never spoken aloud to anyone. Things he barely admitted to himself. She'd mined emotions from him that he'd buried deeply in his past and his work and whatever else might smother them. Emotions he hadn't allowed himself to feel, let alone express. And strangely, in dredging the unpleasantness to the surface, he'd found real relief. Freedom.

Shoving away this troubling realization, Jace turned his attention to the task at hand. The house call to check on Daniel. He was still incensed by the memory of Daniel's ungrateful outburst at the picnic, but Jace stowed his anger inside his duty as a physician. He pulled the buggy up to the Hogle house. The porch lamps glowed and the house was well lit. For a moment, Jace feared Daniel had taken a turn for the worse.

Jace rapped on the door. Without a word, Gertrude led him through the quiet hall to the parlor, where Daniel sat on the sofa beside his uncle, the pastor. Dolly sat opposite them. Their grim expressions gave Jace the distinct feeling he'd interrupted a serious family discussion.

Matthew Webster appeared from the next room, halting at the sight of Jace. Resuming his pace, he strode to Dolly, then dropped the afghan he carried into her lap.

"It's late, so I'll check Daniel's condition, then be on my way," Jace said.

Daniel remained silent during the brief examination, only nodding and shaking his head to answer Jace's questions. Beneath the watchful eyes of his audience, Jace completed the exam, satisfied to discover Daniel suffered no lingering symptoms, not even a headache.

"You've recovered nicely," Jace said. "I'll check on you once more tomorrow. Notify me if there's any change in the meanwhile." Jace gave a nod to the others. "Good night." He closed his medical bag, then turned for the door.

"One moment, please, Doctor," Pastor Hogle called.

Jace stopped short, his spine tingling with dread.

The pudgy man stood, hands on his lapels. "Just before you arrived, we were discussing my nephew's accident."

"He was lucky. The concussion could have been worse."

"Daniel told us that while that woman—your fiancée—was kneeling over him, he experienced something strange."

"Strange?" Jace glanced to Daniel, and the coward averted his eyes.

"She did something to him," Gertrude declared, leaning forward.

"I didn't say that, Gert," Daniel snapped.

Gertrude slumped back in her seat next to Dolly.

"What is it you did say, Daniel?" Jace frowned, shifting his weight. "What have you to say about the woman who rushed to your aid? The woman who held ice to your head, which reduced your swelling significantly, and therefore, the severity of your injury?"

"She was kneeling while applying the ice," Pastor Hogle clarified. "And she used her own glove, did she not?" He stepped closer. "I've heard disturbing stories of self-proclaimed mystical healers and practitioners of witchcraft and how they use personal items to—"

Jace blinked incredulously. "Are you suggesting that Miss Sutter cast a spell on him?" He teetered between laughter and rage for all of a moment. The pulse pounding at his temples pushed him swiftly toward rage. "That her actions led to his prolonged impairment, when, in fact, her quick thinking may have saved his life?"

Pastor Hogle pursed his lips, taking a few moments to form a reply. "I'm suggesting you refrain from allowing that woman to act as a nurse to your patients. My nephew is quite distressed."

"I'm fine," Daniel said. "I merely mentioned I'd felt something strange."

"You did feel something strange, Daniel," Jace shot back. "It was a horseshoe to your skull." He pointed at Daniel. "You should be counting your lucky stars that you're alive, instead of attempting to discredit Miss Sutter with ridiculous accusations." Jace dragged his look of disgust across the other faces peering up at him. His eyes fixed on Matthew's triumphant expression, and he felt his stomach lurch. "So should the rest of you." He turned and strode from the house.

The door slammed behind him, but he didn't care. He stomped from the porch toward the buggy. Clenching the reins, he gave them a snap and tore down the road. Would these people never leave Maddie in peace? Ignorant fools, the lot of them for shunning and blaming her.

Maddie was a remarkable, resilient woman, but perhaps it was silly to hope that she might one day transform Misty Lake's irrational hatred of her into something manageable. She deserved so much more. Watching her today with Caroline and the Strope brothers, Jace had realized how easy it would be for Maddie in another town, away from her past and the poisonous talk, far from those who made her life miserable.

Jace couldn't help wondering if he, himself, had hurt Maddie by taking her into his bed. Despite her vow that she would never marry, she could certainly do so if she wished. She could leave Misty Lake and start a new life. People started over all the time. Men would flock to her.

The sharp ache in his chest confirmed what he already knew. He didn't want her to leave. Now he was not only a jealous man, he was a selfish one, too. It was not a self-discovery in which he took any pride or pleasure, and he gritted his teeth in shame for the remainder of the short ride home.

Chapter 18

Maddie's mind buzzed with the memory of last night, and her body still hummed. She'd arrived at the office that morning eager for more, but she and Jace had barely had a moment alone since sun up. A steady influx of patients had kept both of them running all day, and Jace was just now saying his good-byes to the last one. He would then spend some time transcribing patient notes in his office, while Maddie moved on to her final task of the afternoon: cleaning and restocking the examination room.

She set to her work, grateful for the distraction. The hours in Jace's presence had filled her with desires she could barely contain. She was fairly bursting with longing to touch him again.

Her wildest dreams about what it might be like to share Jace's bed paled in comparison to how wonderful it had been. Not even when she healed, when she poured her heart and soul into another living being, had she ever experienced anything as intensely intimate as she had in that bed.

No wonder she'd fancied herself in love with him. She shook her head against such foolishness, accepting that she'd mistaken lust for love. Even now, the mere picture of him, hunched over his desk, engaged in the task of writing notes, filled her with longing. What was more, she found the anticipation of acting on her lust again overwhelmingly thrilling.

With a deep breath, she refocused herself, straightening the supplies on the counter in the examination room. Jace was a stickler for order when it came to the room where he performed his most important work. Everything had to be arranged just so for easy access, and Maddie took great care to ensure the room's condition measured up to his high standards. This chore would keep her busy until Jace drove her home.

She restocked the shelf with fresh linens, then proceeded to sweep the floor. Her work was interrupted by a call for help from the hall.

"I need the doctor!"

Maddie hadn't seen Evan Yates since he'd moved to Chicago two years ago, but even with the bushy mustache he now wore, she recognized him immediately.

Jace rushed from his office, almost colliding into Maddie as he skidded to a halt. "I'm Doctor Merrick. What is it?"

"My wife. The baby isn't expected until late next month, but something is wrong. Hurry, please," he said.

With a reassuring squeeze to Evan's shoulder, Jace said, "I'll get my bag." He turned to Maddie. "Can you get yourself home?"

"Yes, of course." She waved Jace toward the door.

"No," Evan said. He turned to Maddie. "You must come, too."

Maddie blinked in surprise. Evan's sister, Phoebe, had died in the wagon accident Maddie had survived. No one in that family had spoken a word to Maddie since. Until now.

"Please, Madeline," he said. "Laura needs a woman with her. She's crazed with fears of childbed fever, and my mother went to Saratoga. She may not be back for hours."

That he wanted Maddie's help with the birth of his child showed how terrified he truly was. Maddie couldn't refuse. "All right." She glanced to Jace.

"Let's go," he said.

She grabbed her shawl and followed behind the men as they headed outside. Jace raced to hitch up the buggy, while Maddie tried to calm Evan with small talk. "So, are you and your wife in town for a visit?"

Shaking his head, Evan stared after Jace, clearly distracted. "We're staying with my mother while we build our own house on the property next door. Laura's been helping me clear brush all week. The exertion must have brought the labor on early."

"Don't worry, Evan. Doctor Merrick will take good care of Laura and the baby," she said, glancing toward the carriage house and wishing Jace would hurry.

A few minutes later, Jace had the buggy hitched and ready to go. Maddie hurried to the buggy as Evan hopped into his wagon and tore down the road.

Maddie held tight as Jace sped to keep up with Evan. The Yates house was situated on the more isolated side of Misty Lake, a few miles from town. The thought of Evan's poor wife, trembling in pain, afraid and alone, turned Maddie's stomach. Women sometimes died during childbirth. Babies died, too.

She glanced at Jace. He drove with purpose, his handsome face set in determination. As always, his confidence helped put her at ease. Maddie felt sure that Jace's skill as a physician would result in a healthy outcome for both mother and baby.

They reached the house. Evan ran to the porch and took the stairs two at a time. "I'm coming, Laura!" He flung open the weathered screen door, nearly snapping it from the rusty hinges. "I've brought the doctor."

Maddie's heart pounded as she and Jace raced inside. They followed Evan upstairs to the bedroom at the end of the hall.

Laura squirmed in the bed, panting wildly. Sweat beaded on her forehead. Tears streaked her pale cheeks. She clutched the sheets at her sides, writhing and whimpering in pain.

Jace set his bag on the foot of the bed, then opened it wide. He set out some bottles and instruments, including ominous-looking forceps. "You may want to wait in the hall, Evan," he said at the man's petrified expression.

Evan leaned over Laura and kissed her cheek. The tender concern in his eyes as he gazed down at his wife caused a lump in Maddie's throat that nearly choked her. Oh, to be loved so dearly…

"I'll be right outside," Evan whispered in Laura's ear.

Laura nodded frantically, overcome by her discomfort.

"All right, now, Laura, let's see how you're doing," Jace said. After a brief exam of her belly, he said, "The baby's positioned properly." He walked to the foot of the bed. Lifting the sheet between her legs, he ducked beneath the tent he'd created to examine her. "You're doing just fine," he said. "It won't be long now."

Whimpering in fright, Laura nodded.

Maddie distracted herself from her own fear by filling a basin with water. She soaked a rag, fingers trembling as she squeezed out the excess water. "My name is Madeline, Laura," she said as she dabbed the cool compress to Laura's sweaty forehead.

Laura conveyed her gratitude by patting Maddie's hand. Her soft grip on Maddie's fingers tightened as another pain tore through her body.

Maddie winced from the force of Laura's grip. And again from the piercing scream that punctuated the end of Laura's contraction.

Maddie's heart ached for the girl, but she didn't dare intervene. Laura required Jace's ability today, not Maddie's. He would guide this child safely into the world. Maddie watched as Jace moved about, preparing for the birth. The massive responsibility he carried each day—by choice and not circumstance—filled Maddie with awe.

The door opened and Evan's mother burst inside. "What's happening?" Evan followed on her heels.

"You're about to become a grandmother, Mrs. Yates," Jace said.

The woman rushed to Laura's side. "Stay strong, darling," she said, patting Laura's knee. Mrs. Yates uttered a few more hasty words of encouragement before she noticed it was Maddie at her side. "What is she doing here?" she asked, turning to Evan.

"I was desperate, Mother. Laura needed a woman."

"Laura was frightened," Jace said. "Madeline is helping to keep her calm."

"That's what chloroform is for," she shot back. "Besides, I'm here now, and we don't need her upsetting things."

Laura stared, wide-eyed, at Mrs. Yates's sudden hostility. The confusion on her pale face turned to alarm.

Relinquishing the compress to Mrs. Yates, Maddie took a step back. She'd do nothing to upset Laura, nothing to jeopardize the delivery. "I'll wait downstairs," she offered.

"Mrs. Yates, there's no need—"

"This is my house, Doctor Merrick. My family. I will not have my grandchild born into a room occupied by Madeline Sutter."

"I'll be downstairs," Maddie said to Jace on her way to the door. She stepped from the room, tears stinging her eyes.

She stopped in the hall to regain her composure. Stiffening at the sound of the door opening behind her, she turned, expecting to see Evan. Instead it was Mrs. Yates who had followed her.

"I'm sorry, Madeline, but I can't have you anywhere in the vicinity of my grandchild's birth." Her voice emitted no cruelty, only grief. Maddie knew she was a painful reminder to Mrs. Yates of a daughter lost much too soon.

Maddie lowered her eyes at the memory of Phoebe's sweet face. The unintentional discomfort Maddie had caused, at what should be a joyous event, filled her with shame.

"I will wait on the porch."

Mrs. Yates shook her head. "You don't understand," she said. "I need you off the premises." Her voice was barely a whisper. "Please go."

Maddie turned, squeezing back tears as she descended the stairs. In her haste to leave, she snagged the sleeve of her dress on a loose nail on the broken screen door. She yanked it free, tearing the fabric and the skin beneath, but she didn't care. She felt utterly wretched as she stepped from the porch and into the blinding darkness.

* * * *

Jace held the baby, marveling at the new life squirming in his arms. He felt honored that he was the first person in the world to touch this tiny child. In Pittsburgh, he'd been so rushed after each delivery, he hadn't the chance to reflect on how remarkable it was. It struck him suddenly that by settling here, in Misty Lake, he'd get the chance to watch this child grow. To see him through common colds and fevers, bumps and bruises, and all the other ailments children experienced.

His last meeting with Doctor Filmore popped into his mind. Filmore's mute anguish in the wake of Jace's finger pointing began to sink in. It was difficult losing patients. But Doctor Filmore hadn't only lost three anonymous patients in that wagon accident. He had lost three girls he'd held in his arms during their first moments on earth, before their own mothers had even had a chance to touch them. Girls he had nursed through illness and watched mature into young women. Daughters, nieces, and children of lifelong friends. While this could never excuse what he'd done to Maddie, Jace could now appreciate how Filmore's emotions had impaired his judgment.

Jace placed the baby in Laura's arms, watching the joy on the faces of the people in the room with him. Evan, Laura, and Mrs. Yates huddled around the new addition to their family, and Jace's chest swelled with pride, and something else he couldn't quite define.

Maddie would have enjoyed this scene, and he would have enjoyed sharing it with her. He bit back his anger at Mrs. Yates for banishing Maddie from the room, when she'd come here only to help. "I'll be going now," he said as he packed up his bag. "I'll stop back tomorrow to check on Laura and the baby."

"Thank you, Doctor Merrick," Laura said. "And please thank Madeline for me."

"You can thank her yourself," he said. "She's right downstairs." He glanced to Mrs. Yates. "Would you call her?"

Mrs. Yates replied without looking up. "She's not here."

"What do you mean? Where did she go?"

Mrs. Yates glanced down at the baby, avoiding Jace's eyes.

He stiffened, appalled. "You sent her out of the house? Alone? In the dark?"

After several beats, the woman finally looked up, her expression cool. "I did what I had to. Now, if you'll excuse me, I must tend to Laura." She turned back to her daughter-in-law. "I'll get you a nice cup of cool black tea, dear."

Jace left the house, emitting a succession of curses as he boarded the buggy. Maddie's crumpled shawl lay on the seat beside him, and he swore again that she'd been forced out into the cold. He drove at a brisk pace, keeping his eyes honed for any sign of her. The birth had progressed rather quickly, and Maddie had a long walk home.

In the dim light of the buggy's lamps, he saw movement on the side of the road up ahead. It was Maddie. He snapped the reins hard. He stopped the buggy when he reached her, then helped her inside. Placing the shawl around her, he noticed a large tear in her dress.

"What happened? Are you all right?" he asked, unable to disguise his alarm.

"It's nothing. I caught myself on the screen door on my way out."

He took a quick breath of relief, but his fury lingered. Something terrible could have happened to Maddie out here all alone. He leaned to inspect the torn fabric at her elbow. "You're bleeding," he said, though it didn't look bad. "We'll stop at the office and clean it up." He tightened the shawl around her trembling shoulders.

With a nod, she nestled into the wool, settling beside him. "Thank you." She spoke casually, as though she'd been out for a stroll and not banished into the dead of night. "Everything went well?" she asked eagerly.

"Mother and baby are fine."

Maddie smiled. "Boy or girl?"

"Boy," he said. He placed his hand over hers. "I thought you were waiting down on the porch."

She shrugged. "Her daughter was in the wagon."

"One of your friends who died in the accident?"

Maddie stared straight ahead.

"That's still no excuse."

Her silence told him that she disagreed. Did she honestly believe she deserved the hostile treatment she received? She inched closer on the seat beside him for warmth or comfort or both. Whatever she was feeling in the wake of this latest rebuff, she obviously didn't wish to discuss it. He obliged her silence as the buggy rolled toward town.

Once back at the office he ushered her inside. "Let's clean up that cut." He led her to the examination room and motioned to the table. "Up."

She hopped onto the table and sat, feet swinging. Her mood seemed much improved, and he was glad she'd put the earlier unpleasantness behind her. Her resilience amazed him, and he admired the hell out of her. He also wanted her. Badly.

Inside the confines of the small room, her lilac scent was stronger. More alluring. Returning focus to the task at hand, he lifted the flap of torn fabric on her sleeve and peered inside. "Not bad at all," he mumbled. He unfastened the buttons at her wrist. His concentration was hampered by the peripheral view of her breasts, rising and falling on each quiet breath.

Blowing out a breath of his own, he gathered a bandage and the supplies needed to treat the cut. He turned to pour some disinfectant onto a cloth. "This won't take long," he said over his shoulder.

"That's good news, Doctor Merrick." She used the sultry voice he'd come to know and like so well. "That leaves us a bit of time for other things."

He grinned, closing his eyes, elated. He turned to face her. "The sooner you quit distracting me, the sooner I'll finish."

She smiled, and he smiled, too.

She hummed impatiently as he prepared a bandage. He rolled up her sleeve, his fingertips brushing her soft skin. With a deep breath, he proceeded to disinfect and dress the cut. Securing the dressing, he tied it off with one final knot. She placed her hand atop his, and he froze, meeting her eyes.

Tilting her head, she watched their hands move as she led his palm from her arm to her breast. She sighed, her eyes fluttering at the contact. Inhaling sharply, he drank in the sight of her lovely face. His pulse spiked with arousal. She was as eager as he. He cupped the luscious weight of her breast, his free hand greedy for the other. Leaning back on her arms, she arched her back to his touch and released a soft moan.

The sound of her pleasure filled the small room, and his shaft thickened with need. She leaned forward, hands in his hair. "I've been waiting for this all day," she whispered into his ear.

The memory of last night had left him starved for more. He captured her face between his hands and kissed her, devouring her. Their tongues entwined in a frenzy. He would not last long.

He dove into the scent of her, kissing her neck, her throat, her hair. His fingers raced to unbutton her dress, and she slipped her arms free, wrapping them around his neck. Lifting her skirts, he spread her legs, pulling her to the edge of the table.

The swift maneuver forced her to release him, and she steadied herself on her arms. Grasping her bottom, he pulled her closer. She wrapped her arms around his neck, her legs around his waist. The feel of her left him dazed. He told himself he'd recoup his wits later. But as he ground against the warmth of her body, he wasn't so sure.

Panting, he stepped back, fumbling with her undergarments. They shed their clothing in a blur. He stood ankle-deep in discarded skirts and trousers as he lifted her to the table. He drank in the sight of her, perfect breasts, perfect face. "You astonish me."

Her mouth opened, her expression so startlingly somber he feared she might cry. "Do you pity me, Jace?"

He blinked, stepping back. She may as well have poured a bucket of icy water on his lap.

"Do you?"

He shook his head in disbelief. "Never. I pity them."

"Why?"

"For not seeing what I see."

She tilted her head, dark eyes glimmering with emotion. "What do you see?"

"I see you." He stepped closer. "Someone special."

She lowered her eyes. "You mean damaged."

He frowned. "I mean special." His harsh tone softened as he lifted her chin. At that moment he'd have said whatever it took to be inside her again, but he still spoke the truth, every word. "You have no idea what you do to me."

"Tell me then," she demanded.

"I'm about to make love to you on my examination table, Maddie." He touched his forehead to hers. "I think that says it all."

Chapter 19

Maddie had to agree, and she smiled at his handsome face. That was all it took to reignite the fire between them. She wrapped her arms around his neck again, her legs tightening around his waist. He thrust into her body, and her eyes fluttered closed in delight. Clutching his neck, she coasted on wings of sheer pleasure.

Jace lifted her from the table and drove into her, harder and deeper. She cried out his name and gave voice to wanton sounds she could not hold back. Sounds that would surprise and embarrass her had she the sense to care, but at this moment, she cared not a whit. So she clung to Jace, and she moaned, and she moaned some more. The sound of her ecstasy rebounded off the walls, the ceiling, the floor.

Jace moved faster, intensifying the urgency and her ascending pleasure. Rocking inside her, he set free a flood of wild sensations that spiraled through her center and careened out of control. She tingled in her limbs, her fingers, her toes. Every inch of her pleaded for the sweet mercy of release. She cried out through ragged breaths, "Please, oh, Jace, please."

She grasped the damp flesh of his shoulders, holding tight. He groaned in response, moving faster. The tension wound through her core, winding tighter. Air hitched in her throat. There was nowhere to go, no spiraling higher. She threw back her head, reeling in pleasure as it all came unfurled.

Jace's body tensed. Clutching her bottom, his deep moan filled her ears as he lifted her to the table and pulled away from her body. Gasping over her shoulder, he came in a surge of hot breath and vibration.

Easing away, he reached for a towel. Her legs trembled as he gently wiped his seed from her belly and between her legs. She closed her eyes as he kissed her, soft and sweet. She drifted into his touch, floating on the tranquil aftermath, ragged and spent.

Nothing outside the small room mattered to Maddie, nothing but the way she felt right now. Regardless of what lay ahead of her, of them, she was, for the first time in years, truly, incandescently happy.

* * * *

When Amelia dropped by the office a few days later, Jace insisted Maddie enjoy some time off with her friend. The wedding was less than a week away, and according to Amelia, there was still much to do. She and Maddie decided to discuss the remaining event-planning duties over lunch, and they soon found themselves sitting at a table by the window of a charming restaurant in town. The conversation flowed with the list of wedding preparations. Amelia gushed about floral arrangements, place card designs, and most importantly of all—to Amelia, anyway—the selection of the cake.

"My mother is so old-fashioned." Amelia rolled her eyes. "She insisted charms be baked inside the bride's and groom's cakes, but I'll not have my bridesmaids soiling their gloves searching for favors."

Maddie smiled. There was a day she'd have frowned on the traditional practice as well, but after plunging her hands into the bloody wound of a dying deer, soiling her gloves with cake no longer seemed quite so distasteful.

They finished their meals over fine tea and fond memories. The sound of Amelia's laughter carried Maddie back to a time when her life was so simple. To a place where girls spent their days planning for tomorrow and what might happen at the next ball or cotillion, oblivious to the fragility of life and the waning time in each other's company. Time they had taken for granted.

"Oh, Mads, remember that afternoon down at the lake, when you feigned a twisted ankle to get Philip to carry you up to the house?"

Maddie nodded. "A trick I learned from you, I might add."

Amelia laughed, nearly spewing a mouthful of tea. "And I learned it from Phoebe, who learned it from Susan." She covered her lips with her napkin, laughing some more. "The Fair Five had no shortage of stratagem when it came to boys." She shook her head, smiling. "So, how are you and Doctor Merrick getting on?" she asked, pulling Maddie from her thoughts of the friends she missed so much.

Maddie swallowed the last bite of her blueberry tart. "What do you mean?"

"Are you enjoying working at his office?"

She nodded. "It's fine."

Amelia sipped her tea, eyeing her over the rim of her cup. "And Doctor Merrick? Is he fine as well?"

Maddie shrugged. "I suppose." For the briefest of moments, Maddie feared Amelia sensed the extent of Maddie's relationship with Jace. For another brief moment, Maddie came close to confiding in her friend. She ached to tell Amelia about the wonderful intimacy she and Jace had shared. Maddie knew Amelia well enough to suspect she and Lester had likely engaged in similar behavior.

But Amelia and Lester were soon to be married, which, of course, was a different story entirely. She wasn't confident her friend would encourage the risk Maddie was taking, and she was enjoying her affair with Jace far too much to risk tainting it with Amelia's disapproval. "He's a fine doctor," she said instead. "I enjoy working with him, and it passes the time."

"I'm glad for you, Mads. Truly. I only wish..." Amelia wiped the corners of her mouth with her napkin. "I fear this sham engagement of yours might do more harm than good." She leaned forward in her chair. "You are eliminating your options."

Maddie snorted. "I have no options."

"Maybe not in Misty Lake, but—"

"Amelia..." Maddie shook her head.

"Philip is smitten with you."

Maddie's jaw dropped at Amelia's candor.

"I'm certain of it. I can see it whenever you're around."

For her part, Maddie couldn't dispute the possibility. She'd sensed Philip's interest herself. "I like Philip, but—"

"But what?"

Maddie struggled for something to say.

"He doesn't see you as the others do, Mads. Despite all the talk, he sees you as the same person he was besotted with when we were girls."

And that was the problem. Maddie was no longer that person. She was no longer the girl whose biggest concerns consisted of choosing which bonnet to wear and which coy flirtation to employ on which beau. Maddie's decisions now held real consequence. True relevance. Life and death hinged on her choices and the weighty repercussions of using her gift. Though her shoulders were slight, she carried a powerful responsibility. And an enormous, life-altering secret.

Philip had no idea who Maddie truly was. And sadder still, neither did Jace.

"We're no longer girls, Amelia."

"I know." Amelia lowered her eyes, reaching for her tea. "So, what are your plans?"

"My plans?"

"Do you never think about your future?"

Maddie shrugged in lack of an answer. "I…"

"For goodness sakes, Madeline, have you never thought about leaving Misty Lake?"

Maddie frowned at Amelia's sharp tone. "You know I cannot leave Grandfather," she snapped back.

Amelia leaned in, studying her. "Are you certain you don't use your grandfather as an excuse?"

Maddie stared, shaking her head. "He's all I have, Amelia. Surely you can understand."

Amelia tilted her head, her expression softening at Maddie's distress. "I'm sorry. I don't wish to upset you. Not for the world."

"I'm not upset. I'm…tired."

Amelia eyes widened as she glanced over Maddie's shoulder to the window behind. "Oh, look, there's Dolly and Gertrude," she said. She craned her neck up and down the street. "And somewhere close by we'll see… Yes, there he is. I knew it."

Maddie followed Amelia's gaze out the window. Matthew Webster stood on the street kitty-corner from the girls, watching and waiting as they entered the mercantile.

"Like clockwork." Amelia shook her head. "There'll be no shaking him now."

"What do you mean?"

"Lester told me that his uncle gave Matthew permission to marry Dolly next year."

Maddie cringed in surprise. "He didn't."

"He did," Amelia said with a nod. "The marriage has not yet been announced, but in the meanwhile, Matthew will do all he can to ensure he's not pushed aside for someone else. And as much as I hate to say it, I don't see that he'll have any real competition. Young men aren't exactly turning cartwheels for Dolly's attention," Amelia added. "That's why I found his interest in Dolly so sweet, at first. His willingness to look past Dolly's appearance seemed a commendable trait."

"And now?"

"I know it sounds strange, but I now sense his interest is born of the opposite impulse. It's as though he sees nothing past her birthmark. As though he wants her because of it, not despite it. As though the mark will guarantee she will always be his."

Maddie considered Amelia's disturbing observation. "How does Dolly feel about him?"

Amelia shrugged. "I can't imagine anyone bothers to ask."

Maddie frowned.

"Matthew barely speaks to her—I've yet to see them engaged in actual conversation. But he set his sights on her and hasn't looked away since." She shook her head. "I don't know how the poor girl tolerates it. He follows on her heels like a hungry puppy."

A wolf seemed a more appropriate description, but Maddie kept that thought to herself as she turned away from the window in disgust.

"He hasn't bothered you, has he?" Amelia asked.

"No. Why do you ask?"

Amelia lowered her eyes and fluffed at her skirts. "No reason."

Considering Matthew's close ties with the pastor and the many ugly looks he'd sent Maddie's way in the last few weeks, Maddie could easily deduce the reason for Amelia's question. Maddie could only imagine how the two so-called "men of faith" spoke of her behind closed doors.

Amelia gave a toss of her red curls and took a deep breath. "Let's not discuss Matthew Webster any longer. Let's talk about me." She smiled.

Maddie smiled, too. "Because we so rarely do that."

Amelia snickered and continued. "I almost forgot to tell you," she said. "We've decided on Niagara Falls for the honeymoon."

"That's very romantic. I hear the falls are spectacular."

Amelia shook her head. "I could not care less about seeing the sights." Her blue eyes twinkled with mischief, reminding Maddie once again of their days as girls. "But Lester has rented us a suite in the quaintest little inn." She cupped a hand to her mouth, more for dramatics than privacy. "We may never step out the door." Amelia waggled her brows, and Maddie laughed hard.

Amelia and Lester would have a wonderful life together as husband and wife. A beautiful future. Despite her happiness for her friend, in that moment, in the barren scope of her own expectations, Maddie had never envied anyone more.

* * * *

The following evening Jace drove Maddie home from the office. A sudden heat wave had settled over the area, and the temperatures continued to climb. Even the gentle breeze on her face as the buggy rolled along held the warm remnants of the day's blazing sun.

Maddie glanced up at the full moon and the stars, the unlimited wonders of the world, feeling so lost. Were there others like her out there? Others possessing her ability? Surely she couldn't be the only person in all existence who could heal as she could. The chasm between her and the rest of the world widened as she reflected that she would likely never know.

With only one day remaining until the wedding weekend, Maddie found herself increasingly on edge. She abhorred the thought of spending an entire weekend in the presence of people who detested her. Then there were the people like Mrs. Yates, who didn't seem to hate her as much as they felt fear and dread in her company.

Though a part of her wished time would stop, leaving her here in this moment with Jace, she also longed to have the ordeal behind her. Amelia's wedding should be a joyous event, but to Maddie, it would be more bitter than sweet. The end of the weekend would bring about the end to her sham engagement and her time with Jace.

Pushing the depressing thought from her head, she focused on the here and now. Jace sat beside her, and she was determined to make the most of their dwindling time together.

Just as she was formulating a few seductive words to whisper in his ear, something snapped loudly beneath them, and the buggy plunged abruptly to one side. Fear trapped her breath in her throat. She squeezed her eyes shut and was falling, hurling through the dark memories in her mind. She grasped Jace, clinging tight.

"Whoa!" Jace pulled on the reins to keep the horse from dragging the disabled buggy any farther. "Are you all right?"

Maddie opened her eyes, trembling. Releasing her fierce grip on his arm, she nodded, trying to calm down.

"The wheel must have broken," Jace said. He stood, balancing on the buggy's slanted floor. "Come on down," he said as he helped her to the road. "You're sure you're all right?"

"I'm fine," she said, feeling a fool for her exaggerated reaction to a simple broken wheel. "I was startled, that's all."

Jace nodded. Turning his attention to the buggy, he knelt to check the undercarriage to assess the damage. He got down on all fours for a closer look. Maddie watched, the beat of her pulse ebbing as she enjoyed the view. The memory of his naked body pumping into hers sent a flush of warmth to her cheeks, and her pulse leaped once again.

"We'll have to ride the horse to your house," he said over his shoulder.

She blinked, gathering her wits.

"I'll arrange to have the buggy repaired tomorrow. I think I can manage to get it into the trees so no one disturbs it until then."

Maddie turned toward a sound in the distance. "Someone's coming."

Jace crawled out, then gazed down the road. A wagon appeared around the bend, trudging toward them. "Perfect timing," he said, wiping the dust from his knees.

The wagon approached and slowed to a stop. With a grateful wave at the driver, Jace strode toward the wagon.

Matthew Webster frowned back.

Maddie was dismayed at the thought of being rescued by Matthew, but the fear of having to board his wagon was far worse. Her heart thundered. She stared at the tall vehicle, the spacious double seats and spoke wheels. Swallowing hard, she froze amid terrific visions of the accident that felt vividly real.

She needn't have worried.

To her utter shock, Matthew snapped the reins and the wagon lurched, sending Jace scuffling backward to avoid being hit. Matthew sped past them down the road, leaving Jace and Maddie in the dust.

"What the hell…?"

Breathing deeply to maintain her calm, she said, "Oh, never mind him. It's a beautiful night. We'll do without his assistance."

Jace nodded, watching Matthew barrel down the road. "I'll take care of the buggy, then get the horse ready."

Maddie waited. Her annoyance with Matthew for leaving them deserted was superseded by her subsiding panic about boarding a wagon. She glanced at Jace as he prepared the horse, relieved to be spared from her cowardice.

"Are you ready?" he asked.

He lifted her to the horse, and she arranged her light work skirt around her straddling legs. Jace hopped up behind her. The heat of him radiated on her back and her bottom, and she clenched her legs tight. Positioning himself more comfortably, he edged closer, his thighs flanking hers. With a kick of his heels, he spurred the horse to move.

They rode under the moonlight, through the sound of chirping crickets. The horse walked at an even pace in rhythmic footfalls on the deserted road. Straddling the bareback horse with Jace behind her, she found the motion of their bodies as the horse moved beneath them undisputedly arousing.

Maddie leaned into Jace, just a tad. The warm breath he released fanned her neck, sending tingles through her veins. He straightened behind her, and she smiled, knowing he felt something, too.

He held the reins with one hand, and the other rested on his knee. She dropped her hand to his and guided it to her thigh. The soft pressure of his touch felt exquisite as his fingers kneaded and squeezed.

Their bodies moved with the horse as they engaged in a tango of sensual caresses that had her burning for more. Jace's lips touched her neck. She released a long sigh, arching her spine. Raising an arm, she coiled it around his neck, fingers raking his hair, urging him on.

Cupping her breast, he nipped at her ear, trailing hot kisses down the length of her neck. His hand dropped to her knee and then rose to her thigh, dragging a fistful of skirt up with it. Slipping beneath the fabric, he skimmed over her stocking to her bare thigh.

"Ooh," she moaned, arching against him. His fingers reached inside her bloomers, and she dizzied with tremors of excitement. He touched her there, and she flinched, afraid she might fall.

"You're safe with me, Maddie," Jace whispered. The tenderness in his voice, the wisp of warm breath in her ear, lured her back into the dream. "Just sit back and enjoy it. I won't let you tumble."

Caressing her softly, he whispered some more. "You're so wet. So damn sweet." He strummed her softly, his fingers circling over her burning flesh as she reclined against his chest. Breathing hard, she closed her eyes, pelvis grinding into his hand. He curled his fingers inside her, and she moaned in the sweet torture of it all.

Spreading her legs farther, she opened to the magic of his hand, the friction of the horse beneath her, Jace's fingers, sliding in and out of her. She writhed against his chest, panting. He pressed his hot mouth to her ear. "Come for me, Maddie."

The four words pushed her over the edge, and she climaxed, gasping into the night air.

Jace pulled her bottom roughly against him, his hardness evident. The thought of pleasing him as fully as he'd pleased her, stoked her desire before it could cool. By the time they reached the house, she was afire with need. "Bring the horse to the carriage house and you can water it before you head back," she said.

Jace hopped from the horse and helped her dismount. She slid down into his arms and into a kiss that left her knees trembling. He led the horse to the barrel of water as she opened the carriage house doors.

As he saw to the horse, she stepped inside. Through the flood of moonlight behind her, she assessed her surroundings. She smiled at a stack of hay bales in the corner. Spurred by excitement, she worked quickly. She arranged the bales, then pulled a blanket from the pile on a nearby stool. She tossed the blanket over the hay bales, then sat, leaning back on her arms.

Jace stepped inside, spotting her on the makeshift bed.

"Grandfather's been asleep for hours," she said. "He'll be none the wiser."

Jace walked toward her, removing his coat. After pulling her to her feet, he kissed her. Hard. She wrapped her arms around his neck and his kiss softened. His tongue traced her lips before dipping slowly into her mouth to swirl against hers.

They dropped onto the bed of hay, and he climbed over her. The crisp scent of him—his skin and hair—was still new to her senses, while the nostalgic smell of hay welcomed her home. The combination of exotic and familiar was exhilarating. Titillating.

Jace made love to her slowly this time. With every searing touch to her flesh, every lingering kiss, she dissolved. Each twitch of pleasure in his face, each unrepressed groan brought her closer. Her body was no longer her own.

They were one being with two heartbeats, a melding of limbs and lips flying toward one destination, one goal. One perfect moment of shared honesty.

She shuddered with the blissful thought, with the peaking ecstasy consuming her body. Crying out, she clung to Jace's damp neck, clutching fistfuls of his hair. Her pleasure drove his, and with one final thrust, he pulled from her body and reached his own wild release.

The carriage house seemed deathly quiet as they lay there atop the bed of hay. Jace's heart pounded against hers for several moments before he finally moved. Rising to sit, he reached for his trousers and began to dress.

"I've never before been so eager to attend a wedding." He chuckled, his eyes filling with wicked humor. Maddie smiled back at him with equal anticipation for the weekend ahead. Then she started to gather her own clothes. She sensed Jace was watching her movements, and tossing a glance over her shoulder, she confirmed his fixed stare. She smiled again, this time to herself, deliberately slowing her progress so that he could take his fill.

Slipping into each garment, Maddie dressed in the moonlight and enjoyed the budding discovery that she liked him watching her. She felt bold and lovely in his simmering gaze. A few more moments passed before she fluffed at her skirt and patted her hair into place.

After folding the blanket, she returned it to the stool by Grandfather's wagon. She stopped, staring at the vehicle. Jace came up behind her and wrapped his arms around her waist. "You'll overcome that as well," he murmured against her hair. "I'm certain of it."

During their lovemaking, in the heat of passion, he'd uttered spontaneous sentiments, but she'd taken none of them to heart. But his words now, the way he held her, were not products of erupting pleasure. What they were, she was not sure, but she'd savor every one of them.

His reference to her fear proved how poorly she'd hidden her panic earlier on the road. "Someday, perhaps." She sighed. "If only I could understand…" She paused, stopping herself from saying more. She turned into his arms and looked into his face. The warmth in his eyes melted her heart. Her resolve.

Oh, how she yearned to tell him her secret. She had trusted him with her body, opened to him with honest abandon. Naked and vulnerable, she'd exposed and offered him her entire physical self. Could she not open her soul and reveal who she was as well?

"Do you believe in miracles?" she asked carefully.

"You were lucky, Maddie. You survived because of the circumstances, because of certain factors that lessened the severity of your injuries."

She stiffened in protest, ready to admit everything. But when she opened her mouth, the words would not come. She tried a different tack.

"Surely you agree that there are some things we cannot explain?"

"No," he replied gently. "There's a logical explanation for everything."

His certainty chilled her, and she sobered from her hopeful stupor. The faces of her tormentors—Matthew, Pastor Hogle and all the others—blurred into the dear countenance of her lover. She lowered her eyes, sinking beneath a wave of disappointment.

With a stroke to her hair, he tossed her a lifeline.

"Except, perhaps, my body's insatiable need to have you."

And once again, just like that, Jace's singular magic buoyed her back to the surface.

Chapter 20

Maddie hummed as she twirled about the room, packing her bags. The bridal party wasn't due at the Crooked Lake House until later tomorrow, but since she'd awoken this morning full of excitement about having yet another night with Jace, she'd decided to put her energy to good use.

She felt so alive, so utterly renewed.

This fact both elated and depressed her. She tossed the dress she held to the bed, then slumped down next to it.

She loved him.

The words chimed in her head, and she jumped to her feet to quiet them. Pacing the room, she tried to dispel the panic that coursed through her veins. She simply could not love Jace. It was unrealistic, and Maddie, of all people, knew her limits. She hugged her arms to her chest as she sought another explanation.

Jace had been kind to her, compassionate, protective. When added to the bliss she'd experienced in his arms these past weeks, it was no wonder she was imagining her feelings for him were something more than what they were. It made perfect sense. She and Jace were merely friends. Close friends. Very close friends...

She blinked hard, willing herself to be convinced. A complication such as this had no place in her plans. She knew full well that after the wedding, her time with Jace would be over.

Of course, that didn't mean she couldn't enjoy what time they had left.

Jace had made arrangements to stay at the hotel as well, and they would take full advantage of the opportunity this would provide. Amelia and her guests would be so engaged in the pre-wedding festivities, they'd never notice if Maddie and Jace slipped away.

Her spirit lifted as she decided to focus on that. With renewed vigor, she returned to the task of packing her bags. But she was soon interrupted by a knock on the door.

"You have a guest, Maddie."

"Who is it, Rhetta?" she called through the door.

"Dolly Hogle," Rhetta said. "She's waiting in the parlor."

Dolly Hogle? Had something happened to Daniel? What else could possibly bring Dolly here? Maddie's pulse quickened as she followed Rhetta downstairs.

"Good morning, Dolly," Maddie said.

Dolly glanced up from her seat with a timid half-smile. "I hope you don't mind my stopping by uninvited."

The lack of urgency in Dolly's voice eased Maddie's anxiety. "Not at all." She took a seat across from the girl. "Rhetta will bring us some tea."

Dolly nodded, looking a tad more comfortable.

"How is Daniel feeling?" Maddie asked.

"Very well." Dolly lifted her chin. "Doctor Merrick said it was your quick thinking that helped him recover so thoroughly." She lowered her eyes, fiddling with the folds of her skirts. "Of course, Uncle refuses to believe that." She glanced up for Maddie's reaction. "He prefers to believe you were trying to do something sinister to my cousin."

Maddie gasped at the girl's unexpected candor.

"Were you?"

"You're a bright girl, Dolly. What do you think?"

Dolly shrugged. "I think it's preposterous," she said. "Though I wouldn't blame you for wanting to hurt him after the way he so callously broke off your engagement." She sighed. "That's my opinion, anyway. Not that anyone cares to hear it." She lifted her chin. "In my household I'm expected to keep my thoughts to myself." Anger pierced through each word the unhappy girl spoke.

"I imagine it's difficult to have so strict a guardian," Maddie said, thinking of poor Elizabeth.

"Especially when you're so ugly no one else will look at you."

Dolly's words left Maddie speechless. As did the grain of truth in them. Before the accident, Maddie, herself, had sought to avoid eye contact with the marked girl. She had treated Dolly the way she was now treated by others.

For whatever reason, when she first saw Dolly again at Amelia's dress fitting, Maddie had no longer been distressed by Dolly's appearance. She wondered why this might be.

"You're one of the few people who will look me in the eye," said Dolly.

"People tend to fear those who are different," Maddie replied sadly.

"I've learned to accept my looks and how people react to my birthmark. You only have one life, and I'm going to make the best of mine."

"That's truly commendable, Dolly."

"What I'm not prepared to do is marry Matthew Webster."

Maddie couldn't blame Dolly, but she wondered why the girl was confiding in her of all people. "Amelia told me of the arrangement," Maddie began cautiously.

"Uncle has had it planned all along." She shook her head. "Gert says I'm fortunate that Matthew has agreed. That he's my only option, since no other man would want me."

"Gertrude is a fool."

A slow smile formed on Dolly's lips. "She certainly is. And I'm her long-suffering sister."

The girl spoke her mind. Who would have thought Dolly's mousy facade veiled a witty and straightforward young woman?

Rhetta set up the tea. Maddie poured, listening as Dolly continued.

"Gert's nonsense aside, I've no wish to marry a man I can't stand. Matthew Webster is the worst sort of person. He takes great pleasure in controlling others, me in particular. He believes his natural skill for intimidation makes him well suited to lead a church. While that may be true, he won't be piloting any congregation I'd want to join. He's so self-righteous. Always watching and judging everyone with those disapproving eyes of his."

Maddie couldn't disagree. The way Matthew looked at her made her skin crawl.

"He's worse than Uncle, I swear it." Dolly shook her head. "And Uncle has promised to tutor him to be a man of the church once we are married."

"I see."

"I'd accepted this fate, but now I have hope there's a man out there somewhere who could love me." She stared into the rising steam from her cup. "You gave me that hope."

"Me?"

Dolly glanced up. "If a man like Doctor Merrick could love you, surely there's hope for me, too."

Despite the initial sting of the unintended insult, Maddie admired the honesty. The words held more desperation than malice, but the hope the girl harbored was based on a lie. "You are certainly right, and I wish exactly that happiness for you," Maddie said, feeling guilty. "But for now, you must tell me why you are here."

Dolly sighed. "My uncle hates you intensely, Madeline."

Although this was old news to Maddie, the force of hearing it aloud hit Maddie hard. She took a breath to regain her composure.

"I'm sorry to speak so plainly, but you must understand. Uncle's rantings about you have poisoned many members of the congregation into believing you're the bane of this town's existence. That there's something...abnormal...about you. He condemns you at every turn. Matthew, especially, has been greatly influenced by Uncle's views. So much so, he's insisting that Uncle take more aggressive action against you." She inched to the edge of her chair. "I overheard Matthew and Uncle arguing last night over Matthew's scheme to split from the church to form his own sect." She tilted her head. "Although an estrangement between Matthew and my uncle would be an answer to my prayers, it would be at your expense. Matthew wishes to run you out of town...or worse."

Surely Dolly was exaggerating. A man hoping for a life in the church—even a desperate one—would not be so foolish as to resort to violence. Still, Maddie was happy to have an ally in the Hogle family. It might make things easier at the wedding, at least.

"I appreciate the warning, Dolly. But there's nothing I can do to change people's opinion of me." She smiled a sad smile. "Of course, I continue to try."

"That handsome doctor of yours is sure trying."

"Oh?"

"When he came to check on Daniel after the picnic, he gave it to them with both barrels." A smile peeked out from the curtain of hair shielding her face. "I must admit, I rather enjoyed it."

"What exactly were they saying?"

"Just as I told you. That you were trying to do something sinister to Daniel."

"Ridiculous," Maddie squeaked.

"That's what Doctor Merrick told them. And that's why I wanted to come see you today. Uncle was furious after Doctor Merrick left. Oh, how he carried on." She sipped her tea. "Gertrude forbids me from speaking to you in public, so I'm telling you now. I do not share their opinions." Dolly set down the cup. "If a man as smart and handsome as Doctor Merrick intends to marry you, I surmised you couldn't be as bad as they say."

Maddie blinked, and Dolly gasped at the words that had just snuck out of her mouth.

"I only meant—" the girl stammered.

"It's all right, Dolly," Maddie assured her. And strangely, it was. Maddie liked this girl. Dolly spent her days following in Gertrude's

"Fortunately, you don't have to eat it," she said, eyebrows waggling as she mixed. "I can help apply it if you'd like. I can't be certain it will help, but what harm could it do?"

"No harm," Dolly beamed. "No harm at all." Her eyes brimmed with excitement. Hope.

Maddie tilted her head. "Dolly, this is a simple poultice of horseradish and sour milk. The mixture has helped fade freckles. Even scars. We can apply it, but you mustn't let the results—whatever they are—dim your spirits. There is more to beauty than what is on the surface."

"Yes, yes," Dolly said, impatiently. "I believe all of that, too, but I still want to try."

"All right, then." Maddie stood. "I must heat up the concoction before we apply it." She glanced at the girl from the corner of her eye to gauge her reaction.

"Whatever must be done," Dolly replied. She followed on Maddie's heels, and they crossed the room to the stove. Dolly waited anxiously as Maddie spooned the slop into a pan and lit the range. The only way to disguise the heat her healing induced was to warm the poultice before application. Hoping the mixture wouldn't curdle, she let it heat through and then placed it on the table to cool a bit.

"Have a seat, Dolly."

Dolly slid into the chair at the small table, then removed her bonnet. She sat stiffly as Maddie dipped her fingers into the bowl and spread the goop onto Dolly's cheek. Maddie massaged gently, closing her eyes. The heat radiated from her tingling fingers. Dolly shifted in her seat but didn't complain. The poor girl was so desperate to be free of the mark she'd probably endure anything.

The thought heightened Maddie's desire to help. She closed her eyes tighter, pressing both hands to Dolly's face. She had to be careful. She hoped only to fade the mark, not erase it completely. A few moments later, she withdrew the pressure and returned to massaging. "Are you all right?"

"Yes," Dolly replied. "It's much warmer than I expected."

"It didn't burn you, did it?"

"No. It… It seemed to penetrate, though."

"Good." Maddie smiled. "That's precisely what it's intended to do." Maddie let the mixture set. "That's enough for now," she said. "You can take the poultice with you. If you can manage it, apply it twice more today and then three times a day after that."

Dolly smiled. "I can manage," she said. "And who knows, perhaps the next time you see me, I'll be as pretty as you are."

"I'm fine, girl, quit your fussing."

Maddie searched his face. "I hate leaving you for the entire weekend."

"Rhetta is here. She'll take good care of me." He gave an affectionate pat to his bottle of port. "So will this."

"You'll be sure to have Gil come for me if you need me, won't you?"

"Yes, yes," he said, waving her away. "Now, off with you. Go have a grand time, and send Amelia my regards."

"I will," Maddie said. She kissed her grandfather's gaunt cheek, then hugged him tight. "Wish me luck," she said with a smile.

"You'll do fine." But something in the man's trembling smile made Jace uneasy. "I love you, girl," he uttered softly as his granddaughter swished away.

* * * *

The Crooked Lake House was a bustle of activity. Carriages lined the drive as the wedding guests arrived for the weekend. Maddie's bags were unloaded, and she was led to her assigned room on the upper floor, near the other bridesmaids. Jace was staying on the floor below and already Maddie was planning her route to his room.

She unpacked quickly, then hurried down the hall to Amelia's suite to help her get ready for luncheon. Caroline greeted her at the door. "It's lovely, don't you think?"

Maddie glanced around, smiling. It was a spacious room, with plenty of light, complete with a large mirror perfect for bridal primping. A plush carpet covered the wood floor beneath the four-poster bed, and floral draperies flanked the glass doors to the balcony overlooking the lake.

Amelia, Caroline, and Maddie enjoyed a tray of tea as they waited for Gertrude and Dolly, who were nearly an hour late. Maddie's blood raced with anticipation at seeing Dolly and the result of her "poultice." How wonderful it would be to discover the mark had faded well enough to conceal with powder. An ugly duckling turned swan...

The door to the suite flung open, and Gertrude charged inside, dragging Dolly behind her. "Look what she's done, Amelia!"

Amelia blinked. "Look what who's done?"

Gertrude pointed a stiff finger at Maddie, chest heaving. "Her!"

"Calm down, Gert—"

"I will not calm down. She's an evil woman. And you're a fool, Amelia, for not seeing what she truly is."

Amelia shot to her feet as Gertrude shoved Dolly forward. "Look what she did to Dolly's face!" Gertrude held back Dolly's hair, exposing her face. "Look!"

Maddie gasped. Amelia and Caroline did too. Dolly's swollen face teemed with welts. Nasty, angry welts that looked painful and sore. Maddie swallowed her horror. Her guilt. Not only was Dolly's birthmark unchanged, but it now appeared more prominent on the raised skin beneath.

Amelia's gaze flew to Maddie.

"It's not her fault," Dolly cried.

"It most certainly is her fault, Dolly, so quit defending her and keep quiet." Gertrude took an imposing step forward. "She mixed up some concoction and rubbed it on Dolly's face, promising to make her mark disappear."

"I did no such thing," Maddie said.

"Did you not apply it?"

"Yes, but—"

"Mads!" Amelia spun toward her, looking angrier than she'd ever seen her. "Whatever were you thinking?"

The censure in her friend's face filled her with shame. "I—"

"Look at the poor girl." Amelia grimaced, adjusting Dolly's curls back into place to cover the unsightly blotches. "She looks atrocious."

A sob rose in Maddie's throat. "I'm so sorry, Dolly," she croaked through her tears.

"That's not good enough!" Gertrude stomped her foot. "My uncle is going to have plenty to say about this, I promise. How you coerced this foolish girl into participating in your trickery, I'll never know, since she continues to defend you. But I do know you did something evil here, just as you tried to do to Daniel at the picnic!"

A hush fell over the room, and in that silence, Maddie heard what they all were thinking. That Gertrude was right. Maddie was an abomination. Looking at Dolly, Maddie couldn't blame them. What had she done? Dolly had trusted her.

Maddie's healing attempts weren't always successful, but they'd never produced results such as this. She moved toward Dolly to examine her, but Gertrude pulled her away.

"Come along, Dolly." Gertrude dragged Dolly to the edge of the room and out the door.

Now everyone would know what Maddie had done to the poor girl. Maddie slumped to a chair, head hung low. The weight of ensuing thoughts sunk her lower.

Dolly needed medical attention. Those welts on her face had to be painful. Jace might prescribe something to help. Jace.... Maddie cringed at his reaction to what she'd done. He'd warned her about getting involved. Of course, he feared Maddie would get Dolly's hopes up and there'd be no difference in the mark. He hadn't expected that Maddie would make it look worse.

"Damn," Maddie uttered. She glanced at Amelia and Caroline, who were clearly irked at her, too.

"I was only trying to help." The words sounded pathetic to her ears, and she despised her self-pity.

"I'm sure you were, Mads," Amelia said. "But in light of the way the Hogles feel about you, perhaps it would be best to keep your distance from them in the future."

"I agree," Caroline said. "Why would you do anything that might make these people angrier at you than they already are?"

Maddie sighed. So Caroline had been informed of Maddie's past after all. Maddie turned to Amelia, who lowered her eyes. The wedding weekend was off to a very bad start, and she began regretting coming at all. She feared Amelia harbored the same regret.

"Amelia, perhaps I should leave—"

"No!" Amelia took a deep breath. "Please, Mads, I need you here."

Maddie nodded. She wasn't sure why Amelia still wanted her, but she was obligated to honor the request.

"Let's put it behind us now, shall we?" Amelia said.

But Maddie couldn't put it behind her. Dolly needed a doctor. "I'm going to find Jace," she said. "He may be able to make Dolly more comfortable."

"Good idea," Amelia said. "Everything will be fine." Her hopeful smile carried a plea. *Please do nothing else that might spoil my wedding.*

Maddie went to find Jace. She walked down the wide staircase to the hotel lobby, peering around. She all but hid behind a potted fern when she spotted a group of people heading toward her. Lifting her chin, she breezed past them and continued her search.

Jace sat in the far lobby with a few other men. His brows rose in surprise when he spotted her in the doorway. She waved him toward her. He glanced around, then snuffed out his cigar. With a nod at the men seated around him, he rose and headed toward her.

"What's wrong?" he asked. "Why aren't you getting ready for luncheon with the others?"

"Something has happened."

His eyes widened. "What is it?"

Since they'd arrived, he'd been on alert for signs of trouble from Pastor Hogle. Usually Jace's protectiveness touched her heart. Currently, it ripped it to pieces. She swallowed her guilt. "Yesterday I applied a poultice to Dolly's face."

His expression stilled. He narrowed his eyes, inhaling for patience. "Go on."

"Well, now her face is covered in welts."

Jace inhaled again. Deeper this time. "What did you use in the poultice?"

"Just horseradish and sour milk."

Jace considered this for all of a moment. "She must be allergic to horseradish. That's a fairly common allergy." Jace glanced around. "Where is she?"

"In her room with Gertrude. Who is furious at me, by the way."

Jace pinned her with a look that said he couldn't blame her. "All right. I'll go see what I can do."

"Shall I go with you?"

He stared incredulously, shaking his head. His jaw was clenched tight. "You've done enough for now," he ground out. "We'll talk later." He started away.

"Jace!"

He turned to face her.

"Please tell Dolly how sorry I am."

"I'll tell her," he said, his expression softening. "For all the good it will do."

She lowered her eyes, and Jace clasped her shoulder for a moment.

"Now go back upstairs and try to stay out of trouble."

Chapter 22

Maddie paced the room, cursing her arrogance. She'd played with fire by attempting to fade Dolly's birthmark, and the poor girl was suffering because of it. Maddie slumped into a chair, overwhelmed by the depth of her frustration. Her gift allowed her to heal fatal injuries but had no effect on something as simple as a birthmark.

She thought of Grandfather, and how she'd failed to cure him. It was most unfair that the one worthwhile result of her accident was so unpredictable. Despite her best efforts, some of her "patients" would live and some would die. And some would be forced to live their lives hiding behind a curtain of curls and self-consciousness.

Maddie sprang to her feet at the knock on the door. With a deep breath, she crossed the room, then pulled back the handle. Jace stood in the hall. "She's fine," he said at once.

Maddie exhaled in relief.

"I gave her a salve to counteract the allergy. The welts are already beginning to subside."

Tears pooled in Maddie's eyes. At least she'd caused Dolly no permanent damage. Not physically, anyway.

"She's not angry at you, Maddie. She made me promise to tell you so. After her face swelled up, Gertrude forced the story out of her."

Maddie lowered her eyes, wiping her tears.

Jace lifted her chin to face him. "She's fine." He nodded firmly, then released her. "We're late. I'll go dress for luncheon, then meet you downstairs."

She nodded.

"Dolly promised to save me a dance tonight. I hope you don't mind," he added as he turned to leave.

Maddie couldn't help smiling. He'd already managed to charm Dolly with his handsome face. This additional kindness had likely swept her off her feet. Understandable. Jace had a soft spot for outcasts. An unexpected accord with people like her and Dolly. Maddie appreciated this wonderful quality in him. No matter how horrid things got, or how low she sank, he always managed to lift her back up.

"Jace," she called.

He stopped and turned to face her.

"Thank you."

He winked. "I'll see you downstairs."

Maddie hastened to freshen up, feeling better than she'd thought possible. She donned her new crimson dress and matching hat and gazed into the mirror. To her surprise, she saw her old self staring back. A fresh and lovely young woman with the world at her feet.

Blinking, she returned from the past and made her way downstairs to the lobby where Jace waited. He looked so handsome. And so self-assured. Admiring his confidence, she straightened her shoulders, determined to follow his example. She had as much right to be here as the others. Amelia had insisted, despite the debacle with Dolly.

They took luncheon on the lakeside patio. The sun shined on the sparkling water, but the patio remained comfortably cool beneath the shade of the colorful awning. Smells of freshly cut grass blended with the aroma of grilling meat from the large cooking pit on the surrounding lawn. Everyone ate and drank champagne, greeting late arrivals, who continued to stream out to the patio from the wide glass doors.

Maddie and Jace sat at a table on the outer corner. People whispered and stared, more so than usual. Maddie felt every prick of their pin-sharp glares. Word of the incident with Dolly obviously had spread through the assembly. Gertrude's smug smile confirmed this. As always, Pastor Hogle kept his back to Maddie, going out of his way not to face her directly. On this particular occasion, she was grateful for his rebuff. She was also relieved that Matthew Webster was conspicuously absent.

Looking around at the unwelcoming faces, Maddie decided she could no longer fool herself that she had any chance of re-entering the closed society of Misty Lake. Very few of her fellow celebrants were happy to see her here, and she secretly longed for the safety of home.

Only one more day. And then she would formulate a new plan for her life. One with realistic expectations of success.

She lifted her chin and focused on getting through it. Guests would enjoy the afternoon at the shore before retiring to their rooms where they'd dress for the rehearsal dinner and dance in the ballroom later that evening. A breakfast reception would follow the marriage ceremony tomorrow, after which Amelia and Lester would embark on their wedding tour to Niagara Falls. Then, thank goodness, it all would be over.

A flush of shame at her selfishness warmed her cheeks as she glanced to Amelia. After a moment, Maddie began to smile in earnest as she watched her friend flit from table to table, mingling with her guests. Amelia fairly glowed with happiness. She was a natural conversationalist, poised and well-liked, a vision of everything a man could want in a wife.

Everything Madeline Sutter once was.

Sighing, Maddie shook off the last of her envy and turned to Jace. "Three months ago I never would have imagined I'd be here."

"It's a big step," he said tenderly. "I'm proud of you, Maddie."

The sincerity in his words enveloped her like an embrace. Just knowing he understood was all the consolation she needed. She gazed into his warm eyes, fighting the urge to wrap her arms around his neck and kiss him fiercely. As if sensing her desire, he reached for her hand and cradled it in his.

She gave his fingers a squeeze. "Thank you, again, Jace. For doing this."

He tilted his head, lips quirking. "A deal is a deal. And you are a ruthless negotiator, my dear." He leaned forward. "Added to that, your case has taught me quite a lot. I know I can use that knowledge to help others who suffer with trauma."

While she supposed she should be pleased she had helped, something in his solemn expression made her feel quite the opposite. "Others like Kathy Fitzsimmons?" she asked.

Jace averted his eyes. "Yes."

A shadow of disappointment crossed her heart. She could stand being permanently ostracized by her neighbors as long as she knew Jace wanted her primarily for herself, rather than for the educational value of her story. She wanted his promise that she meant more to him. Not forever, for she knew that was a silly girlish fantasy. But for tonight at least. "I've learned much from you as well." Caressing his hand, she circled her fingertips inside his palm. "Knowledge I hope to use on you later."

His eyes widened, and she could swear he was blushing. "I will consider it, but you must promise to be gentle," he whispered, grinning. "If I need medical attention after you demonstrate your skills, there'll be no one to attend to me but me."

Before Maddie could make a saucy reply, Caroline approached, dragging David behind her. "We're going out for a boat ride," she said. "Care to join us?"

Jace glanced to Maddie. "I think we'll stay here and enjoy our champagne."

Several other guests headed down to the lake, where a line of rowboats awaited. Pastor Hogle and his family paraded by their table on their way to the shore. Maddie stiffened beneath their disapproving eyes as they ushered Dolly past. Up until now Pastor Hogle had avoided looking at her, but suddenly he was making a point of letting her know her presence would not be ignored.

"Fools," Jace uttered.

Maddie smiled in spite of herself. "Indeed. Did you know that Pastor Hogle has arranged a marriage between Dolly and that protégé of his, Matthew Webster?" she asked. "Dolly told me about it yesterday."

Jace's brows shot up in surprise.

"Yes, she's very young, isn't she? And she's not at all pleased by the arrangement. In fact, she's quite angry with her uncle for making this match."

She considered telling Jace about Dolly's warning, that the girl feared her fiancé posed a threat to Maddie. But it all seemed a little melodramatic now that Maddie thought back on it. Dolly was at an age when emotions seemed more intense than they were in reality. In all likelihood, she had unintentionally exaggerated the man's dislike. Maddie bit her lip as she pondered what to do. Her thoughts were soon interrupted by a shout from the doorway.

"Doctor Merrick!"

Carl Belden waved from across the room. A small crowd gathered around the balding man as his waves to Jace grew more urgent.

Something was wrong.

"Excuse me for a moment," Jace said before he hurried to the man. Mr. Belden's arms flailed in his distress as he spoke. Jace listened intently. Nodding, he patted the man on the shoulder, then returned to the table.

"I'll be back shortly," he said. "Mr. Belden's horse has been injured, and he wants me to have a look."

"Of course."

Jace made his way toward the men, then disappeared inside the hotel. From their somber faces it appeared the situation was serious. She uttered a prayer that Jace would deem the injury minor and all would be well. The last thing anyone wanted to hear at a wedding was the shot of a gun, putting a sick animal out of its misery.

As much as Maddie wished to help alleviate the horse's pain, she resisted the urge to follow. She'd had good luck healing animals, true.

But after what had transpired with Dolly, she didn't dare make a move to assist.

"Are you enjoying yourself, Miss Sutter?"

Philip had appeared from out of nowhere. Looking dapper in his fine blue suit and his slicked-back hair, he smiled before taking a seat beside her.

"I am," she said, returning his smile. "It's lovely here by the water."

"My cousin certainly seems to be enjoying herself."

Amelia swooped happily over the blue-stone patio, the sound of her laughter wafting around. She glowed in the warm attention. Watching her fluttering about reminded Maddie of the days when she and the Fair Five had dreamed of their weddings. They'd spent hours imagining and planning their futures. She shook away the memory as best she could. It would not do to succumb to grief today.

"You'll save me a dance later, won't you?" Philip asked. "I promise my dancing has improved since the last time we waltzed."

Maddie laughed, remembering how clumsy Philip had been as a boy. Tall and lanky, he'd been a miserable partner who'd often stomped on her toes. Looking at him now, it seemed hard to imagine this man was that same awkward boy. "I'd be happy to dance with you," she replied honestly.

Philip leaned back in this chair and stared off at the water. "I'll miss the beauty of the country." He turned back to her, looking grave. "I'll miss it more than I'd thought possible."

Maddie sensed he referred to more than the sparkling vista. She shifted beneath his heart-wrenching gaze, wishing Jace would hurry back. "When do you return to Boston?"

"Tomorrow afternoon." He puffed his chest. "I've just purchased a house in the city and have much to do before I move in."

"That's wonderful, Philip," she said. "Amelia tells me that you're doing very well at the bank."

Philip's smile dimmed. "Forgive me, Maddie, but I must tell you— seeing you again has been the highlight of my visit to Misty Lake."

Maddie lowered her gaze to her glass of champagne.

"I don't mean to make you uneasy," he said. "I just couldn't leave town without saying it. And I hope you and Doctor Merrick will be very happy."

Maddie met his eyes. His lost expression tugged at her heart. "Thank you, Philip."

"You deserve some happiness after what you've been through. No matter what the fools in this town say about it. Please remember that."

"I will," she assured him, her hand trembling slightly as she reached for her champagne.

Maddie glanced over his shoulder to see Jace heading toward them. She sat straighter as he arrived at the table.

"Doctor Merrick."

Jace gave Philip a nod.

"Is everything all right?" Maddie asked.

"The horse has a sprain."

"Oh, no," she said.

"Bad news, for sure." Philip tsked as he stood.

"Yes," Jace replied somberly. "We'll see what transpires with the swelling, but more than likely the animal will have to be put down."

Maddie swallowed.

"Well, if you'll excuse me," Philip said. He left the table, and Jace took his seat.

"Why was I not surprised to see Philip sitting in my place?"

Maddie couldn't help enjoying Jace's jealousy. "For your information, he wanted to wish us luck. With our impending marriage," she added, though she wasn't sure why.

Jace frowned, turning to watch Philip striding across the patio. Jace turned back to Maddie. "Did I miss anything else?"

She shook her head. "No one has bothered with me, if that's what you mean."

"Good," he said, pretending he was pleased that they'd been snubbed by the other guests. "More time for us."

She smiled, her spirits lifting. When he looked at her as he did now, the whole world fizzled away. Wrapped in the warmth of his eyes, she was safe, shielded from the hostility all around her.

Amelia announced that dinner would be served promptly at seven o'clock. The orchestra would perform in the grand ballroom, which opened to the veranda for dancing beneath the stars. It all sounded so wonderful and romantic.

"How about a walk along the shore before we dress for the evening?" he asked.

Maddie glanced around. Guests had begun dispersing, some heading toward the lake, others heading into the hotel. Pastor Hogle and his family were crowded in a boat on the water. "I'd like that," she said. Jace pulled out her chair, and she took his strong arm.

They strolled along the water's edge, a soft breeze on their backs. "It's pretty here," she said, breaking the silence.

"It is."

"Do you miss the city?"

"I don't miss the emergency ward," he said flatly. "Here, I'm discovering my work on a more personal level."

"So, you're pleased that you decided to practice here?"

"I feel that I'm making a difference in people's lives."

"That's important to you."

"More than I care to admit."

The simple statement revealed much about what made Jace Merrick tick. His need to matter. His father had spent his life healing the sick only to be remembered for the lurid circumstances of his death.

"It feels good to help others," she murmured, longing to say more. The urge to confess her secret to Jace was growing as strong as her need to withhold it.

"That feeling was lost to me during my work in the city. Here I'm able to learn each patient's case and history and follow up appropriately. I'm even beginning to see that making the right diagnosis is only the beginning of my task. I have to earn my patient's trust with compassion— and I must listen to what they *aren't* telling me if I want to provide the best care."

Maddie blinked in surprise, and he laughed.

"I owe that to you, of course," he said, his smile fading.

She stared into his face, swallowing hard. She appreciated his gratitude. But it wasn't love.

"Most importantly, I'm learning to accept my limitations."

"You have no limitations," she said.

He snorted. "While treating patients in Pittsburgh I did everything medically required. Followed every procedure. Only to realize this strict adherence to procedure may not always be best for the patient." He shook his head. "A dying child should spend those final days at home in the arms of his mother, not confined in a hospital. Regardless of what's medically recommended." He smiled a sad smile. "Recommended by me."

"I hope to devise individual treatments for my patients and specially tailored courses for prevention and management of disease. Little Joey Cleary, for instance, is doing well on his weekly visits."

"That's wonderful." Maddie lowered her eyes. "I feared your association with me might hamper the success of your practice."

He shook his head. "And I feared I would always be compared to Doctor Filmore. Despite his despicable handling of your case, the man's reputation was pristine. People revered him."

"Yes, they did."

"I'd like to wring his neck for what he did to you, Maddie."

Fire blazed in his eyes, and she warmed in his desire to protect her. She'd spent so long on her own.

His face softened with a smile, and her heart swelled with love. Real love. This was no playful dalliance, no girlish crush, no desire for attention. Her reflection shone in his eyes, and she saw with surprising clarity the woman she had become.

The silly belle she once was had been lost to her past, and she couldn't help wondering, what precisely about her former self did she miss?

Chapter 23

The rehearsal dinner was a lavish affair. Maddie took a calming breath and tried to enjoy it. Linen-covered tables arranged in the shape of a horseshoe bordered the room with Amelia and Lester seated front and center. Candle sconces glowed on the walls. Courses of Julien soup and baked salmon preceded stuffed quails and partridges, filet of beef and potato croquettes. Toasts were made in the couple's honor as finely attired guests indulged in endless bottles of wine.

The families of the Fair Five were seated a safe distance from Maddie and Jace. As of yet, none of them had approached her. She hadn't expected they would, and she couldn't blame them. She knew how painful it must be for them to see her, to be reminded that she'd lived to attend this happy occasion when the girls they loved had not.

She shrank with remorse inside her beautiful new gown, taking refuge behind the tall floral centerpiece. All at once she wanted to flee from the room. From herself. The urge intensified when Pastor Hogle rose to offer a prayer.

Lifting a glass in his hand, he followed with a toast that rambled into a sermon. Something about paying for one's sins, good and evil, and striving to recognize the difference and not be deceived. Maddie clenched her satin skirts as the Pastor's eyes burned into her. Jace squeezed her hand in reassurance, and in that slightest of gestures, she loved him even more.

If only he could love her back. She chided herself for the futility of the thought. Jace did not want to have those feelings. He believed romantic love would interfere with professional goals. And even if he was convinced otherwise, there could be no real future for them together. Not with the secret she kept.

Music filled the grand ballroom and dancing commenced. As promised, Jace danced with Dolly. The blissful smile on the girl's face warmed

Maddie to her toes. From over Dolly's shoulder, Jace flashed Maddie a wink. She smiled back at him, beaming with pride.

To Maddie's surprise, when the music ended, Dolly approached her. "Madeline, I wish to tell you something."

Maddie glanced around to see if any of the Hogles noticed the girl's bold move.

"If you're worried about Matthew, rest assured. He's not here."

"He's not?"

Dolly shook her head. "Uncle sent him to Altamont under the pretense of a dire errand."

"What do you mean?"

Dolly smiled. "I did it, Madeline. I stood up to Uncle this afternoon. I told him if he forced me to marry Matthew, I would hate him forever."

Maddie stared, stunned.

"I couldn't believe his reaction. It was...so unexpected." Tears welled in Dolly's eyes. "He told me that after losing a daughter, he could not bear to lose a niece, too."

Maddie swallowed hard at the pastor's words. Elizabeth had been the man's only child. His open hatred for Maddie had made it easy to forget the deep pain behind it.

"He will break the news to Matthew upon his return from Altamont," Dolly said with a smile.

"I'm so very happy for you, Dolly." Maddie spied Pastor Hogle craning his neck in their direction. "You'd better rejoin your family now," she said with a pat to the girl's hand.

Dolly walked back toward her family, and Maddie couldn't miss the jubilant bounce in her step as she made her way back across the dance floor.

"Dance with me?" Jace appeared beside Maddie and extended his hand.

Maddie took it, and he led her through the crowded room and out to the deserted veranda for the next dance.

He held her close, and her body reacted as it always did in his arms. Magically. Her pulse skittered and her senses peaked. The heat of him radiated through her, a pleasant contrast to the soft chill of the breeze on her flesh. Beneath the stars, they swayed to the music, their bodies moving as one.

It was a perfect dance, and she'd remember it always. If nothing else, these past few weeks had provided her with a mountain of moments like these, moments that would sustain her for the rest of her days. It would all end tomorrow, but she wouldn't think of that now. Jace was hers until then. She snuggled closer to his shoulder. The wonderful scent of him engulfed her, and she closed her eyes, inhaling it in. She savored his essence so she would never forget, all the while knowing her memories would have to be enough.

* * * *

Jace moved against the warmth of Maddie's body, his mind drifting off with the rhythm of the music. The shapely feel of her drove him mad as he fought for composure.

But the agony of arousal was a welcome distraction. The icy treatment Maddie had received all evening was difficult to bear. Even as people openly shunned her, she'd held herself together. She was a remarkable woman, and for reasons that had nothing to do with her unfortunate past. She was bright and compassionate, and possessed a strength and resiliency that amazed him. He'd never known anyone like her.

The thought that she soon would revert to her isolated life gnawed at him. He envisioned her, wiling away the hours in her room, carving those wooden boxes. At least throughout the duration of their ruse, she'd gotten out of the house. Forcing herself to face people every day hadn't been easy, he knew, but it was good for her.

Her well-being concerned him, not as it might with a patient, but as a man who cared for a woman. As much as he wished it weren't so, he could not deny this. His failure with Kathy had prompted his interest in Maddie. But pursuing that interest had created something more.

There was also the indisputable fact that he would miss seeing her every day. He'd adapted well to her presence around the office, and he would miss the afternoon coffee they shared. He suddenly realized how quiet the house would be without her. How lonely *he* would be without her.

"I was thinking, Maddie, that you might consider staying on at the office," he said.

She looked up at him, eyes wide. "You were?"

He nodded in as business-like a manner as he could muster.

"My patient records are well organized, and you keep a calm head during emergencies. I meant it when I told you that you would make a good nurse. I don't always enjoy your opinionated approach to office management, but I'll sorely miss your help."

She smiled. "Is that so?" Her teasing tone came complete with a coy toss of her hair. The woman was a vixen. Moonlight shone on her creamy shoulders and neck. Her intoxicating scent wafted around him like invisible hands, pulling him toward her. Jace wanted nothing more than to have her again.

"What else, specifically," she asked, "would you miss?" Her lips quivered with a brazen grin.

"Your fine penmanship," he teased back.

"Is that all?"

"If you're fishing for more compliments, you'd do better to toss a line in the lake." He gestured with his head toward the water.

She smiled from ear to ear. "Oh doctor, what a delight you can be when you let down your guard." She leaned closer. "You enjoy having me around, Jace Merrick, admit it."

He shook his head, and she laughed.

"You are a menace," he growled.

"Perhaps." She shrugged. "But you like me anyway."

He twirled her around, their bodies pressed tightly together. Music flowed out from the open doors. The smell of the lake and crisp night air filled his senses, and he felt so alive. Awakened.

For the briefest of moments he envied Lester and Amelia. The commitment of marriage was something Jace found implausible. Nothing could hold his interest as medicine did. He was certain of it. Tonight, though, with Maddie in his arms and the music playing, he wondered suddenly if it were possible that a man such as he could ever make a woman happy.

He thought of his parents and their neglected marriage. His mother had suffered the silent misery of her husband's inattention and his unwavering commitment to his profession. And Jace was equally committed. He knew of no other way. He couldn't imagine subjecting the vibrant woman he held in his arms to the same pain his beloved mother had experienced.

Maddie deserved a man who could focus on her. A man who could give freely of himself, not in drips and drabs, but completely.

He should stop the dance now—release Maddie and get on his with his life.

Maddie glanced up at him, and his lusty reaction chased off the thought. Her eyes gleamed in the moonlight. She was so beautiful. Unable to resist, he nuzzled her hair, inhaling the aroma of flowers and rain. A thrum of sensations pulsed through his veins. He had one more night, one more chance to enjoy this thing they shared. Whatever it was. And, heaven help him, he would take it.

He stopped, reaching for her hand. Ignoring her surprised expression, he led her around the corner of the veranda, then pulled her into the shadows. He kissed her. Hard.

The soft moan behind her lips spurred his desire to have her. He ran his hands down her sides, over the swell of her hips. She pressed her body to his, urging him closer.

"Jace?"

"Hmm?"

"I've something to tell you."

Caressing her bottom, he kneaded and squeezed. Conversation was the last thing on his mind as he pulled her to his hardness. His time with her was running out with each passing moment, and it was all he could do not to toss up her skirts and take her, hard and fast, against the wall. "Later." He nibbled her ear. "Let's talk later."

She nodded, lolling her head to the kisses he trailed on her neck. Her skin tasted so good. He seized her mouth, wanting more. Delving into the warm depths of her, he kissed her with a force he couldn't control.

The sound of laughter carried from around the corner. He drew his lips from her mouth and pressed them to her ear.

His attempt to whisper came out in a growl. "Meet me in my room at midnight."

"Midnight," she sighed, breathless.

He reluctantly released her, then led her toward the door. Her lips shimmered with his kiss as they stepped inside the ballroom. And he was weak with desire.

* * * *

Maddie had less than an hour before she was due to meet Jace. After attending to some last-minute wedding details with Amelia, she slipped out the side exit of the hotel, clutching the apple she'd plucked from the bowl of fruit displayed in the lobby.

Despite her best efforts, she'd failed to talk herself out of helping Mr. Belden's injured horse. The disaster with Dolly was still fresh in Maddie's mind, a nagging warning she couldn't ignore. But the crisis with the horse was worth the risk. She was given this ability for a reason, and if there was a chance she could save the poor animal, she had to take it.

Hoping no one would spot her, she gauged the distance to the large barn where the horse was stabled. She glanced around, counted to three, and then hurried across the moonlit lawn. The chirp of crickets echoed on the lake. Frogs croaked near the shore. Quickening her pace, she arrived breathless and undetected at the barn.

She pulled open the heavy door, then ducked inside. After allowing a moment for her eyes to adjust to the shadowy dimness, she treaded a path of moonlight streaming in from the small windows above. The pungent smell of manure grew stronger as she neared the long row of occupied stalls.

She located the injured horse, distinguishing it by the white dressing that was wrapped above its right front hoof. Unable to bear weight on the injured leg, the horse stood with its hoof raised slightly off the hay-covered floor.

Maddie tilted her head in sorrow. "You're a handsome fellow, aren't you?" she cooed. Reaching over the stall door, she held out the apple, grimacing as the horse limped toward her. With a whiff, the horse snatched the treat from her hand. "Poor boy." She stroked his soft neck as he chewed.

A horse in the adjoining stall whinnied, and Maddie all but jumped from her skin. She inhaled a deep breath of hay and manure. "I'm more skittish than you are," she murmured against the injured horse's wet nose. Her hesitation to act increased with her mounting fear of discovery. Her botched attempt to help Dolly heightened this fear. Maddie could leave now—leave this poor creature to its fate—and return, safe and sound, to her room. She took another long breath for courage. "Promise not to tell?"

As if in reply, the horse reared its large head. Its dark eyes met hers, and she knew what to do. She peeled off her gloves, then unlatched the stall door.

* * * *

One excruciatingly long hour after their dance, Maddie still hadn't arrived at Jace's room. Maintaining discretion was imperative, but what the hell was keeping her? He shrugged on his coat and headed toward the staircase to Maddie's room. His body tightened with anticipation. Kissing her as he had, touching her again, had spiked a longing inside him that had only grown stronger as the hour had passed.

Shoving away any stubborn misgivings about the risk they were taking, he hurried through the lobby. Maddie wanted this as badly as he did. And he wanted nothing more than to give her what she wanted. What was wrong with partaking in a brief affair between like-minded adults? They were both committed to remaining unmarried, so it stood to reason they'd commit to each other. For the weekend, anyway.

He jogged up the stairs, rounded the corner, and came face to face with Amelia.

"Jace," she gasped.

He felt like a child caught in mischief, and his throat thickened as he sought something to say. "I…"

"No need to explain yourself to me," she said with a wave. "But I would like a quick word with you, if you don't mind."

"Not at all," he said, though he very much minded.

"I've known Maddie for a long time," she began. "And she's explained the circumstances of your engagement." Amelia regarded him closely. "Or rather, your pretend engagement. I've also noticed the way she looks at you," Amelia continued. "Maddie has been through a lot, and I've no wish to see her hurt."

"Neither do I."

"I'm glad to hear that," she said with a nod. "So before you proceed to her room, I hope you'll consider what's best for her?"

Jace narrowed his eyes. "And what's that?"

"Maddie must leave Misty Lake, Jace. You know this as well as I do. For goodness sake, you saw all of them down there tonight. It's the only way she can have the future she deserves."

"Isn't that up to her to decide?"

"Yes." She nodded, red curls bouncing above her stern eyes. "But she won't consider it if she's in love with you."

Jace stiffened. "She's not in love with me."

Amelia tilted her head. "Are you sure about that?"

Jace stared in silence, not sure of anything. Of course Maddie was drawn to him. She was lonely, and he was the first man to show her any attention in three long years. But love?

"I know it's none of my business, but Maddie is my friend. If you're not prepared to make a future with her, perhaps you shouldn't let your involvement with her go any deeper. Being as it's well past midnight, and you're about to sneak into her room, I can only assume that's what will occur if you continue this course. You care for her. Anyone can see that. But you must do what is right for her."

"She won't leave her grandfather. And even if she would, where do you propose she go?"

"Boston."

Jace blinked at the ready response.

Amelia lifted her chin. "Philip loves her. I suspect he always has. My cousin has confided to me that, if given the opportunity, he'd like nothing more than to take Maddie to Boston and make her his wife."

Jace clenched his fists so hard he was sure he'd drawn blood. "Is that so?"

"Yes. I only tell you this now because I wonder if that wouldn't be the ideal thing. To finally get her away from this town and the people who torment her." Amelia's face filled with distress. "I'm beginning to fear for her safety. Dolly mentioned some threats." Amelia touched Jace's arm. "Perhaps if you persuaded her…"

Jace didn't know what to say. Threats or no threats, Amelia was right. Jace had known all along that Maddie should leave town, but he didn't want her to go. Even if he claimed her for his own, she could never be happy here. These fools wouldn't allow it.

He pictured Maddie and Philip together, and his chest clenched along with his fists. He had no doubt Philip was in love with Maddie and would do his darndest to make her happy. The thought should have comforted Jace in some slight way, but instead, he felt suffocated.

"Think about it. Please." Amelia gave his arm a soft squeeze. "You're a good man, Jace Merrick. You'll do the decent thing, I'm sure."

She descended the stairs as Jace stood anchored in dread. He wanted to shout after her, protest with all his might that she was wrong. Common sense kept his feet planted and his mouth closed. He shook his head, hating the feelings churning in his gut. He should have known better than to let things progress so far with Maddie, but it was too late for regrets.

A stab of guilt for his selfishness nearly pierced him in two. Because deep in the pit of his conflicting emotions, he didn't regret a thing.

Chapter 24

Maddie closed the stall door behind her, then slipped on her gloves. Gathering her skirts, she bolted from the barn. She wasn't certain she'd succeeded in healing the horse, but the animal definitely seemed friskier. So much so, that while reapplying the dressing above its hoof, she'd feared earning a kick in the head for her trouble.

She hurried across the damp lawn. When she reached the side door to the hotel, she stopped for a moment to catch her breath, then slipped inside.

"Miss Sutter?"

Maddie froze. "Philip," she said. "You startled me."

He stepped toward her, and the strong smell of brandy came with him.

"I was just out for a breath of fresh air," she said, tightening her wrap around her shoulders.

He glanced toward the door behind her. "Alone?"

She nodded.

"If you were mine, I'd never leave your side." The blunt words were disarming. As was the sincerity in his glassy eyes.

"Philip…"

"Forgive me." He smiled, shaking his head. "I've had too much to drink." He reached for her hand and kissed her glove. "Good night."

He strode away, no doubt embarrassed by his forwardness. A trickle of guilt coursed through her, though she wasn't sure why. She'd done nothing to encourage Philip. It wasn't her fault that he hoped for more than she wanted to give. And while she felt sorry for this sweet young man, she couldn't squander precious time thinking of him now. Jace was waiting.

It was well after midnight, and she was already late. Her body hummed with excitement, anticipating her imminent rendezvous. But first she needed to change her soiled shoes.

How she hated lying to Jace. She'd come so close tonight to telling him her secret. In his arms—in the magic of that moment—it had seemed so right to share with him this thing she could never share. She'd almost convinced herself that he'd understand. That he would keep her secret between them, and perhaps help her make sense of it. He was so good at making sense of things.

But he could not make sense of this. And he would despise her for it. Whatever they shared now would die a certain and terrible death in the wake of her revelation.

When she reached her room, Jace was standing just inside the door.

"Where the hell have you been? I've been waiting here for twenty minutes."

His angry tone took her aback. "I was detained by Philip downstairs."

Jace frowned. "Hurry up. Get inside before anyone sees us." He urged her inside the room.

"Is something wrong?"

"We must talk," he said, closing the door quietly behind them.

The room darkened from the lost light of the hall. Behind them moonlight pooled in the center of the room. On the bed. "Talk?" Tossing her wrap to a chair, she walked slowly toward him. She had no intention of wasting time talking. "I was hoping we'd do more than talk." She smiled, slipping her arms around his neck. In a flash, his tense shoulders relaxed, and his response whetted her appetite for more. Shadows and moonlight danced across his handsome face. "In fact, I prefer we don't talk at all."

"Maddie…"

"Jace." She all but purred as she raked her fingers through his soft hair.

He reached for her hands and lowered them to her sides. "We must talk."

She sighed, exasperated. "What is it?"

His lips pursed, then parted, but nothing came out. She rolled her eyes, waiting impatiently as his lips pursed, then parted again.

"Jace?"

"I think you should leave Misty Lake."

She blinked, uncertain she'd heard him correctly.

"You deserve so much more than…" He waved his hand between them. "This."

Her heart plummeted.

"You deserve someone with whom you can start a new life. Someone in a position to take you away from here."

She narrowed her eyes, shaking her head. "What are you saying?"

"Philip."

She stared, unable to speak. Unable to breathe. Moments passed before she could summon her voice. "You're suggesting I pursue Philip?" The impact of hearing herself speak the words aloud was staggering. She turned away from him, grasping her hands together to keep them from shaking.

"Just listen to what I have to say."

She squeezed shut her eyes. Her pulse pounded furiously at her temples.

"Philip can take you away from Misty Lake. Think of it, Maddie. A whole new life in Boston, where people aren't poisoned by all the nonsense and rumors that haunt you here."

"Philip?" she repeated, turning back to him. "You're telling me to marry Philip?"

"He loves you. Anyone can see that."

She stared at him, weak-kneed. Scalding tears burned her throat. She swallowed hard, nearly choking. For weeks, the thought of ending their time together had sliced to the bone, but this—his handing her off to another man—hurt so much more. She wanted to die on the spot. "And what about you?"

His shoulders slumped. "I care for you. I hope you know that. What has occurred between us was my fault, and I can't take it back. But I want only what's best for you now."

She stifled a bitter laugh. She was a fool for imagining that Jace's feelings for her might one day amount to more than an oddly incendiary combination of lust and pity.

She lifted her trembling chin, her chest aching with the sobs she was determined to contain. "You're forgetting about Grandfather."

"You needn't worry. I'll watch over him. I promise you that. He'll be so pleased and relieved to know you're well cared for in Boston. And you would know he is well cared for here."

"As usual, you've come up with a sensible solution for everything."

"Maddie—"

"I appreciate your well-conceived plans for my future, but I will decide what is best for me." She thumped her fist to her chest. "*I* will decide. Not you." She took a deep breath for composure. "I'm not one of your patients, Doctor Merrick. You know nothing about what is best for me. No more than you know what is best for yourself."

"What's that supposed to mean?"

"It means you're a coward." She straightened her spine, hating him. "Perhaps someday you'll find the courage to step out from that shield of common sense you hide behind. Until you see that logic and science don't define everything in this life, you'll never truly live." She shook her head in disgust. "Good night."

He stared at her, looking abashed.

"Good night," she repeated.

He turned and walked out the door.

* * * *

The next morning Maddie woke up with a headache. She'd cried herself to sleep as the endless night faded into dawn, and now she wanted only to pull the covers over her head and disappear. Jace didn't want her. She squeezed shut her eyes but couldn't block out the sight of his face.

With a deep breath, she opened her eyes to the ceiling of the fine hotel room. She glanced to the large window, squinting against the bright cheeriness of the day. She rubbed her temples and counted to ten. The exercise soothed her and helped clear her head. The weekend was nearly over, and she would survive it. She would survive her broken heart. She'd survived far worse.

After flinging the covers aside, she bolted upright. She'd get through this damn day, and then she'd never lay eyes on Jace Merrick again.

Despite her fury, the thought devastated her. She'd miss him so much.

There was also the agonizing knowledge that she'd caused this whole mess single-handedly. She'd pursued Jace right from the start. She'd seduced him. He'd tried to warn her—to stop her—from making what he knew would be a terrible mistake.

She snatched her bridesmaid gown from the tall armoire, then tossed it onto the bed, hating the very sight of it. Somehow she muddled through the movements, washing and dressing for the wedding.

She hurried down the hall to Amelia's room. Temporarily distracted from thoughts of Jace, she managed to smile her way through the frenzy of helping Amelia into her bridal array. Amelia looked lovely in the corded silk dress. Her red hair was beautifully arranged beneath a tulle veil. A simple bridal wreath of orange blossoms completed the piece.

The ceremony went by in a blur. Amelia looked radiant, Lester looked happy, and Jace barely uttered a word. Maddie cried throughout the ceremony, though most of her tears were for herself. The couple was departing for their honeymoon to Niagara Falls immediately after the ceremony, and Maddie couldn't wait to depart for home.

She'd made it through the wedding and honored her promise to Amelia. No one could ask anything more of her. She missed Grandfather.

She longed for the safety of her home—her room. And for distance from Jace. The man she loved.

She glanced at him from the corner of her eye. Then she wiped at her tears and offered a final wave to the newlyweds. The jubilant couple had just boarded the carriage that would carry them off to their new life, where they'd live happily ever after.

Even though she hadn't spoken them out loud, these three words made her tears fall harder. In the midst of the crowd, she felt so alone. Everyone cheered as the carriage rolled from the drive and toward the road. People chased it, calling out their farewells. The carriage disappeared down the road, and the quieting crowd began to disperse.

Philip stepped into view and gave her a nod. She returned a small smile, quickly looking away. She hadn't the strength right now to deal with Philip. She stiffened as she noticed Pastor Hogle and Daniel huddled nearby. Behind them, Mr. Belden led his horse from the stable.

They all turned their attention to Maddie, and a shiver of impending doom crawled down her spine.

Pastor Hogle's hostile eyes bore into hers. He pointed his finger at Maddie. "There!"

She flinched, her heart pounding.

The meandering crowd parted as Pastor Hogle charged toward her. Gravel crunched beneath each angry step. "Look what she's done!"

Jace took a step forward. "What is it now?"

Pastor Hogle pointed to the horse. "She healed that animal!"

"I saw her!" Gertrude yelled. "I saw her sneaking out of the stables last night. Lucinda and Dolly saw her, too!"

"We did. We saw her!" Lucinda cried.

The pastor's chest swelled as each girl substantiated his claim. "You said yourself, Doctor, the horse would have to be put down. What have you to say now?"

Jace shook his head at the man's ranting. "That this latest attack against my fiancée is perfectly ridiculous."

Pastor Hogle turned to the crowd, addressing his audience, as if from his pulpit. Fire blazed in his tone. "We all know what she did to my niece." He gestured toward Dolly, who lowered her eyes. "She laid hands on the girl, and we all saw the result."

Maddie shook her head. "That was an accident!"

Pastor Hogle spun to face her. "Another accident caused by you!"

Maddie gaped as the crowd inched closer.

"This is nonsense!" Jace stepped toward the pastor, fists clenched. "And it's slander. She didn't go near that horse."

"Oh, yes she did!" Gertrude cried. "Just look at these shoes!" Gertrude held up the pair of soiled shoes she must have confiscated from Maddie's room. "They've been in the stable for sure."

Maddie felt faint, too faint to run.

"You took her shoes?" Jace stared incredulously. "Good God, this has gone far enough." He turned back to Maddie. "Let's go."

"Reveal yourself and admit your tricks," Pastor Hogle shouted at Maddie. "Admit the wicked things you've done."

Fear trapped in Maddie's chest. She couldn't move. Her eyes darted across the row of shocked and expectant faces.

"Maddie, let's go." Jace wrapped his arm around her, as if that might help. But his protection was fruitless. She had no defense.

She shook her head, consumed by her rioting panic. "I—"

"Miss Sutter!"

Everyone turned toward the approaching rider in the drive. Dust and stones scattered as the rider skidded to a halt. "Miss Sutter!"

Maddie craned her neck over their heads toward the familiar voice in the distance. Gil jumped from his mount, then pushed his way through the crowd.

The tense silence stretched to eternity. Maddie's pounding heart now thundered with dread.

"Step aside." Red-faced and breathless, Gil shoved past Pastor Hogle. Gil's grim expression turned her blood to ice.

She felt Jace's grip on her arm, steadying her trembling knees. She clutched his arm for support. "What is it, Gil?" she croaked. "What's happened?"

Gil took a deep breath, compassion suffusing his face. "Come quickly, Miss Sutter," he said. "It's your grandfather."

Chapter 25

Maddie ran through the house to her grandfather's room, and Jace followed on her heels. Mr. Sutter lay in the large bed, his vacant eyes fixed toward the ceiling. She gripped her grandfather's hand as Jace swiftly examined him. Jace peered into his eyes but knew what he'd see. "He's unresponsive, Maddie."

She swallowed hard. "What does that mean?"

"He's dying."

Her mouth quivered open, but she formed no reply. Shaking her head, she turned back toward the bed. She sank, bowing her head against the man's chest. Her slender shoulders racked with quiet sobs.

"We'll keep him comfortable, but there's nothing more we can do." Jace straightened the man's bloated legs, then placed a pillow beneath his knees.

"I never should have left you, Grandfather," she uttered. "Forgive me."

Jace touched her back, but she shrugged him away.

"Leave us alone!" She shook her head. "Just leave us alone." She pressed her grandfather's fragile hand to her cheek. Murmuring softly, she brushed back the hair from his face.

Jace watched, deflating in powerlessness. Of all the emotions he experienced as a physician, this sense of impotence was the worst. Unlike his father, Jace could accept the disheartening and frustrating limitations of medicine. But it never got easier.

He turned his efforts to keeping the patient—Adam Sutter—comfortable as he passed this world. This good man, whom Jace had grown to like and admire, would be the first person he'd lost in Misty Lake.

He would leave the room for Maddie's sake, but he would not leave them alone. Adam would die soon, and he didn't need Jace. Maddie would. She would need him then to help her through the grief of her loss. And he would be here for her when she did.

* * * *

The hours passed slowly as the distance between Grandfather's labored breaths grew longer. Each sound he made became weaker. Maddie knew, as she always had, that she could not help him. Why had she been given this ability to heal if she couldn't help the one person in her life that she loved the most?

Memories of her grandfather's life filled the silence, floating like shadows before her blurry eyes. The savvy businessman, the strong man who'd carried his granddaughter atop his proud shoulders, the handsome charmer who'd made women swoon.

She glanced to the photograph of her grandmother and parents on the mantel. Like her, Grandfather had lost much. And yet, even during the years of his declining health, he had never complained.

Jace sat in the corner of the room behind her. She'd insisted earlier that he leave, but he hadn't gone far. Sometime during the fog of her grief, he'd returned to the room, and she hadn't the energy to order him out. She told herself that Grandfather might need him, though she knew deep in her heart, this wasn't true. She might need him.

Grandfather made small sounds, not sounds of pain, but little sounds that told her he sensed her presence. From someplace deep inside his withered body, he knew she was there. She clasped his hand between hers. "I'll be fine, Grandfather," she whispered into his ear. His fingers twitched, and tears rolled down her cheeks. "I'll be fine."

A long breath of air whooshed from his chest, and then he went still. Maddie gulped hard as she shot to her feet.

Jace rushed to check Grandfather's pulse. He pressed his stethoscope to Grandfather's chest, then drew back, his eyes brimming with sorrow. "He's gone."

She sank to the chair. Covering her face, she sobbed into her hands. She slumped forward and rocked on her knees, crying for all she was worth. She cried for Grandfather, the man she loved so much. The man who had raised her after the death of her parents, the man who had done his best for her. And she cried for herself. Because despite all her unanswered prayers and fruitless hopes, Grandfather was gone.

And come tomorrow, she'd be alone.

* * * *

She felt as though she were living in a dream when Jace finally led her to her room. She sat in the chair by the window as he spoke quietly to Rhetta out in the hall. A few minutes later, he returned to her side. He handed her a small glass of brandy. Without a word, she drank it down, welcoming the bitter taste and soothing haze that flowed through her.

She sat numbly in the window seat, staring out as the day turned to dusk. They didn't speak. There was nothing to say.

Jace urged her into bed. He pulled up the quilt to cover her, and she settled onto her side. Facing the wall, she buried her face in her pillow and sobbed like a child. A lost, frightened child.

The mattress slumped with Jace's weight as he lay down behind her. Gathering her into his arms, he nestled against her back. He held her in silence, his body molded to hers. She calmed inside the cocoon of safety and warmth.

His gesture of comfort was almost too much to bear. She realized now that he'd never intended to hurt her. It was her own fault for letting herself fall in love with him. He'd tried to warn her against forming a relationship with him right from the start. She'd been so determined to seduce him that she never considered how the affair might affect her after it ended. She was too foolish, too tempted by things that were never meant to be, things that weren't hers to have, would never be hers.

And now Grandfather was gone.

She fell asleep on that despairing thought, desperate to escape the pain of the day. A part of her hoped she would never awake. But she did awake. In Jace's arms.

She managed to ease from his embrace, turning toward him. He slept quietly, and she took the brief moment to study his face. The urge to touch him, to feel the slight shadow of stubble on his unshaven cheek overwhelmed her. As if sensing this, his eyes fluttered open.

"You're awake," he said, rubbing sleep from his tired eyes.

"I've much to do." She crawled over him, scampering to her feet. "I'd better get downstairs."

Jace left her to freshen up. After speaking briefly with Rhetta downstairs, Maddie proceeded to the parlor, where Jace sat, drinking coffee. He set down his cup as she entered.

"How can I help?" he asked, rising.

She shook her head. "You've done enough," she said. "Grandfather wished to be buried in the family plot with my parents. He'd insisted that only Rhetta, Gil, and I attend his burial."

Jace looked disappointed. "I can stay—"

"No, thank you," she said. "Gil has gone for the casket." She reached for the letter on the mantel. "Grandfather left this with Gil. It's addressed to you."

Jace took the letter. "What is it?"

She shrugged. "I have no idea," she answered, honestly.

Jace tucked the letter into his coat pocket.

"Thank you, Jace. For last night."

"Maddie—"

"I'll be fine," she said. "And I want you to know I've decided to leave Misty Lake." She stared into his handsome face. Lifting her chin, she steeled herself against the lure of his striking blue eyes. "Now that Grandfather has passed, there's nothing keeping me here."

* * * *

Maddie carefully arranged the large bunch of daisies on Grandfather's grave. After only five days, she missed him so much. Tears blurred her vision as she stared down at the grave, the scent of freshly turned earth filling her nose.

She gazed skyward, searching the expanse of crisp blue and the billowy clouds. There were so many questions and mysteries, and she felt helplessly small. She knew grandfather was out there, his spirit, his soul. She could feel him as plainly as the sun on her face and the breeze through her hair.

All around her, her family lay in eternal rest. The parents she'd barely known and now Grandfather. She would leave this place, but their love would follow her. A tear rolled down her cheek. Her history would follow her, too. The pain of losing her friends was a part of her now, and that ache would be with her always. But not all of the changes wrought by the accident were unwanted. Maddie knew she had gained in compassion and depth of character what she had lost in human companionship.

She also knew that, were it not for the accident, she would have married Daniel. Which meant that she might never have had the chance to fall truly in love. As badly as things had ended with Jace, she could not regret that.

She wiped at her eyes and stood. She had much to do and could tarry here no longer. Leaving Misty Lake was for the best. Whatever excuse Jace gave as to their broken engagement was unimportant. No one would care. They'd be happy just knowing they were finally rid of her.

She would go to Boston and start a new life for herself. With her inheritance from Grandfather, she had more than enough money to do it. She wouldn't ever need to work if she didn't wish to, but she thought she would attempt to find employment anyway. It might be a good way to find friends.

What she would not do was seek out Philip. He had sent a brief note expressing his condolences, and she knew he would welcome her with open arms with only the tiniest encouragement. But Maddie had no intention of using Philip to escape her misery. Somehow, she would muddle forward on her own.

* * * *

Jace paced his empty office. He'd tried to catch up on some work, but he couldn't get Maddie from his mind. He strode to his desk, then reread the letter from Adam Sutter.

Watch after her, please. You're all she has now.

He frowned. Now that her grandfather was gone, she was alone. Jace was confident she'd be left in peace to grieve. She was in mourning, and people would respect that. With any luck, she'd manage to leave town without being bothered.

He paced through the house. Reminders of Maddie were everywhere. Each room reflected the changes she'd made to make his simple office a home. The withered lilacs on the mantel, the potted fern by the door. She would make a fine wife.

The thought wrenched in his gut. His work—his patients—required a constant commitment. There was no room in his crammed world for anything more. No time to cultivate and sustain a marriage. Certainly no time for love.

But Maddie should not be forced from her home. His eyes fixed on the small wooden box she'd given him. The precious symbol of all she'd been through.

"The hell with this," he muttered as he strode from the room. He shrugged on his coat, then charged out the door.

The miles to Maddie's house passed quickly as the buggy rolled along. Somehow he'd become her protector, her friend, and he would not desert her now. When he arrived at the house, he was still uncertain what to do.

Rhetta led him to the parlor. Several minutes passed before Maddie finally appeared.

"Tea won't be necessary, Rhetta," Maddie said stiffly. "You may proceed with your plans in town."

With an awkward nod, Rhetta left them alone.

"How are you?" he asked.

"I'm busy," she said. "I'm in the midst of packing."

"So, you're really leaving?"

"As soon as possible."

"Tell me you're leaving of your own accord. Not at my urging. Not at theirs. Don't allow others to chase you from your home."

She looked him in the eye. "I'm not leaving for you. I'm not leaving for them either. I'm leaving for me." She lifted her chin. "This house is my home. Outside its walls, I'm a stranger. A pariah. I'll never be a part of things here. I'll never be a member of the women's quilting bee or church choir. Misty Lake will never again be my home," she said. "It just took me a very long time to accept that."

"Why did you visit the stable that night?"

She stiffened, turning to fidget with the folds in her skirt. "I brought an apple to the injured horse."

He regarded her closely. He was not sure if he believed her, but she didn't seem to care. He tried again.

"You were going to tell me something that night we were dancing on the veranda," he ventured. "What was it?"

She shook her head. "It no longer matters." She lifted her chin. "Why did you come back here, Jace?"

"I have something to say to you, and I want you to listen." He pointed to the sofa. "Please sit."

"I don't have time—"

"Sit, Madeline."

She rolled her eyes, plopping down across from him. "What is it?"

"I want you to stay."

Her brows shot up in surprise. "First you want me to leave. Now you want me to stay?"

"You can stay and continue to work with me at the office."

"As your employee?"

"As my wife." The words stunned him as much as they did her.

Her mouth fell open. She stared, brows narrowing slowly as she eyed him suspiciously. "Just what did that letter of Grandfather's say?"

He took a deep breath. "He asked that I watch after you."

She frowned. "I see."

"I want to do that, Maddie. I'll keep you safe. And we are a good team. A marriage between us makes perfect sense."

Her face flushed crimson. "And things must always make sense," she spat.

He sighed, feeling defeated.

"I can't marry you. But thank you for asking. And for trying to honor Grandfather's wishes." She stood, smoothing out her skirts.

"Maddie—"

"I can't." She shook her head. "Good-bye, Jace."

He nodded sadly as the hard truth reverberated in his ears. She would not be his. Not on his terms anyway. And so he had to let her go. "Take care of yourself," he whispered.

"I intend to."

Jace turned, forcing his feet to move toward the front door. He stepped out to the porch and came face to face with Matthew Webster.

Jace froze where he stood on the threshold. His surprise turned to anger during the course of one breath. A warning spiked in his veins. Pulling the door closed behind him, he took a step forward. The three words Matthew growled were more frightening than the gleaming pistol he drew from his vest.

"Send her out."

Chapter 26

Jace raised his hands to hold Matthew at bay. "Take it easy, Matthew," he said as calmly as he could manage. His heart pounded. "Just take it easy."

"Send her out!" Matthew's crazed eyes widened as he waved the gun in front of Jace. "Now!"

Jace should have predicted this. He should have paid heed to Amelia's fear for Maddie's safety. Clenching his fists, he took a deep breath, trying to gauge the depth of Matthew's instability. "I don't know what this is about, but I think you should put down the gun so we can talk it through."

"There's nothing to discuss. I intend to rid the world of that abomination—that murderer. Send her out!"

The rage underlying this senseless talk was terrifying. It was clear that Pastor Hogle's prejudice had incited a disturbed man to violence. Now this madman was set on killing Maddie—the woman Jace loved.

That this revelation struck him now—at such an ill-timed moment—stunned Jace almost as much as the revelation itself.

Nevertheless, it fortified something inside him. He would protect Maddie, no matter the risk to himself. "Are you prepared to kill me first? Because that's what you'll have to do to get past me."

Matthew frowned. "I'll do whatever I have to. I have nothing to lose." He took a step forward. "She cost me it all."

Jace considered attempting to disarm Matthew, but the distance between them was still too great. His only recourse was to stall for time and inch closer.

"What has she cost you?"

"Everything!" The man's voice cracked beneath the weight of his emotion. "She turned Dolly against me!" Tears welled in his eyes. "The pastor, too! I wanted revenge for what she did to Dolly's face, but Pastor refused. He denounced me as some kind of lunatic." Matthew shook his head in disgust. "That's what he called me before he cast me from the church." He swiped angrily at his eyes. "Now he won't let me have Dolly!" His face turned to steel. "I intend to make that woman pay for ruining everything."

The man was beyond reason. His eyes darted wildly.

Jace had seen men in the emergency ward in similar states. Men so removed from reality, so unhinged by their delusions, they posed a danger to others, even themselves. Most of those men were strung out on whiskey, opiates, or other mind-altering substances. This was different.

Matthew was deranged by hatred.

The door behind Jace opened.

"Jace?"

"Get back inside, Maddie!" he yelled over his shoulder.

"What's—"

"Stay put!" Matthew ordered.

Jace heard Maddie's loud gasp but resisted the urge to rush toward her. Any sudden movement might set Matthew off.

"Come out here." Matthew motioned with the pistol for Maddie to step forward.

She edged stiffly to Jace's side. He stepped in front of her, shielding her body with his.

"What do you want?" she called out.

"I want you gone."

"Maddie, get inside," Jace commanded through clenched teeth.

"Don't move!" Stepping backward, Matthew retreated down the porch stairs, the gun aimed firmly at them. "Now come down off that porch."

Jace didn't move. His thoughts raced. Could he somehow get her safely inside without killing them both?

"Now!" Matthew jabbed the gun in the air.

Jace held Maddie at his back, guiding her down from the porch as directed. He glanced over Matthew's shoulder to see Pastor Hogle riding up the drive. Whether Matthew's former mentor would defuse or ignite the situation, Jace hadn't a clue. But Jace was desperate for help, and for the first time, he was happy to see the man.

Matthew frowned as Pastor Hogle dismounted.

"This house is in mourning, Matthew. What are you doing here?" He rushed toward Matthew, slowing when he saw the gun. The pastor's alarm reinforced the hopelessness of the situation. He was clearly as frightened and surprised as Jace and Maddie were.

Matthew puffed his chest proudly. "I'm doing what I've been called upon to do," he replied. "What you haven't the courage to do."

"This is madness," Hogle whispered, hands outstretched and trembling. "She must be punished for what she did to Dolly."

"Dolly is fine, Matthew. She—"

"But you won't let me have her!" Matthew waved the gun toward Maddie. "All because of Madeline Sutter!"

"Matthew—"

"Dolly is mine! She was chosen for me. Her mark proves it."

Pastor Hogle nodded frantically. "Yes, yes, we will work it all out."

"Liar!"

"I will reconsider, Matthew. Just put down the gun and—"

"Shut up!" Matthew narrowed his eyes. "I've heard enough of your words. Enough of your sermons and lectures and lies. I devoted my whole life to you. I did all that you ever asked. But you betrayed me and spurned my devotion. As though it all meant nothing. *You* said she killed your daughter. *You* said she must go."

"I meant to encourage her to leave town. Not to harm her."

"She is leaving," Jace shouted. "Her trunks are already packed."

Pastor Hogle's face brightened. "You see, Matthew. She's going—"

"That's no longer enough. She must be removed from the world."

"You're confused." Pastor Hogle spoke calmly now. "You're confused and not thinking clearly."

"And you are a coward! You're not fit to lead anyone."

Pastor Hogle flinched. He stared, shaking his head sadly. "What has become of you?"

"I've become what you made me." Matthew turned the gun to Pastor Hogle, his lips twisting with fury. "And you cast me away." He cocked the trigger.

Pastor Hogle lunged at him, but it was too late. Maddie screamed as the gunshot rang out.

And Pastor Hogle fell, bleeding at Matthew's feet.

* * * *

Maddie cowered in Jace's arms. His tight grip on her slackened as he pushed her behind him. Matthew straightened, staring down at the man he'd just shot. "I didn't plan to shoot him," he cried. "I came to shoot her!" He aimed the gun at Jace, his hand unsteady. "Get out of the way, or I'll kill you, too."

"No!" Maddie pushed away from Jace, struggling to break free of his grasp. She would die before she let him hurt Jace. "He has nothing to do with this!"

"Maddie—"

Jace pulled her back, but she wrenched from his hold. "It's me you want, not him. Do to me as you will, but hurt no one else."

"Matthew…" Pastor Hogle writhed on the ground, his hand extended in a desperate plea.

Matthew stared down at the man, his expression teetering between rage and despair. "You betrayed me, Pastor. You left me no choice."

Something in Matthew's face changed as he tilted his head. Tears streamed down his face. All at once he looked so young. Hopeless. Afraid.

Maddie's fear mixed with pity. Her heart froze solid in her chest.

Matthew took a small step toward Hogle, standing over the dying man, considering him in mute anguish. Then, in one swift move, Matthew raised the gun to his own temple. "This is for you, Pastor," he said before pulling the trigger.

Maddie screamed into her palms as Matthew dropped to the ground.

Jace cradled her in his arms, and they both sank to their knees. Maddie sobbed into his shoulder, shaking uncontrollably.

"It's all right," he soothed, although he was trembling, too.

He rose slowly, lifting her to her feet. "Go inside." He urged her toward the house.

She glanced back to the horrifying sight of the two bodies sprawled on the ground. Heeding Jace's directive, she stumbled up the stairs to the door. She grasped the doorknob for support, turning back to Jace.

Knowing Matthew was dead and nothing could be done, Jace rushed to Pastor Hogle. Gil appeared suddenly, running from around the side of the house.

"I heard shots…" he began and then he stopped, stunned, gaping at the bloodied bodies on the ground.

"Help me get him inside," Jace said. He spotted Maddie still at the door. "Maddie, can you get my bag from the buggy?"

She nodded, summoning her wits. She ran past them to Jace's buggy, then followed as Jace and Gil carried the unconscious man to Grandfather's room. They placed him on the bed.

Jace worked furiously to unbutton the pastor's coat.

"It's a belly wound," Gil mumbled, shaking his head.

Jace rummaged through his bag. "I need clean linens," he said. "And some whiskey."

Gil nodded. "Rhetta went into town. I'll get them." He tore off for the supplies as Jace filled a syringe.

Maddie watched, mind racing, as Jace sedated the pastor to make him more comfortable. The man was in and out of consciousness, but his moans of pain quieted as the drug took effect.

Maddie hugged her arms to her chest, staring down at the lifeless man on the bed. His open white shirt was saturated with blood. He looked dead.

"Will he survive?" she asked.

"The bullet went through but nicked an artery." Jace shook his head grimly. "He'll bleed out within the hour."

"You can't help him?"

"He's bleeding internally. I can't stop it."

Maddie glanced back at the pastor. Life drained from his pale face as blood seeped through the compress from the hole in his stomach. She thought of Grandfather and all he'd suffered. Now another man would die in this room. In this bed. One man who had loved her—and this man. This man who despised her and had caused her so much misery.

Perhaps he had gotten what he deserved for his sins against Maddie—and Matthew.

The thought gave her no comfort. Because as much as she might believe this, as much as she hated him for what he'd done, she couldn't stand idle while he died. She could save him. As she'd saved Joey Cleary. Despite the boy's blood malady, she'd healed his punctured vessels, and she could heal this man, too. No matter the cost, no matter the consequence, every fiber of her being told her what she must do.

She turned to Jace, touching his arm. His blue eyes met hers. The tenderness in his gaze warmed her to her bones. Her heart melted like butter as she bid him a silent farewell. Regardless of the outcome, he'd never look at her the same.

She blinked hard for courage before she changed her mind.

"Do you trust me, Jace?"

* * * *

Jace tilted his head at her strange question. "Of course I trust you. More than anyone else," he said.

"Allow me to help him."

He nodded, patting her hand. "Send Gil for the Hogle family. With any luck he'll survive until then."

She shook her head. "I can help him," she said. "I can stop the bleeding."

"No one can stop—"

"I can."

She edged past him, not bothering to explain.

Pastor Hogle's eyes fluttered open. "Keep her away," he uttered before he went out again.

Maddie removed the blood-soaked compress that covered the wound, then carefully set it aside.

"What are you doing?" Jace asked.

"You must trust me. Please."

Leaning forward, she placed her bare hands directly on the bleeding hole in the pastor's gut. Adjusting her touch, she pressed her palms into the bloody flesh.

"Applying pressure won't help."

She ignored him. Jace watched in confusion as she closed her eyes. He stepped closer, a shiver crawling up his spine. She stood, eyes closed, in a trancelike state, so deep in concentration it was as if she'd disappeared. Tears poured down her pale cheeks.

The pastor stirred beneath her hands but never opened his eyes. Jace leaned forward, blinking in disbelief. The blood seeping through Maddie's fingers began to flow more slowly.

What the hell was she doing? Jace's heart pounded. He couldn't move. He couldn't think. He could only watch in awe as the bleeding stopped before his eyes. His throat tightened with the sickening taste of bile.

Maddie removed her hands, then replaced the compress to cover the wound. She stepped back as Jace nudged her aside. His hands trembled as he lifted the compress. His eyes flashed wide. He stared, not believing what he saw.

He blinked again, certain he was losing his mind. His eyes weren't deceiving him, though, and the reality of it hit him like a barreling train.

The wound had healed.

Chapter 27

"Christ Almighty." Jace spun to Maddie, heart pounding. He stared at her, dazed and speechless, as he struggled for words. "What…?"

Maddie took a step toward him.

He took a step back. "How…?"

She shrugged, shaking her head. "I don't know—"

"How?" The anger in his tone boomed through the room as he strode toward her.

"I don't know! After the accident something happened. I was massaging my injured leg, and I felt something strange. It healed. I don't know how."

He shook his head, trying to shake away the absurdity of what he was hearing.

"I wanted to tell you."

His eyes pinned hers. "You wanted to tell me?" he shouted.

She swallowed any futile reply.

"But instead you deceived me. You kept me in the dark. All this time." Her deception sickened him, tainting all that they'd shared. This woman he thought he knew so well now stood a stranger before him. His troubled mind reeled.

Shifting his weight for stability, he braced himself against his next thought. "My patients?" he asked.

She lowered her eyes.

"You were healing my patients?" He stared, stunned as this registered. "You were healing my patients under my nose." He glared, fists clenched. "Playing me for a fool!"

She shook her head. "I just wanted to help." Tears welled in her eyes. "I couldn't tell you. I wanted to protect you. I just wanted…I wanted… to be normal."

"But you're not normal!" Anger erupted inside him. The words spewed forth of their own volition. "None of this is normal!" The glaring truth of this pained him physically. Mentally. And everywhere in between. His turmoil unleashed a ruthlessness he couldn't contain. "All this time I was defending you. Trying to convince people they were wrong about you. That you weren't some freak of nature. But you are!"

Her gasp of anguish hurtled him back to his senses. But it was too late. He blinked, chest heaving. The shattered look on her face told him that he'd gone too far.

She squared her shoulders, and the unrelenting strength in her surfaced. She lifted her trembling chin.

"I am no freak," she declared firmly. "I am a woman with an ability you do not understand. And you've just confirmed that I was entirely right to hide it from you."

She tore her gaze from his, then ran out the door.

* * * *

Tears burned Maddie's eyes as she fled from the house—from that look on Jace's face. The image of his horrified expression chased her through the field, even more so than his mortifying words. That look… She could bear such revulsion in the eyes of anyone else—everyone else—but not him.

She ran faster through the tall grass, ascending the small hill to the cemetery. Reaching the fence enclosing the headstones, she clung to a weathered post, sinking to her knees.

It was over. Her secret was out. She'd had no choice, and she'd done what she'd had to do. A man was dying, and she'd saved him. She stifled a bitter laugh. She'd do well to be on the first train to Boston before Pastor Hogle came to from the sedative.

Not that his reaction mattered to her. She could not care less about any of them. Except Jace. Poor, logical, sensible, Jace. She'd turned his world on its ear. He would spend the rest of his days hating her and trying to figure out how she'd done it. How a simple girl's fingers had stopped an artery from bleeding and closed torn flesh in a matter of moments.

All along, he had considered her as some oddity to study. Well, she'd certainly given him ample material to analyze now.

The loss of Jace, his friendship, his kiss, of being held safely in his arms, ricocheted through the hollowness inside her. She yearned for his comfort in this moment, so much that it felt as if she might die without it. But she wouldn't die. She would survive.

She glanced to the fresh plot of earth that marked Grandfather's grave. The memory of his words chimed in her ears. "You'll have to find your guts, girl, but you'll find them."

She settled back on the grass, calming. She had to leave town as soon as possible. She'd finish packing her belongings tonight and depart first thing in the morning. Until then, she'd stay out of sight. While she gave not a damn about the Hogles and what would ensue when they discovered what she'd done, she hadn't the stamina to face Jace again. Not that she thought for a moment that he would seek her out.

She would never forget the horrified look on his face when he realized what she was capable of. And she knew with utmost certainty that for as long as he lived, he'd never forget it either.

* * * *

Jace sat, staring at Pastor Hogle's sedated form on the bed. The man slept soundly, but Jace's restless nerves kept his heart racing in his chest. What had Maddie done? He shook his head to clear his mind. She had somehow healed the gunshot wound.

He frowned. Just as she had probably healed the horse the other night. And Joey Cleary. And who knew how many others. He ran a stiff hand through his hair. "Goddamn it," he ground through clenched teeth. The upsurge of anger pulled him to his feet. He stormed to the parlor and grabbed Mr. Sutter's bottle of port. In one long swallow he guzzled down what was left.

All these weeks, he'd thought he knew her. He'd thought he loved her. But she was a stranger. He knew her no better today than he had the first time he'd laid eyes on her in the forest. The sweet taste of the port lurched in his throat. The deer... He'd hit that deer with a kill shot that morning, and she'd healed it.

He slumped into a chair, head hung low. Everything he knew about life, about science and reason, Maddie had scattered like withered leaves to the breeze. But he felt more crushed by her deception than anything else. She hadn't trusted him enough to tell him the truth. She'd let him go on defending her and caring for her. Loving her.

And now he had Pastor Hogle to deal with. Although the pastor was heavily sedated, it was not as if Jace could simply tell the man the wound was a graze.

What the hell would become of Maddie now?

Walking through the quiet house, Jace went back to the bedroom to check on the pastor. As expected, the man still slept soundly. Rhetta had returned from town and notified Jace that Gil had gone for the pastor's family. Maddie was nowhere in sight.

Jace pushed thoughts of her from his mind. He hadn't time for them now. Once the Hogles arrived, he'd have to tell them something.

At the sound of the family's frantic arrival outside the door, Jace took a deep breath and stepped out to face them.

Gertrude clutched Daniel's arm, on the verge of hysterics. As always, Dolly stood quietly behind them.

"He'll survive," Jace announced.

Unified sighs of relief filled the room. Gertrude clutched Daniel tighter.

"Matthew is dead," Jace said.

A heavy silence fell over the family as Dolly took a step forward. She lifted her chin. "At least Madeline is safe from his lunacy now."

"Save your worries for Uncle, not her," Gertrude scolded.

Jace frowned, suppressing his instinct to defend Maddie, even now in the midst of this mess. "You can all wait in the parlor," he said. "I'll let you know when he wakes. He can't be moved for some time, but he will recover." Jace could sort out the details of explaining the pastor's recovery later, but first he needed to see how much the man remembered.

* * * *

Pastor Hogle's eyes fluttered open, but he didn't move. Jace watched as the man blinked hard, trying to focus. Jace had given him a strong sedative, and as the pastor blinked again, as though the room spun around him, it was obvious he was still disoriented from the effects of the heavy dosage.

"Where am I?"

"You're at the Sutter house," Jace said.

"Am I dying?"

"Not anymore." Jace reached for his stethoscope, then checked the man's heart rate and pulse. He'd lost a great deal of blood, but his weak pulse had grown stronger.

"Did he kill her?"

Jace stiffened, hanging the stethoscope around his neck. So, the pastor remembered that much. "If you're referring to Madeline, the answer is no. He shot you instead." Jace frowned, unable to suppress his bitterness. "Right before he turned the gun on himself."

Pastor Hogle squeezed shut his eyes. "Oh, Matthew," he uttered.

"Quite a disciple you created." Jace couldn't help himself. This whole incident was the pastor's fault for poisoning a young mind without giving a thought to the potential consequences.

Pastor Hogle glanced to his bandaged stomach. "Did you remove the bullet?" he asked.

"There was no need to remove it." Jace thought about what the hell to say. He was a doctor and had never before lied to a patient. He'd taken an oath. "It went straight through. You've lost a lot of blood, though. You must rest. Let the sedative work off. Your family is waiting outside, and you can see them later after you're more clear headed." Jace started for the door.

"Doctor Merrick?"

Jace stopped and turned to face him.

"I was dying. I felt it."

He nodded. "Yes, Pastor, you were."

Pastor Hogle's eyes fluttered closed as he succumbed to the drug.

* * * *

A few hours later, Pastor Hogle awoke with one question. "What happened?"

Jace shrugged, not quite sure how to reply. "Tell me what you recall."

"Matthew shot me."

"That's what happened."

"But…" Pastor Hogle placed his hands on his stomach. "I feel no pain. No pain at all."

"I wish I could explain it to you, but I'm not sure I can explain it to myself."

"She did something, didn't she?"

Jace frowned. "Goddamn it, her name is Madeline!" He clenched his fists. "And yes, she did something. She saved your life."

Pastor Hogle shook his head to banish the possibility. "I thought I was dreaming."

"You weren't dreaming. You were bleeding to death. And Maddie healed the hole in your gut."

Pastor Hogle's brows rose in amazement. "How?"

"All I can tell you is that you're alive right now, because of her."

"Demon."

"You self-righteous son of a bitch," Jace said between clenched teeth. "Even now, after what she did for you, how can you still accuse her of malice?"

"I'll tell them all what she is—"

"You can do that, yes," Jace said, struggling to rein back his anger. "And after you explain what she did to save your life, you can tell them what you did to end Matthew's."

He winced, averting his eyes.

"Your hatred did this. Your rancid grief. You poisoned a weak and vulnerable mind with your accusations and slander. You'll have to live with that."

Pastor Hogle shook his head. "I tried so hard to make sense of my Elizabeth's death." Jace stared, surprised as the man wiped at his eyes. "Why did Madeline Sutter get to live when my Elizabeth didn't?"

"It was an accident." Jace took a step closer. In this moment of truth, he'd disclose it all. It was hell past time someone did. "Your daughter was driving the wagon. If anyone was responsible, it was she."

The pastor's eyes flashed wide. "That's a lie! I never allowed her to drive."

"Precisely."

"Elizabeth wouldn't disobey me." He shook his head, but his eyes lacked conviction.

"Unfortunately, that day, she did."

The pastor shuddered with a pained sob.

"And you blamed Maddie because she survived," Jace said. "She allowed you all to blame her, to preserve your daughter's memory."

"Doctor Filmore came to see me after my sermon that day," he murmured.

"What?"

"After the day she showed up in church. Filmore told me he'd made a mistake by declaring her dead and wanted to set things straight." He lowered his eyes. "I convinced him a man of his high competence would never make such an error." His voice sank in remorse. "At the time, I believed it."

Jace took a deep breath. "You were wrong."

He closed his eyes, and a tear rolled down his cheek. Turning away, he cowered against the pillow in his grief.

Jace made no move to console him. He didn't want to console him.

"Maddie did a remarkable thing, but it's far from malevolent."

"But how—"

"I don't know," Jace said, shaking his head. "All I know is that you were dying. And she could have kept her ability to herself and just let you die. But instead she risked everything to save you—a man hell bent on destroying her. A man whose death would have made her life easier. Without you carrying the torch of hatred, people here might have found their way toward acceptance. That's the woman you call a demon." Jace restrained the emotion welling inside him. "I don't know how, or even why, she saved your life. But she did a miraculous thing—a good thing."

Jace heard the sound of his own words, as if someone else had spoken them. What a hypocrite he was, what a coward. How could he, of all people, reject such convincing advice? Whether he was attempting to persuade the pastor or himself remained unclear. He knew only the truth in it. And what he felt in his heart. "You owe Madeline your life," Jace said.

The pastor opened his eyes, looking stricken. "And how do you propose I repay that debt?"

"By doing what's right," Jace said. "Maddie has been gifted with an ability neither of us understands. I am a man of science. If I can try to accept it, shouldn't you, as a man of faith, do the same?"

Chapter 28

Jace left the pastor to rest and slipped out the back door. He needed some time alone. He needed to think. Walking off his restless energy, he drank in the familiar sights, the trees and the birds, in some unquenchable thirst for normalcy. The world around him remained unchanged, and yet everything was different. The tightly knit fabric of his life had unraveled.

He strode across the lush lawn until he reached the lake. As he stared out at the rippling water, the whirl of his thoughts settled on what he'd witnessed in that room. What Maddie's small hands had accomplished.

Jace's father had spoken of people who called themselves healers—cases where ailments were cured by the mere touch of a hand. Jace had dismissed these occurrences as hoaxes, coincidence, or the sheer will of the patients themselves. Mind over matter.

The human brain was a powerful organ laden with thoughts and ideas—and untapped potential.

Maddie had accomplished the extraordinary. Could her talent have derived from the trauma of the accident? Was it possible the pain of losing her friends and her survivor's guilt could have created an internal force of emotions that manifested in something tangible—physical?

He shook his head. Not that it mattered. He could still barely believe it. It all seemed like a dream. Recalling his ugly reaction felt more like a nightmare.

He'd been confused and afraid of what Maddie had done, and in his addled state, he'd taken his shock out on her. He cringed, hating that he'd hurt her.

He'd accused her of betraying him, but how could he blame her for keeping her secret from him? She'd known that he—most of all—would recoil from her ability. She knew her gift was an affront to everything in which he believed. He was her only friend, and she'd feared his reaction.

And he'd brought that fear to life. No wonder she hadn't trusted him. The crushing weight in his chest was made heavier by his shame.

She'd healed his patients, but in all honesty, could he truly fault her for that? She was not one to stand idle while people suffered. Would he prefer that she had? Jace was certain her intention had not been to deceive him. He had forced her into an impossible position by insisting that she work at his office on that day he'd first kissed her. He'd known then she was special. He almost laughed at the understatement.

Jace thought of his father as he tried to make sense of this astounding thing Maddie had done. He suddenly grasped that it was not for him to explain what he did not understand. Nor was it his responsibility to tear everything apart, wasting his life, in fruitless attempts to make sense of it all.

As his father had.

Maddie once told Jace that he was only human. A man. A good man. The words had brought him such consolation that day. The mere memory of her tender regard warmed him still.

Surely, she hated him now. The bitter chill of the present hit him like a gust of wind. Matthew could have killed Maddie today. The thought filled him with a fear that rocked him to his core.

All his life Jace had feared romantic love because it was illogical, an irrational response to physical desire. Maddie had taught him that fear was a damn poor excuse for not getting on with things. Suddenly, it was all crystal clear. Maddie's remarkable ability to heal would not destroy him.

Losing her would.

* * * *

The commanding knock on her bedroom door told Maddie it was Jace before he spoke a word.

"Open up, Maddie," he ordered.

So much for her hope to avoid him. She inhaled an angry breath. Armed to the teeth, she flung open the door. "What do you want?"

He brushed past her into the room. "Explain something to me."

"I can't explain it," she shot back. "If I could I—"

He moved closer. "Explain to me how a sham engagement became something I want to make real?"

The honest expression on his handsome face stunned her. She softened, her eyes welling with tears. "What—"

"Marry me, Madeline."

The words lifted her from the depths of her gloom, but she resisted his rescue. Jace acted on reason—and reason alone. She tilted her head, plummeting quickly. "Because you wish to study me like a rat?"

"Because I love you, goddamn it!"

She shook her head in disbelief.

He grasped her shoulders and held her before him. "I don't know how you did it," he said. "And I don't care."

"You don't?"

He shrugged. "All right, so I'm slightly intrigued," he said with a smile.

She smiled, too.

"But all I truly care about is you. I love you, Maddie. For the woman you are. Not the woman you were before the accident or the woman you're trying so hard to become—but for who you are now."

She stared up at him, speechless.

"You sacrificed everything. You saved the pastor at the expense of exposing your secret and reclaiming your life. That took true courage."

She shook her head. "I never gave that a thought," she said honestly. "My only thoughts were of you." She touched her head to his chest. "I sacrificed you."

He kissed the top of her head. "You once told me that until I realized that logic and science don't define everything in this life, I'd never truly live."

She drew back, gazing into his eyes.

"I am finally ready to live." He pressed his forehead to hers. "And I want to live my life with you."

She trembled on the verge of a dream. "I love you, Jace Merrick," she said, hugging him tight.

He kissed her hard.

"What about Pastor Hogle?" she asked, breathless.

"I don't believe he'll tell anyone what occurred in that room. But it no longer matters. We are leaving Misty Lake as soon as I'm packed."

"But what about your practice?"

"I can practice anywhere. What I can't do is risk your safety again. I won't."

She smiled, loving him more.

"No one will hurt you again. That includes me," he said. A shadow of sadness crossed his face. "I never meant those ugly things I said to you, Maddie. You have an ability. A gift for healing."

"As do you," she said. "And I'm sorry—"

"You don't need my forgiveness. Or anyone else's, don't you see? The accident wasn't your fault. The only forgiveness you've ever needed was your own."

He kissed her forehead, and she nodded against the press of his lips.

"I've a theory that perhaps that's where this power comes from. Your guilt manifested into something—"

"Jace." She shook her head, laughing through her tears. "You're not trying to analyze it already, are you?"

He smiled. "No. We've a lifetime for that." He kissed her again. "My sweet Maddie," he uttered against her ear. "My sweet, remarkable Maddie."

She hugged him for all she was worth.

"The Hogles and I are departing soon. We're taking the pastor home, but I'll be back as quickly as I can."

"May I join you?" she asked.

He shook his head. "While I'd like nothing more, I must take the pastor in the wagon."

She considered this for barely a moment. She'd almost lost the man she loved. Her fear of riding in a wagon again was nothing compared to that. She straightened her spine, feeling ready for anything.

"Save a place for me, darling." She flashed him a smile. "I'm not afraid anymore."

Epilogue

One Month Later

Maddie and Jace enjoyed a glorious honeymoon in Saratoga Springs. Although their wedding had been a simple one compared to Amelia's, the intimate ceremony overlooking Misty Lake had been special just the same.

Maddie sat on a bench in one of the beautiful gardens of Congress Park, resting her leg and waiting for Jace. He'd gone to fetch lemonade from a vendor cart they'd strolled past earlier, and she wondered now what was keeping him.

Gazing out at the colorful flower beds, she recalled the events that had transpired in Misty Lake. Pastor Hogle had recovered completely, and as Jace had predicted, the man's only mention of Maddie in the aftermath was that she had helped Jace in saving his life.

The simple statement was enough.

Doctor Reed was currently filling in for Jace during their extended honeymoon. Jace had left it to Maddie to decide whether to return to Misty Lake. While she was leaning against going back, she'd yet to make up her mind. But wherever she and Jace landed, they'd work together in his office, especially while treating people suffering with trauma.

Jace had read the journal she'd written after the accident and felt certain the method she'd used to overcome the after-effects of her trauma would help ease the suffering of others. Maddie was eager to help him refine the technique. She also was eager to find others like herself, people with strange and remarkable abilities that could not be explained. Together, she and Jace would work on that, too.

She straightened on the bench at the sight of Jace in the distance. Her heart beat faster each time she looked at him. He rounded a tall row of hedges, and she noticed the small child walking beside him. She waited curiously as they approached.

"This is Annabel," Jace said.

Maddie glanced at the slight child, who could not have been more than seven years old. Her cheekbones protruded beneath her pale skin, and dark circles rimmed her hollow eyes. Her blond hair was so thin Maddie could see patches of scalp around the large pink bow perched on her head.

Maddie swallowed her sorrow, forcing a smile. "It's a pleasure to meet you, Annabel," she said. "And I must say that's a lovely dress you're wearing."

Annabel bowed her head, looking lost inside tiers of pink ruffles and lace.

Jace patted the girl's bony shoulder. "Annabel and her family are in Saratoga for the healing effects of the springs," he said. "Her mother was kind enough to allow her to walk with us for a bit."

"That was kind of her, indeed," Maddie said in honest praise of the woman who spared some of her precious time with this child. She glanced back to the girl, who stood shyly at Jace's side. "I hear there's a fountain beyond those trees over there."

Annabel glanced over her shoulder to where Maddie pointed.

"And I understand it's a magic fountain."

The girl's dim eyes brightened as Maddie continued. "The story is that if you toss a coin into the enchanted water, your wish will come true." Maddie leaned close. "Would you like to give it a try?"

The girl nodded, her excited grin filling her ashen face with light.

Maddie reached into her reticule and fished out a penny. "Now, your wish must be very special if you want the magic to work," she cautioned as she placed the coin into Annabel's frail hand.

Annabel nodded again. "Thank you, miss," she whispered, clutching it tight. "I think I know a good one."

Maddie glanced up at Jace, and he gave her a nod.

She stood, her heart swelling with love. "I have a good one, too," Maddie promised as she peeled off her gloves. "Why don't you take my hand, sweetheart?" she asked the girl with a smile. "And we'll go make our wishes together."

Meet the Author

A three-time RWA Golden Heart nominee, **Thomasine Rappold** writes historical romance and historical romance with paranormal elements. She lives with her husband in a small town in upstate New York that inspired her current series. When she's not spinning tales of passion and angst, she enjoys spending time with her family, fishing on one of the nearby lakes, and basking on the beach in Cape Cod. Thomasine is a member of Romance Writers of America and the Capital Region Romance Writers. Readers can find her on Facebook and follow her on Twitter: @ThomRappold.

Keep reading for a special sneak peek of the next book in the Sole Survivor series:

THE LADY WHO SAW TOO MUCH

Cursed with prophetic visions and desperate to atone for a death she could have prevented, Gianna York swears she will never again ignore the chance to save a life. When she is hired by autocratic Landen Elmsworth to serve as companion to his sister, Gia repeatedly sees the image of her employer's lifeless corpse floating in Misty Lake. As subsequent visions reveal more details—including the possibility of foul play—Gia soon realizes her best chance to protect this difficult man is by becoming his wife.

A Lyrical e-book on sale June 2016.

Learn more about Thomasine at
http://www.kensingtonbooks.com/author.aspx/31713

Chapter 1

She was about to be tossed to the street. Gianna York folded her trembling hands on her lap, lifted her chin, and did her utmost to maintain her dignity.

Prolonging the torture, Mrs. Amery tidied one of the tall stacks of papers covering the surface of the large desk between them. "I'm sorry, Gia, but my decision is final." The woman's usually stern voice softened beneath her crushing words. "You've done a fine job these past months, but in light of your recent disclosure, I simply cannot keep you on any longer."

Gia slumped in her seat. She'd expected the worst when she'd been summoned to Mrs. Amery's office so early this morning, and that's precisely what she'd been handed. She stared down at her lap as she fought to contain her dismay.

"Our students are impressionable young women, as you well understand. The precarious situation in which you've placed yourself by fleeing your home as you did, leaves me with no other choice. And I'm afraid it leaves you with limited respectable options."

Bristling at the unnecessary reminder, Gia rued the moment of weakness during which she'd divulged this part of her past. Lesson learned. From here on out, she would lie. The thought made her angrier. Not at Mrs. Amery, who'd always treated her fairly, but at herself. It wasn't weakness but pride that had prompted Gia's confession. Her stubborn attempt to challenge society's perception of what she'd done had failed miserably. If a woman as forward-thinking as Mrs. Amery couldn't be swayed... "I understand," Gia uttered.

Mrs. Amery sighed. "It's a bitter pill to swallow, I know, but all is not lost. I may have a solution."

Gia glanced up, surprised.

"I've learned recently of a position that might interest you. Of course it's not as a teaching assistant nor here at the school, but—"

"Where?" Gia leaned forward.

"Misty Lake."

"Misty Lake?"

"A small town in the country a mere half-day's ride from here. The position is for a companion to a young woman from an upstanding family who summers there. The poor girl suffers with a crippling shyness, and her family feels a companion might help alleviate her condition. Their trust in the Troy Female Seminary has brought them to me for a recommendation." Mrs. Amery tilted her head. "I've told them only of your quality work here, nothing more," she said sternly.

"I appreciate that."

"I know it's not ideal, but if you still refuse to consider returning to your family, I truly believe it's your only recourse."

Gia stiffened at the mention of her family. Returning to Boston meant abiding by their conditions, and Gia knew all too well the terms of those conditions. Blind obedience. Total conformity. Mind-numbing medications to "restore her health" and "quiet the spells" from which she'd been afflicted since the accident, but rendered her senseless in the process.

No. She refused to go back to that life.

Gia had survived the icy water for a reason. And while she'd never understand why she'd lived while her brothers hadn't, she'd conceded, after much painful resistance, that all that ensued was a part of that reason. Gia had to accept this. Even if her parents couldn't.

Gia straightened in her chair. She could be a companion. She could be whatever was required of a companion, so long as it paid sufficiently.

"And it pays quite well," Mrs. Amery added as if reading Gia's thoughts. "The position must be filled immediately, so if you decide to accept, you must depart at once."

"I'll do it," Gia said.

"Very well then." Mrs. Amery reached into the desk drawer. "The Elmsworths are expecting you tomorrow." She handed Gia an envelope. "All the information is there. Along with travel expenses."

Gia stood, feeling better. A quiet summer in the country would not be so bad. While she'd miss the girls here at the school, she was fortunate she'd have a roof over her head. Beggars couldn't be choosers. "I'd better start packing."

Mrs. Amery nodded. "I'm due at an appointment upstairs." She plucked up a file as she rounded the desk. With a sympathetic smile, she patted Gia's arm. "Good luck to you, my dear." She hurried from the room, deserting Gia to the fate contained inside the envelope in her hand.

Blowing out a long breath, Gia opened the envelope. Fingering through the contents, she bypassed several crisp bills before slipping out a gold-embossed card. The fine parchment bespoke wealth and status, as did the bold print. With her thumb, Gia traced the raised letters of the ornate script. *Landen J. Elmsworth.*

A chill of foreboding crept up her spine. The print shifted, fading slowly from focus before her blurry eyes. Her heart pounded. With a fortifying breath, she braced herself against the inevitable—and all that came with it. Fear and dread gave way to total helplessness as the vision emerged like a slow wave of nausea.

Closing her eyes, she sank to the chair. She clutched the parchment in her palm, the buzz in her ears growing louder, drawing her in. Brisk air filled her lungs. Gooseflesh formed on her skin. The smell of pine loomed amid tall trees and shadows. Entranced by the sound of babbling water, she waited as a picture took shape in the darkness.

A man lay at the bottom of a rocky creek, face down in the shallow water. His long black coat clung to his lifeless body. The crimson scarf around his neck drifted like a thick stream of blood on the mild current.

And then as insidiously as it had appeared, the vision was gone. Gia opened her eyes. Panting, she unfurled her trembling fist, then stared down at the crumpled card. She hadn't experienced a vision so vivid in months. Nor one so ominous. Especially of someone she'd yet to meet.

She leaned back in the chair, still reeling. Visions of strangers came rarely but were no less disturbing. She shoved the card into the envelope and tried to stay calm. The thundering pulse at her temples refused to recede as each detail of the vision pelted her brain.

She remained seated for several long moments before attempting to stand. Rising on shaky legs, she composed herself. Exhaustion in the wake of the vision struck hard. She clutched the chair for support. She'd almost forgotten how draining it could be—it had been so long. Why this was happening now, after all this time, she didn't know. But of one thing she was certain.

Landen J. Elmsworth, whoever he was, was going to die.

* * * *

Gia stared at the gable-roofed house, urging her feet to move. She dreaded meeting the man she'd seen dead in her vision, dreaded meeting his family. A part of her longed to ignore the vision, run miles in the opposite direction and try to forget it. While she was unsure if she could prevent her visions from becoming reality, she was determined to try. She had to.

The memory of Prudence Alber's death pierced her chest like a dagger. Gia had stood idle, and a young girl had died. The heavy weight of her guilt kept her rooted in the gravel drive in front of the large house, too ensnared in the past to move. She took a deep breath, then stepped to the porch. She had to do something to make up for what she hadn't done for Pru.

Somehow—some way—she would save Mr. Elmsworth.

Gia rang the bell. After announcing herself, she was led by a tall housemaid through the foyer and into a finely decorated parlor. "My name is Florence, Miss York. Please make yourself comfortable while I get Miss Elmsworth."

Gia took a seat on the small settee, glancing around. The spacious room was styled to perfection with elegant furnishings and bright hues and only a hint of the musty smells so common in summer retreats. Outside the large windows, the lake sparkled amid mountains and trees, a scenic painting come to life.

There were several such lakes in the area. Were there as many creeks as well? Gia pushed from her mind the thought of her vision and the challenge ahead. She had to stay positive. A few moments later, Florence returned. A young woman followed demurely behind her.

"Miss York, this is Miss Alice Elmsworth." Florence urged the girl forward.

"I'm pleased to make your acquaintance, Alice," Gia said. "May I call you Alice?"

Alice nodded, staring down at her shoes.

"I will bring tea," Florence said

Alice watched Florence exit the room. From her forlorn expression, Gia half-expected the girl would follow. "She won't be but a few minutes," she uttered instead. She said nothing more as she took a seat across from Gia.

Beneath Alice's clenched hands, her knees bounced with nervous tension. The timid creature appeared as though she wanted to be anywhere but in the presence of this stranger who'd been hired to be her companion. Gia sighed, feeling increasingly uncomfortable for causing the girl's palpable distress.

Gia fidgeted in her seat, wondering how best to approach the situation. They waited for tea in excruciating silence until Gia could bear her own discomfort no longer. "May I ask how old you are, Alice?"

"I turned twenty in March," she replied without looking up.

"I turned twenty in March as well."

Alice glanced up, and Gia smiled. "Six years ago."

Alice smiled too. A brief little smile that came and went so quickly, Gia almost missed it. Alice shifted in her seat, relaxing a bit, but the strain in her voice remained. "You attended the Troy Female Seminary?"

"That's right. But I'm originally from Boston." Gia worked in her mind the tale she'd concocted to explain her relocating to Troy. "After the death of my parents, I took up residence at the seminary," Gia said, feeling guilty for the lie.

"My parents are deceased as well," Alice said. She lowered her gaze to her lap, but not before Gia glimpsed the pain in her eyes.

If possible, Gia felt guiltier. She was also perplexed. So, Landen Elmsworth was not Alice's father as Gia had presumed. Her uncle, perhaps? Florence entered the room with a tea tray, and Gia was grateful for the distraction.

Alice and Gia drank their tea amid bits of conversation that consisted of little more than Gia's questions and Alice's yes or no answers. Although it was obvious the girl lacked the usual self-esteem that came naturally to most young women of her class, Gia sensed that a treasure trove of fine qualities lay buried beneath Alice's severe anxiety. When she wasn't avoiding eye contact by fidgeting with her hands or the folds of her skirts, her large blue eyes shined with wit and intelligence.

Unfortunately, the effort involved in exhuming these qualities would exhaust anyone attempting to draw them to the surface. Gia imagined the girl in a crowded ballroom. Alice would disappear into the wallpaper. Gia understood, now, why her family had resorted to hiring a companion. The security of having someone at her side might help build Alice's confidence.

"Alice!"

A male voice boomed through the foyer.

"Alice!"

Alice straightened in her seat. "We're in the parlor!"

The sound of heavy footsteps stomped toward the room, and then he was there, posed in the doorway. Gia stared. The black coat, the dark hair. The wide shoulders. Was this him? The man in her vision?

He stepped into the room, addressing Alice as if Gia weren't there. Anger blazed in his blue eyes. "I just saw Mrs. Folsome in town," he said. Alice set down her tea.

"She told me you declined the invitation to her dinner party next week." Alice shot to her feet, hands on hips. Her entire demeanor changed as she challenged the man, face to face. The timid mouse was a tiger at heart.

"I told you, Denny, I do not wish to attend."

Denny. Gia exhaled in relief. For some reason, she felt inexplicably grateful that this particular man was not the man in her vision. Not that she'd wish such a fate on anyone, but the thought of this young, virile, and stunningly handsome man's end seemed a terrible waste.

"And I told you, you must make an effort," he said to Alice. "You are twenty years old now. Much too old to spend your days holed up in the house."

Alice motioned with her eyes toward Gia. "We will discuss this later," she said through clenched teeth.

Ignoring the cue they had company, he said, "There is nothing to discuss. You will attend Mrs. Folsome's dinner and that is the end of it." He turned toward Gia, finally acknowledging her presence in the room. "You're the companion?"

His blunt question sounded more like an accusation. Gia nodded.

"Then please explain to this stubborn miss the importance of socializing."

Reluctant to engage in their familial dispute, Gia opened her mouth, but nothing came out.

"Denny!" Alice gaped. "You have yet to introduce yourself to Miss York, and you're already barking orders at her."

He frowned, lips pursed tight. For a moment, Gia thought he might protest. But with a sigh of resignation, he affirmed that Alice was right. "My apologies, Miss York," he said as he yanked off his hat. He tossed the hat to a chair and a stern look at Alice. "But my sister has a habit of distracting me from my manners."

He turned toward Gia, and she swallowed hard beneath his bold scrutiny. He moved closer. The tense slant of his brow slackened, as did the taut line of his mouth. His perfect lips parted, luring all lucid thought from her head. "How do you do?"

Even the smooth sound of his voice had turned pleasing. She licked her suddenly dry lips and managed a nod.

His gaze held hers as he extended his hand. Clasping her fingers, he gave her hand a slight squeeze, all the while appraising her with those placid blue eyes. The heat of his touch pulsed through her veins. He released her, but she remained gripped by a strange giddy sensation. The reaction was girlish and silly, and as overpowering as her visions.

She stared into his face, lost in a moment of mesmerizing desire. Like a cuff to the head, his next words jarred her back to her senses.

"I am Landen Elmsworth."

Made in the USA
San Bernardino, CA
22 January 2016